SHE WAS A WOMAN GROWN . . .

"That's right," she said, with a tone he didn't quite understand, full of pain somehow, "I am a woman. I am not the child you knew."

Rorke couldn't deal with following this line of conversation. He couldn't think of Gwyneth as a woman.

She was Damon's sister. That was how he had to see her.

"For all I can see," he lied, "you are the same maddening, defiant, and outrageous child you ever were. Even worse, now you are apparently without your wits, or do you have some explanation for what the hell you are doing in the siege camp outside Manvel, dressed as a boy, sneaking into tents, putting yourself into twenty different kinds of danger—"

"The only danger I've been in so far has been due to you!"

"You are in no danger from me."

His mind instantly leaped to the truth, that she *was* in danger from him.

And she was danger *to* him.

He couldn't even look at her and think straight. He kept remembering how strong and supple her lithe body had felt beneath him. . . .

Dear Romance Readers,

In July 2000, we launched the Ballad line with four new series, and each month since then we've presented both new and continuing stories set everywhere from medieval England to the American West—the kind of passionate, romantic stories you love best, written by the most gifted authors. At the back of each book, we'll tell you when you can find subsequent books in the series that have captured your heart.

This month, Willa Hix offers the second and last installment in her highly romantic *Golden Door* series. What happens when a British rake forced into the circus business meets a high-wire artist who acts as if *she's* running the show? In **Gone Courting**, you'll find out! Next, the always talented Sylvia McDaniel returns to the sultry heat of New Orleans with **The Price of Moonlight**, the second in her steamy *Cuvier Widows* series. Is the handsome man who happens onto the plantation of a stunned widow the answer to her prayers—or a temptation she can't resist?

The fabulous Tracy Cozzens continues her *American Heiresses* series with **White Tiger's Fancy**, as an impulsive young woman schemes her way into a big game hunt in India—and finds the daring hunter has captured her heart. Finally, reader favorite Suzanne McMinn concludes her sweeping *The Sword and the Ring* series with a tale of childhood love and grown-up decisions in **My Lady Knight**. Enjoy them all!

Kate Duffy
Editorial Director

The Sword and the Ring

MY LADY KNIGHT

Suzanne McMinn

ZEBRA BOOKS
Kensington Publishing Corp.
http://www.kensingtonbooks.com

> *To my fabulous hunky husband—always*

ZEBRA BOOKS are published by

Kensington Publishing Corp.
850 Third Avenue
New York, NY 10022

All Kensington titles, imprints and distributed lines are available at special quantity discounts for bulk purchases for sales promotion, premiums, fund-raising, educational or institutional use.

Special book excerpts or customized printings can also be created to fit specific needs. For details, write or phone the office of the Kensington Special Sales Manager: Kensington Publishing Corp., 850 Third Avenue, New York, NY 10022. Attn. Special Sales Department. Phone: 1-800-221-2647.

Zebra and the Z logo Reg. U.S. Pat. & TM Off.

First Printing: December 2002
10 9 8 7 6 5 4 3 2 1

Printed in the United States of America

One

England, 1356

The morning was mist and mystery. The castle of the lord of Manvel shimmered through it, the walls emerging in dreamy increments through the thick air.

Wagons creaked and sloshed over the muddied ground, still sopping from last night's rain. Horses' hooves thudded and boots marched in time with the turning wheels. Breaths rose and fell and quickened.

Her feet were tired, her belly empty, but Gwyneth of Wulfere's heart was filled with hope and her pace was undaunted. There were worse things than sore feet. She could be spinning, hemming, embroidering, brewing, and enduring relentless talk of marriage negotiations with the duke of Lothian. She would not marry the loathsome Lothian for any quantity of wool, silver, and spun cloth, but no one was listening to her, particularly not her brother Damon who was her guardian, plague, and prison warden.

He thought he knew what was best for her, and for all the freedom he had granted her for so many years, now there was no more of it. He was her brother, but above all he was a man, and like all men, he thought he knew what was best for the women in his life. And so she had no choice but to disobey him, she told herself as insidious guilt crept through her at her secret escape. Despite her frustration, she loved her brother, loved her entire family. They would worry when they discovered she was missing, but what else could she do?

Gwyneth was not like Belle, her sister-in-law, who had found enduring love with Damon. And neither was she like Elayna, her older sister who had found a like passion with her husband, Graeham. They had opened their hearts in a way that Gwyneth never could, or at least, never *would*.

Love was a shackle that took away a woman's freedom forever.

Instinctively, she reached up to touch the bottom edges of the woolen cap that covered her head and hid the mass of thick dark hair much as the shapeless, coarse tunic hid the feminine form of her body. She was a boy for now, but she hoped the disguise was temporary, just until she proved that she was ready, willing, and able to face battle. The world outside her sheltered home of Wulfere was changing, and even the illustrious Order of the Garter had dabbled with the admission of women.

Gwyneth had spent years working and training with the sword. She had studied well the exploits of other women warriors—Eleanor of Aquitaine, Jeanne of Navarre, the countess of Ross. . . . She had dreamed that years from now the name Gwyneth of Wulfere would be among that list. Why not? She was good enough, tough enough, strong enough.

Damon had ripped the very tapestry from beneath her boots with the matter of the loathsome Lothian. She had mentioned the Order of the Garter, and he had gone livid. His face had raged red, whitening the thin scar that sliced down one side.

"You are my sister. You are a lady. The world is a dangerous place, and there is no place more dangerous in the world than battle," he had decreed in his low voice that could be quite frightening in its steely resolution.

It was the demeanor that had brought him through countless battles of his own.

He had seen too many of his comrades die—in France, where he had spent five years in the king's service—and here at home, in sieges such as the one about to take place at Manvel.

It was one thing, he had gone on, to play at swords in the bailey of Castle Wulfere but quite another to face war's reality. It was his place as her brother to protect her from exposure to its harsh horrors.

She had argued, of course. There was no more dangerous fate to her mind than to be placed beneath a husband's thumb, nothing she was less prepared to face. What man would ever grant her the freedom she not only craved but needed to survive?

But even Damon did not understand. He was a man. He was free.

And he had already been a grown man, a warrior,

when their mother died. Gwyneth had been but five years of age, and in the years that followed—while Damon had been away at war—their father had been in a sickbed.

Gwyneth had been left much on her own. During that dreadful period when their evil cousin Julian had held sway over all their lives as, unbeknownst, he had been slowly poisoning their father and leading a band of criminals that had terrorized the countryside as well as Castle Wulfere, she had developed a decidedly unladylike attraction to arms. It had at first been a reaction to her very real lack of control over her own life, but very soon it had become an obsession.

Her teachers were castle guardsmen, her playmates the sons of armorers. She played camp ball and swung maces and wrestled.

And all the while, she had turned into somebody else, somebody who didn't have to be afraid—at least, not physically. Her skills had set her free from the constraints of the world's expectations for a girl as well as from the vulnerability that had surrounded her early when she'd lost her parents.

By the time Damon had returned home, there was little he could do to tame the stubborn, wild thing she had become. To reach her, he had indulged her love of swordsmanship over the objections of his own best friend and chief man-at-arms, Rorke of Valmond, whose reluctant job it had become to supervise her formal training.

Into her hands Rorke had placed glaives that outstripped her and broadswords that outweighed her. He'd raced her up against quintains that knocked her out and ordered her to collect cow dung for mangonel practice.

He'd tried everything to make her quit. *Ready to dip candles yet, little lady?*

His deep voice still reverberated in her memory, but beneath it all, she had known the truth, that he had admired her tenacity and her strength, and she had admired him in return. He was, after all, the epitome of knighthood.

He was all-powerful, untouchable, invulnerable—everything she wanted to be.

When he had abruptly abandoned Castle Wulfere three years ago for some mad quest that even Damon had shook his head over, he had not even told her good-bye. She had refused to admit, even to herself, that this had hurt. It would have been weakness, and she was not weak.

Neither did she want to know that her hero was weak, that he was not all-powerful, untouchable, invulnerable.

That she thought of him now as she joined her first siege, she also refused to ponder. It was natural to remember him now, but she wouldn't allow it to continue and she pushed from her mind the man who had trained her, and disappointed her, as she examined her situation.

It was far from perfect, but it was a beginning.

She had slipped in amongst the squires and grooms as the band of men—foot soldiers, bowmen, and knights led by Damon—had set out from Wulfere at dusk. It would be her first experience with real battle, and it was worth more than gold simply for that.

Distant shouts, followed by a trumpet call, cut through the thick air. Finally, through the protective haze of the shrouding mist, the castle guards had spied their advance. They were lucky they'd made it undetected thus far. The village lay behind them, its few remaining inhabitants dazedly falling to the inescapable force, their capture muted by sleep and fear, surrendering and thus saving their thatched cottages from the repercussions of defending their treacherous lord.

Most had clearly fled in advance, leaving their cottages empty, in full knowledge of the lord of Manvel's undoing as he had absconded to his castle after being caught in a plot to put together a band of barons to overthrow the king. Those few who had remained now threw themselves on the gathering army's mercy to save their homes from fire.

Damon and the other lords who had joined him through the night to advance together had ridden past the village undeterred.

The castle would not be taken so easily.

Blood pounded through her veins faster at the mere thought of seeing trebuchets, mangonels, and battering rams in full battle action—and she had sworn on the memory of her blessed heroine Eleanor of Aquitaine that she would be right in the middle of it.

Before her, Damon's standard blew in the light breeze. The growing morning sun glinted on the lances and banners and standards of others who had joined their trek through the night. There were at least a score of lords with their knights and countless bowmen and foot soldiers.

Gwyneth mixed in with the squires and grooms and serving boys, slowly making her way farther from Damon's standard. Now, in the light, she had to worry about being recognized.

She would have to blend in with the others, the strangers around her.

Her plans had been made quickly. She would call herself Tucker in honor of the miller's son in Fulbury, the village at the foot of Castle Wulfere. Tucker had been her good friend before he had drowned in the millpond last Saint Swithin's Day.

Her family believed her to be leaving at dawn to return home with Elayna, who had been visiting Wulfere. Gwyneth had told Elayna that she had changed her mind about going to Penlogan.

Of course, she had told her brother and Belle just the opposite.

She'd even had to lie to her two younger sisters, Lizbet and Marigold, to avoid getting them in trouble by involving them in her plans. It had been especially difficult to lie to Lizbet. She was closer to Lizbet than anyone on this earth.

But even Lizbet would not support her rash plan, and Gwyneth couldn't bring herself to place her sister in the position of having either to lie and help her or to tell the truth and stop her.

There was no way to know now if it had all worked as she'd hoped, that between Damon's late-night departure and Elayna's early morning one somehow no one had realized that Gwyneth was neither here nor there.

If they had realized it, she would have little time. They would no doubt send a messenger to alert Damon by nightfall.

Gwyneth sent up a little plea, squeezing her eyes shut for emphasis. If she was caught, it would be over. Damon would have her wed to the duke without delay and her chance to prove herself on the field of battle would be lost.

She opened her eyes when she bumped up against something hard that grunted—which turned out to be the soldier in front of her.

"Watch yer step, boy," the soldier ground out irritably and gave her a shove using his fist shield.

The first thing she thought was, *he's all nose.*

He had a big, misshapen beak, and beneath his helm, his eyes blazed out at her, slitted and hard and somehow knowing.

Or at least they seemed knowing to Gwyneth.

Did he suspect she was no boy at all?

He wasn't one of Damon's men. She had moved some distance from her brother's band of soldiers now.

She kept her gaze level on the soldier as she stepped around him, her heart beating hard. She felt idiotic when she realized he'd already forgotten her, his attention turned to the soldiers around him who were quickly breaking out tents and poles from one of the wagons, pitching camp where they stood, and it was then that it struck her that while she felt as if all eyes were on her, suspecting her, in truth, she was simply in the way, surrounded by knights and soldiers and even serving boys who knew what to do while she hadn't the slightest idea.

For all her skill in arms, she was not trained in the art of making camp.

Determinedly, she set down her pack. She'd brought little: a comb, a change of clothes, a supper knife along with a few pieces of parchment and writing tools so that she could write her family. Even if she got away with the ruse of making her brother think she was with Elayna—and Elayna think she was at home—they would figure it out eventually.

She would write them to let them know she was safe . . . eventually.

Gwyneth wished again that she'd made it out with some arms and armor. She would have loved to have come garbed as a squire. But it would have been impossible. She'd tried to assemble a suit of armor once by pilfering it one piece at a time from the armory, but Damon had caught her.

Plate armor was expensive, so it was missed. She had to settle for passing as a camp boy. She would find a way to be part of the action.

On the field in the midst of battle, anything was possible.

Not wanting to stick out now, she picked up a wood-handled hammer and joined in with the group of men before her who were setting up one of the lords' tents. One of the men held a spike to the ground, and she drew back to pound down on it with all the force she could muster. She hadn't figured out whose standard they were behind at the moment, and it didn't matter. It wasn't Damon's.

The tent would be for the lord's comfort, whoever he was. The foot soldiers, bowmen, squires, and camp boys such as herself would sleep on the ground, exposed to whatever weather this late spring held in store.

But she was not complaining. She had a big, warm bed at home with a maid to plump her goose-down pillow, and she had no desire to return to its luxury.

She hammered with some force, thinking of Edwin of Lothian and of Damon.

Somebody howled, and when the man holding the spike looked up she realized it was the big-nosed soldier she'd bumped into earlier—and that she'd made the mistake of striking his thumb.

"Damn ye clumsy oaf!" the soldier bellowed. "What be yer name, boy?"

Gwyneth swallowed. "Tucker," she said. "I'm sorry for—"

The soldier cut her off.

"What are ye doing?"

"Setting up the tent?" She hadn't meant it to come out as a question, but his hard stare unsettled her so much that it did.

"Why're ye hanging about here? Who are ye?"

"I told you, my name is Tucker, and—"

"Ye're a page, a serving boy, what?"

She bit her lip, thinking fast. Most lords had dozens of pages and serving boys.

"A serving boy," she gambled.

"Who do ye serve?"

"I, uh—" She waved gamely at one of the standards ahead of them some distance. "Him."

"Is that so?" he asked with a queer tone that told her she'd made a mistake. "I don't remember seeing ye before. And I've been with his lordship these past two years."

"Um, I must have made a mistake. You know, these camps are so confusing. The banners all look the same. If you'll just excuse me—"

He was staring at her with that uncomfortably knowing look again, but he made no immediate move to stop her as she backed away.

The tent was fully erected now, and she slipped around the corner of it, thinking to escape her mistake, when she almost ran full-face into Damon.

Holy mother of Eleanor!

The flaps that made up the tent door were beside her, and she darted inside. *Had Damon seen her?*

Her pulse pounded in her ears. The newly erected tent was empty, but she could hear men just outside. Soon they would unload possessions, a camp bed, chest, and other things, and they would begin to bring them inside. She had little time, maybe a few moments at best, but she counted them out carefully.

Waited, waited, waited.

She had to be sure Damon had passed. She wasn't going to let anything, or anyone, stop her. She'd come too far already. Closing her eyes, she breathed a sigh of relief that Damon hadn't burst in after her.

He hadn't seen her—or if he had, he hadn't recognized her.

She dared to peek out of the tent. The air was thick and cool, but she felt hot. Damon was nowhere to be seen. More relieved, she darted from the tent—

A fist gripped the neckline of her wool tunic, almost snapping her neck as she was yanked backward then spun around to face her captor.

The soldier's nose was even more misshapen up close. She wondered how many times it had been broken.

"Ye're not going anywhere," he growled. "Not till I talk to his lordship. First, ye're claiming to serve him; then ye're not. Then I find ye coming out of his tent where ye've no business at all." He narrowed his slitted eyes even more. "How do I know ye're not up to some ill? What were ye doing in there?"

"What ill would I—"

"I don't know. Who do ye really serve? Maybe ye're a spy for Manvel. How do I know ye're not?"

"It was a mistake, honestly, if you'd just believe me—"

"Ye'll tell it to his lordship," the soldier said. "I have my orders. Anyone lurking around, anything suspicious—I take to him. And ye're suspicious." His frown grew fiercer as he studied her. "There's something peculiar about ye, something definitely peculiar—" He stopped, still looking at her as if she were a puzzle he couldn't figure out.

Gwyneth swallowed, looked around at the other men nearby, rough soldiers just like this one, and she could see they would be no help.

The tent was finished, and they were waiting for the big, bumpy-nosed soldier. He was obviously the one in charge.

"Oh, no, there's nothing peculiar about me," she vouched firmly. "And I'm no spy. I'm here to work, that's all."

"Then there's work to be done," the soldier said, nodding toward the edge of the wood beyond the hilly meadow leading up to the castle.

There were men and boys running back and forth, hauling armfuls of brush from the forest to the water-filled ditch that surrounded the castle.

They were met with sporadic showers of arrows from the crenels above. The defense was only half-hearted. The lord of Manvel no doubt had given orders to save their ammunition for later.

But it was a dangerous job, and her heart beat a little faster than before.

"Come on then," the soldier ordered. "We've got to fill up the moat. His lordship's busy now, making siege plans with the other lords. Ye'll have to come with me." He frowned at her, and he released his grip on the nape of her tunic. "Don't even think about trying anything feebleminded, like running away." His slitted eyes all but seared her. "I'll have yer hide fer supper if ye so much as give me one bit o' grief."

She believed him. She had no doubt he'd be happy to squash her like a bug at the slightest provocation. He looked as though he'd enjoy it, too.

She'd have to convince his lord that she was nothing but a poor boy who'd joined the siege force along the way. It should be no trouble; she was no threat to his lord, or to anyone.

But that was a task for later. She realized she was just standing there, staring at the soldier. He gave her a shove to make her follow the other men who had already taken off toward the wood.

She took off after them and even found herself smiling as she ran.

It was a long way from Queen Eleanor's courageous ride into Crusade, but it was a start.

The moat would take days to fill. Gwyneth felt as if her back were breaking by the end of the day after carrying armfuls of logs and brush, and pushing cartloads of dirt, up the sloped meadow, then racing down again for more. Most of the time, she forgot that the bumpy-nosed soldier and his comrades were watching her like trained falcons ready to dive in for the kill if she made a wrong move.

She didn't care. She was actually having fun.

She would be here, doing this, whether anyone was keeping an eye on her or not.

As they worked, the siege camp came to life. Tents, food, weapons were unpacked and assembled with amazing efficiency.

While bowmen set up mantlets, temporary defenses of huge shields near the castle walls, the construction of the belfry was begun to provide access directly over the walls. Hundreds of soldiers could be housed within it.

A team of carpenters and engineers erected trebuchets aimed at the castle's weakest points while another team built the "rat," the covered framework that would protect the soldiers pushing the battering ram.

Throughout the day, intermittent arrow showers peppered the growing camp, but for the most part, the lord of Manvel was ominously silent. The heavy drawbridge of the castle was drawn up, the gate closed, the iron portcullis shielding it. Until the siege formally began with the first fire of weapons from the attacking forces, the lord of Manvel could still surrender without shame.

But the wooden shutters protecting the bowmen in the crenels as they fired down suggested Manvel had no such intentions.

Even now, carpenters on the walls of Manvel continued to erect even more elaborate side screens around key tower positions, with convenient gaps in the flooring where hot sand or oil could be dropped onto the attackers.

Manvel planned to fight.

Riders had approached the gate several times since morning, shouting their warning to surrender. There had been no reply from Manvel.

At the end of the day, during the last round of arrow showers, the boy next to her had taken a hit in the chest. He'd stopped for a breather and never took another breath again.

He'd died right there at her feet in a horrifying pool of blood.

They'd given them beef pies at midday. She'd been so hungry, she'd consumed three.

She'd retched every one of them up on the ground next to the dead, bleeding boy.

Now she sat in the middle of the camp, staring up at the castle walls, watching the dark shapes who watched them from high atop the walls of Manvel. Around her, the air rang with hammers and shouts, even at this point sometime past sunset, as last-minute work continued in the dying light. Dusk folded in on them as she sat there, bone-weary.

They'd done important work; filling in the moat was a principal strategy for easing their forced entry into the castle. She'd studied enough stories of sieges to know that.

But this was no siege story from an illuminuated manuscript, no tall tale told round a great hall.

This was real, and so was that boy's death.

Nobody had known his name. She didn't know if she wondered about his name because she needed to know it, or because it kept her from thinking about the blood.

Was Damon right when he'd said she wouldn't have the stomach for battle?

She pushed away the doubts because she didn't know what to do with them. The boy's death had put a pall on everything.

Her belly growled, but she wasn't sure—even now—if she could keep food down.

She picked out other sounds as she sat there: pigs, cows, goats. Fresh meat was vital to keep the siege force healthy, and they had brought it with them. She noticed now the serving boys passing out cups of something from the makeshift kitchen fires scattered about the camp. Foot soldiers and bowmen lined up, then crouched about on the trodden, now-muddied meadow to eat.

Already, as the dusk deepened into night, they were setting their cups down where they sat and lying back to fall asleep on the hard earth.

Gwyneth was shocked at how shaky with exhaustion she felt when she forced herself to her feet.

Aching, she walked slowly, twisting and darting between the large, sweaty, smelly soldiers. She had an idea she must be unpleasantly ripe, too.

She hadn't even thought of cleaning up, and now that she had, she dismissed the idea without the slightest regret. Ladies had to smell nice.

Luckily, she was Tucker now, because she was way too tired to care about smelling nice.

Pushing a stray lock out of her face, careful to keep her long, thick hair tucked up in her cap, she lined up to receive a cup of whatever they were handing out, determined to keep it down.

She couldn't believe it, but somehow, some way, the bumpy-nosed soldier, whose name she'd learned was Ryman, had let her out of his sight.

Or so she thought. That was when a hard fist took hold of her forearm and hauled her out of the queue.

"Not so fast," came the low, rough voice she'd come to recognize already.

She figured she'd still hear that voice in nightmares when she was ninety.

"I was just going to get something to eat—"

"Yer lord wants to speak to ye."

He dragged her out of the food line, around the lumps of sleeping bodies, toward the tent they'd erected earlier. He pushed apart the flaps, giving her one last strong shove to put her inside.

She stumbled over the threshhold.

There was no one in the tent. She looked around, bewildered.

"There's water in that bowl over there, and

there's yer pack," the soldier told her. "Clean up. His lordship wants to get a good look at ye."

The tent flaps slapped shut, thankfully. She was alone—but for how long? She didn't take time to look around, so afraid the lord would return and see her changing tunics—and see the bound material that hid her blooming breasts.

Off went the dull brown tunic; on went a dark green one.

The green one was clean, but that was all it had over the brown one. They were both serviceable and poor, but it was the best she could get away from home with on short notice.

She didn't care much about clothes, anyway. Fashion annoyed her. All that trouble over what? Fabric, stitches?

Who cared what one's clothes looked like?

She splashed water from the bowl onto her face, her neck, then wiped herself down as best as she could with the coarse towel the soldier had left behind. She was clean, or as clean as she was going to get.

She touched the hair that kept coming down from the cap, pushing it back into place. Her hands shook slightly.

What did Ryman's lord want with her?

Something niggled at the edges of her consciousness, and she went back to her pack. Something was missing. Several somethings.

The parchment, the quills, the ink. And her small, sharp, deadly dagger.

"Looking," a deep voice inquired from the direction of the tent entrance, "for these?"

She felt slightly faint from the panic that leaped up her throat, combining with the fatigue and hunger, and something else that teased at the edges of her consciousness—

Ryman's lord stood just inside the tent, his body bathed in sputtering candlelight. In his hands he held the things that were gone from her pack.

She could do nothing but stare for a long beat. His form was massive, she noted numbly, as she lifted her eyes from his hands to shoulders.

But then what could she expect of a man who commanded a soldier such as Ryman? The lord's face was hidden in shadows and yet—

Her pulse seemed to grow louder till blood roared in her ears. The hidden thing at the edges of her consciousness moved into the light of aware thought. She whirled, stunned, needing a moment to turn away—a moment to pray that this wasn't happening, that she had to be wrong.

She felt him coming closer.

Panicked, she took in the furnishings as if somehow she might see something that would help her. There was a travel bed and a table with chairs, and another worktable spread with maps and armor and food. She heard the sound of her things being dropped onto the far end of the table, and then—

She felt a hand on her shoulder, and then that hand propelled her by his very touch to turn again and confront him.

Her downcast eyes took him in from the bottom up.

He wore a fine blue tunic over gray leggings and black boots. Every line of the garments showed off a fine physique. He was a man of enormous strength.

"My lord—" she began, leveling her voice with care.

"Yes, my serving boy?" he said quietly.

His voice was quiet but hard. And yes, so familiar, too. She wasn't wrong, though oh how she wanted to be. Three years.

But she was not wrong.

She forced herself to lift her gaze farther, finally to his now-unshadowed visage.

"The serving boy," he went on in that burning-dead voice of his, "that I didn't know I had."

His gaze was as fiercely enigmatic as ever. Her pulsebeat went liquid and she indulged her first instinct—flight.

Two

Rorke of Valmond had had better days than the one he had just passed. He'd been paying absolutely no attention to where he was going, allowed his horse to step into a hole, had fallen off and slammed onto a pile of mangonel artillery. He was sore as hell, and the truth was, he didn't even know what he was doing here. He didn't care about this fight. He didn't care about much of anything these days except his quest—his madness, as he well knew most people called it.

He had no patience left for the boy who had taken one look at him and tried to bolt out of the tent.

But looking down into the terrified eyes of the boy as he held him fast, he felt a twinge of something long unknown to him—*sentiment*.

He added the painful moment to the sum total of painful moments that had led him to this night.

He'd been traveling for nearly a score of years, first as Wilfred of Penlogan's man, then as his own man with squires and soldiers of his own, with only a brief stint as Castle Wulfere's chief man-at-arms to break his wanderings in all that time. He was used to sleeping in a new place every night and facing a new battle every day. He had been a knight in the king's army once.

Now he fought his own personal war, his true enemy always just beyond the next village, the next hill, the next forest—

Somewhere.

Along the way, he often found other battles, battles he fought for the sake of fighting, like this one at Manvel. At one time, Rorke had fought for the king with his heart. Now he fought with his body and his mind because there was a battle and he wanted to fight. Because he could not find the real man he wanted to fight.

Because he had no heart, only a body and a mind and a will that kept him going.

He reminded himself that there were those who thought there was as little left of his mind as there was of his heart. The wriggling boy and the clamor of something old and unallowable still gripping him made him wonder if they were right.

So did the stupid mistakes he had made this day that had landed him with a sore body and an aching pride. He was not himself, was not focused the way he had once been.

He was ripe for killing, that was how he would have put it in the old days, in France, when he still had his heart, mind and body in one piece.

But he would not be bested by a slip of a boy. He was not that far gone.

"Stop fighting me, you little fool," he said. "I have no patience for your antics, and they do you no good."

The boy's eyes, so huge in his elfinlike face, burned up at him through the shadows.

They stood just inside the entrance to the tent. Outside, Rorke could hear shouts of men still settling in for the night, cooks clanging pots at the fires all around, horses snorting.

There was little quiet in a siege camp, and it all made Rorke feel very tired suddenly.

"I have questions for you," Rorke said. "We'll start with who you are."

"You had no right to go through my pack or take my things," the boy said, ignoring Rorke's inquiry. "And you have no right to hold me. I came to set up the wrong tent, 'tis all."

"Oh, really? And pray tell, whose tent should you have set up—Tucker, is it?"

"I, uh—" The boy Tucker looked everywhere but at Rorke.

Strange, how he could seem so innocent and so deceitful at once.

"Who sent you here?"

"That soldier, the one—"

Frustrated, he let go of one of the boy's arms to take his chin in hand, lifting it until he forced the boy to look straight at him. He still kept a firm grip on the boy with his other fist, still ignoring the pain the movement streaked through his sore chest.

The boy's cap was going crooked, and thick, brown hair peeked out of it. It was untamed, snarled—clearly uncombed.

He smelled of dirt and sweat and sun and . . . panic.

Rorke was momentarily taken aback by the desperation in the boy's eyes. Saints in hell, he knew more about desperation than he wanted to know on his own. He didn't want to know about this boy's pain, or whatever it was that shone so brightly in his huge eyes.

He focused on the boy's fierce bravado, the jutted chin—which seemed almost familiar, but then not. That bravado seemed to carry him despite the fact that even as Rorke watched, the boy shuttered that painful, bright panic deep within those big eyes, leaving only the innocent ferocity visible.

He was a fighter, this strange boy.

"Answer my questions," Rorke demanded. "You claimed to serve me. Why?"

"'Twas a misunderstanding," the boy explained tersely. "I was but trying to help, and the soldier, Ryman, mistook my intentions—" The boy broke off, chewing at his generous lower lip, eyes askance, as if trying to think of what to say next.

As if he were afraid and trying very hard not to show it.

Was he afraid of Rorke, or afraid of being found out? The more he looked at the boy, the more suspicious he seemed to Rorke. There was something odd about him, as Ryman had noted.

"Who sent you into this camp claiming to be my serving boy? Answer."

He shook the boy.

The boy squeezed his big eyes shut and clenched his stubborn jaw, turning defiantly away from Rorke's gaze.

Rorke shook him again, harder, and pulled his chin back toward him.

"No one," the boy cried, his big eyes flying open. "It was a mistake."

"It was no mistake. It was a lie."

The boy's face was still streaked with dirt even though he could see some attempt to wash had been made, but beneath that his skin was sun-browned and healthy despite the overall slenderness of his frame.

"Confess, it was a lie."

Rorke watched the fire burn fiercer in the boy's eyes, relieved to see it. For some reason, he didn't like the idea of seeing the boy's natural spirit cowed, even though he'd been trying to do just that.

Still, the sentimental reaction scared him. It was a softness that he didn't need, not now.

The boy couldn't be trusted. There was something wrong about him, Rorke just didn't know what.

Again, he felt the twinge of familiarity that made no sense.

He gave the boy one last jerk out of frustration—with himself as much as the boy.

"Yes, it was a lie!" he gasped in response.

"Then it is time," Rorke ground out, "for the truth."

Truth was not going to get her anywhere, but neither had the lie she'd told. Gwyneth's mind spun wildly as she tried to come up with something in between.

Something that would appease a man she had

never known to be appeased by anything. Rorke had ever been a hard taskmaster, and she doubted he'd changed, at least not in that respect.

But something had changed. His eyes, always so light and deep at the same time, were more tormented than ever . . . and empty somehow.

That bothered her in a way she couldn't take time to comprehend.

"Let go of me, or I'm not telling you anything."

She didn't know what she expected, but it wasn't his laughter.

"A slip of a lying boy, telling me what to do." He shoved her away from him, farther back into the tent, away from the flaps.

She just barely managed to keep her balance.

"You're telling me what to do," she said, sticking with her bluster. At least he'd let her go. It was an improvement.

But still he stood between her and the door of the tent. Between her and freedom.

"Because I can make you do what I will," he pointed out, still sort of smiling—or as much as Rorke ever smiled.

It was a grim sort of lift to his lips, as if it were uncomfortable, foreign. He was not a man prone to laughter.

"With me," he went on, "it is no bluff."

"You can try to tell me what to do," she replied, chin pushed out, knees wobbling a bit. She considered her odds of making it past him if she tried. "Don't expect to succeed."

She eyed the door and the distance to it. He hadn't recognized her, after all these years and dressed as a boy, at least not so far. But the less time she spent in his presence, the better. She'd already lost the dagger in her pack.

There was another in her boot, of course, but pulling it now seemed fruitless. She would need her wits to get out of this tent, not a knife.

"You are bold, boy," he said, the smile—grim as it was—gone as quickly as it had appeared. "Tell me, who is your master?"

"No man is my master," she said instinctively, then worked to pull her thoughts together. She'd made one mistake already, claiming connection to the lord whose tent turned out to belong to Rorke. She would not make another. She found the middle ground between truth and lie. "I ran away. I came on my own, with no lord, just fell in with the men as they came by on the road. I meant no harm, to you or anyone else. I'm sorry to have been a bother, and I will just—"

"You ran away? From whence?" He stepped closer, looming over her, his face shadowed harshly. "You are no serving boy. You speak well, as one with education."

"I *am* a serving boy," she countered, knowing she needed to become insignificant if she were to get away. She was inventing quickly now. "I am but an orphan. My parents fought in France—"

"Both of them?" Rorke had a brow cocked, the dark blond hairs catching the candlelight.

"My father," she corrected haughtily. "I meant my father. He was a soldier. He died, and my mother— she was sick. She died a few months ago. She had been sick a long time. I'm alone. I was—I was educated by my mother, who was learned in letters because her own father had at one time worked as a tutor, but of late I have been working as a tavern boy, and when I heard about the siege, I thought it was my chance to take up the sword, like my father."

She was proud of this tale.

For a moment.

It wasn't so awfully far from the truth. Her father, before his terrible illness and death, had indeed been one of the great warriors of his day.

"And who was he? Perhaps I knew him." Rorke's arms were crossed. "I was in France for many years myself."

"Richard." Gwyneth spouted the first name that came to her head. "Richard of Atwood."

Was there a Richard of Atwood who he would know? She hoped not.

"Where did he fight? Was he at Crécy? Calais?"

"Yes, both."

Rorke watched her with enigmatic eyes. She couldn't tell if he believed her.

"What lord did he serve?"

Eleanor's toes. She couldn't think, and she didn't want to say the wrong thing and get in worse trouble than she was already in.

"I don't know," she said instead. "I was very young, and he died. My mother settled elsewhere after that time, and—"

"Where?"

She swallowed thickly. Too many questions.

"Penham."

The hamlet's name came out of memory. She

had heard it mentioned, some guard's overheard comment once at Castle Wulfere. She didn't even know where it was.

"Penham," he repeated. "Penham-upon-River or the Penham near Norwellyn?"

Great piles of fly-covered dung! Did it matter which she chose?

"Penham near Norwellyn."

She was relieved when he went on.

"And your family? Your other relatives?"

"None," she lied, cutting off that line of questioning. "None at all. All dead." She glanced toward the tent flaps.

Why did not he just let her go? He was watching her, like a feral cat that was going to pounce any moment. She was no danger to him, but he had no idea what a huge danger he was to her.

One day.

She had made it through only one day at the siege, and she'd retched her guts out on the field and been caught in Rorke's tent.

This wasn't working out the way she'd imagined it.

The door of the tent was near and yet so very far. He stood between her and it, but the moment had come. She had to get out, before it was too late.

Her knees were weak, her belly empty, and suddenly she felt angry, angry, angry. This was the man who had shown her the art of war, who had impressed her and awed her and made her want to be just like him. And he was the man who had ridden away from Castle Wulfere without a good-bye.

He had been her only ally, albeit a reluctant one, in her quest for knighthood, and he had left her.

So who was he to come back into her life just in time to ruin it?

He was frowning at her.

"Boy, are you going to faint?"

"No, I am quite fine," she said between clenched teeth, thinking. "Actually, I am hungry, if it matters aught to you." She glanced at the food on the table. To offer it to her, he would have to move . . . away from the door. "Your man did not let me sup before he pulled me back to your tent."

The grim flex of Rorke's jaw told her he found her cheeky response annoying, and yet, as she had hoped, he moved. She watched him carefully, biding her time, not wanting to act too soon or too late.

Or too stupidly.

"Well, then, if 'tis the fault of my man that you hunger, I must have it matter to me," he said, watching her all the while that he stepped closer toward her. "Satisfy yourself, please."

The path between herself and the door was clear. He was near, too near, but if she was lucky, she could make it, disappear into the darkness and the crowded camp—

The boy was going to make another run for it. Rorke watched him, and waited. He would not let this boy Tucker—if that were indeed his name—get away, but he wanted to see how hard he would fight.

He knew for a fact that the boy was not from Penham near Norwellyn because there was no Penham near Norwellyn. There was no Penham-upon-River, either.

The only Penham Rorke knew of was the tiny hamlet east of Bristol. Clearly, Tucker—if such was his name—had no idea where the real Penham was located.

And deceit came easily to his tongue, as if he had no choice.

There was a desperation to him that Rorke did not want to, and yet was increasingly forced to, uncover. The boy was lying. But about what else and why, Rorke had no idea and no time to consider.

The moment came.

The boy sprang into action.

Rorke barely had to move. He simply reached out to the side, clapping his arm around the boy's shoulders with one great swing, and whirled him back around. Rorke sucked in his own burst of discomfort at the movement against his sore ribs.

Other impressions followed. Wavering, shocking. Impossible.

The boy was pinned to Rorke's chest, his slender body trembling, the feel of him beneath the shapeless tunic somehow discordant with his outward appearance.

Rorke yanked the boy's chin up and the wool cap flew off. They stood there, staring at each other, frozen.

She was the first to move.

Three

He caught her with as little effort as before, forcing her down atop the thin, narrow mattress of the travel bed as she kept up her fruitless struggle. He was on top of her, pressing down against her.

Damn him, he was heavy. He was suffocating her.

Gwyneth jammed her knee where it would do the most damage. For a blinding pulsebeat, she could have sworn he was going to strike her in return. Without even thinking, she screamed.

He moved just enough to clap a hand over her mouth. He was breathing hard now, wincing, but was horribly, deadly calm beneath the anger.

"Lady," he rasped, "you force me to unpleasant measures, and you will regret it, that I swear."

She couldn't tell him how much she already regretted.

It had all started out too easily. She had walked away from Castle Wulfere without so much as a peep from a doormouse.

It had been her last stroke of luck. Stupid, stupid, stupid.

How could she have let this happen? Oh, but she knew, and it was her own fault.

She had been caught, unveiled by the damnable

hair Damon had bribed her with Rorke's training to grow. She'd kept it shorn as the boyish girl-child she'd been with her page's tunics and her stick swords, and had kept it her own deepest secret that she'd actually come to pleasure in the silky length it had later attained.

Her one mad vanity had done her in.

She despised beautiful gowns, had no use for ornate jewelry. But her hair—she loved her hair.

She should have shorn it the way Elayna had hers the year she'd sneaked away in a minstrel's cart to become a copyist. Of course, her new life as a copyist had never materialized. Before Elayna had gotten even halfway to the city, she'd been lost and wounded in a dark, misty forest where she'd rediscovered her long-lost love.

Together, Elayna and Graeham had returned to Penlogan and uncovered the mystery that had touched three men: their brother Damon, Elayna's now-husband Graeham, and most of all Rorke.

It had been Damon who had spent a year locked in a French dungeon, falsely accused of the murder of Rorke's beloved Angelette.

Then it had been Graeham's father, Wilfred, who had been set up as the murderer. Damon had been released and Wilfred executed. Too late it had been revealed that the true murderer was Wilfred's priest, Father Almund, now dead, aided by Rorke and Damon's comrade-in-arms, Ranulf, who had used the false accusation of Wilfred to usurp the lordship of Penlogan.

He had disappeared over a cliff after being unmasked by Graeham and Elayna.

That Ranulf had been presumed dead had not been good enough for Rorke. Three years ago, he had set off from Castle Wulfere on a mission to find out for certain if Ranulf was dead . . . or alive.

The mission of a madman, many had whispered, for how could a man go over a cliff and live?

This night was the first time Gwyneth had seen Rorke since the day he had left without saying good-bye, and so far, she didn't like what she saw. Maybe he was crazy like everyone said. He looked crazy enough right now.

He managed to use the free hand not gripping her mouth to push the snarled hair from her face. Staring, staring, staring.

The exact moment her identity hit him felt as if it lasted forever.

Then, from the corner of her eye, she caught a shadow of movement at the door of the tent. A huge, dark shape.

"My lord? Is everything all right? Is there trouble with that boy—"

"Nay, Ryman," Rorke said, his voice quiet and deadly even though he still breathed heavily. "No trouble with the boy. In fact, he's gone now. Don't think we'll be bothered by him again. I'm just having an unexpected bit of sport with this wench instead."

He never took his eyes off Gwyneth's. She could see the shock of recognition moving aside as fury took its place.

There was a beat of silence.

"Ah, well, of course, then good eve to you, milord," came Ryman's reply, and his tone sounded surprised, as if the last thing he expected was to find his lord with a woman, and yet pleased at the same time.

The tent flap closed and he was gone.

Gwyneth took advantage of the opportunity of having Rorke's hand pressed so viciously against her mouth to bite the inside of his palm.

She might as well have been a flea biting a stallion.

Rorke moved his hand, but there was no chance for her to respond, to run. No chance at all. He moved his hand to first roughly push the hair out of her face, clearing her vision and revealing her fully.

He shoved back and tore at the ties of her tunic, pulling it apart to reveal the bound wrapping that hid her breasts.

"Dammit, dammit, dammit," he whispered, his anger harsh in his voice, his gaze lifting back to her face. "What the hell do you think you're doing here, you foolish little idiot?"

How could she even breathe with the material bound so tightly about her?

Rorke didn't think further, only acted, drawing the dagger he'd taken from her earlier and, with a sharp move, slipping it against her chest. She gasped, the sound choked by the tightness of the bonds. Bonds she'd endured all day in the field, working with the men as one of them. Before she could even attempt to stop him, he sliced through the thin material.

There was a flash of white flesh and then she clamped her arms over her chest, instantly hiding the soft mounds he'd released, but not before he saw chill air tighten pink nipples.

She was cold, and he was suddenly hot.

"What are you doing?" she cried.

"Helping you," he said roughly, surprised at his own shaking voice, "to be honest. That's a start."

Her fingers, shaking too, he realized, fumbled at the strings of her tunic;then she took a deep breath, seeming to work to steady her nerves. She finished tying the tunic and gripped her hands into fists.

He pushed off her and stood, and she scrambled back against the wall of the tent where the bed jammed against it, tugging again at the ties of her tunic, drawing the clothing back into place. But beneath the loose-fitting garment, now where there had been flatness there was roundness.

Rorke was having trouble thinking. His hellacious day was not over yet.

"Damn all the saints, you cannot be so stupid," he ground out, concentrating away from that full roundness. "But you are. You're here. What the bloody hell—" He stopped, shook his head, almost still thinking if he looked again—clearly—he would not be staring down into the captive, mutinous eyes of his best friend's sister. "You're incredibly stupid, do you know that? Do you know what could happen to you here? This is a siege camp!"

His words were harsh, but true, and born of frustration and anger and a gut-level concern. He was hit as heavily as he'd been hit by her identity with thought after thought of all the terrible things that could have happened to her in the siege camp.

Thank God he had found her first—or, Ryman had found her.

Ryman had looked after her all day on the field. Nothing had happened to her yet. And heaven help him now because he had to make sure nothing did.

It was a responsibility he intended to turn over to her brother as quickly as possible.

"No, my goodness, I had no idea," she responded with icy smoothness. "Thank goodness you explained. A siege camp, is it? Well, then I'll be careful. So don't worry. I'll just run along and—"

She actually made to get up, but stopped when he strode menacingly back to her.

"You idiot," he repeated as his mind still churned. "Sit the hell down and don't move a muscle."

She looked as if she would strike him dead if that were at all possible. But since that wasn't, she did the next stupidest thing, which was to try to run again.

He struggled to contain the unexpected strength of her as he caught her flying body going by.

She was small, always had been, but not delicate. There had never been anything delicate about Gwyneth of Wulfere. She got one of her hands free and landed a blow on his cheekbone as she tried to make good her escape once more.

"Enough!" Finally, he grappled her arms down again, pinning her back onto the bed.

Her tousled head flung back and forth in frustration with the force that held her fast. And dammit, all he could think for a whole blasted moment was that she was . . . beautiful.

He didn't know who he was more angry with at that thought, her or himself, and it was a struggle to control his raging feelings.

"Enough," he said again, more subdued, and he held her there on the thin mattress of the tent's traveling bed as her panting lessened and her thrashing finally ceased.

The heat of her body seemed to grow uncomfortably warm against him. He scowled to himself, incredulous at the realization that Gwyneth—boy, girl, child—was creating this reaction.

The sensation only added to the bafflement and irritation of the entire situation.

He had to keep telling himself to stop noticing that she was so terribly beautiful. It was the hair, the damned hair, he thought suddenly. The instant it fell down on her shoulders, it had turned her into some kind of wild nymph, cast a spell on him, turned his head upside down.

Though if he were honest, he'd have to admit her eyes were bothering him even before. But he'd thought she was a boy then. Now she had that damned hair and those damned breasts and—

"Get off me!" she shouted at him, pushing at him with her fists.

"Will you obey me, Gwyneth of Wulfere?" he growled back.

"Will you get off me?"

"When you give me some answers. Starting with, what the hell do you think you're doing here?"

She didn't reply, only turned her head and stared at the wall of the tent, her mouth set in rebellious lines he remembered only too well. God's bones, she was the same trial she'd been all those years ago, one he'd only endured then as a favor to a man to whom he owed much loyalty—her brother, Damon.

He would endure her now for the same reason.

But he could only endure so much.

"When you let me go, you will get answers," she said tightly.

He should have expected that she would not drop the confrontation. When had she ever made anything easy?

"Say that you will do as I direct." He was not ready to trust her in spite of his own growing need to put more than the breath of distance between them that separated them now.

He could not allow himself to feel this physical response to her. She was still a child, wasn't she? It could only be the long period he had gone without a woman's touch that would allow this shameless desire.

The lines of her body stiffened again, and yet finally, finally, she whispered, "Yes, damn you," in the most unyielding tone he could imagine, and he pushed off her again, eyeing her warily all the while because he suspected she was lying.

She sat up, her hair tangling around her, and he became suddenly, acutely, aware that he could not deny the obvious.

This was no child.

This was a young woman. Three years.

It had indeed been three years, and those three years had changed her.

In their struggle, the ties of her tunic had loosened again, and the shadow that emphasized the swell of her breasts on either side was hard to ignore. He forced his gaze to lift and he found himself staring into her eyes, vivid and dark, their rebellion mixed with that mysterious pain, and he realized again how familiar, and yet not, that she was.

She was wild, strong, and, he suspected, still very innocent. But she was more than that now. There was something he'd never noted before, that deep pain—or had it always been there and he simply hadn't looked closely enough?

That thought bothered him, and he fought the reaction. She was trouble, and that was all that mattered.

"Cover yourself," he grated, realizing that she did not realize her state.

Frustrated when she didn't move fast enough, he tore the ties together himself, which made things that much worse because his knuckles skimmed her warm, soft skin and his breath caught and their startled gazes snapped together and—

He swore and took a huge step back.

"That's right," she said with a tone he didn't quite understand, full of that pain somehow, "I am a woman. I am not the child you knew."

He couldn't deal with following this line of conversation. He couldn't think of her as a woman.

She was Damon's sister. That was how he had to see her.

"For all I can see," he lied, "you are the same maddening, defiant, outrageous child you ever were. Even worse, now you are apparently without your wits, or do you have some explanation for what the hell you are doing in the siege camp outside Manvel, dressed as a boy, sneaking into tents, putting yourself into twenty different kinds of danger—"

"The only danger I've been in so far has been due to you!"

"You are in no danger from me."

His mind instantly leaped to the truth, that she *was* in danger from him.

And she was a danger *to* him.

He couldn't even look at her and think straight. He kept remembering how strong and supple her lithe body had felt beneath him, and about that shadow between her breasts, and about how even though she smelled like a man, she looked like a woman and that combination was so insanely arousing. He hated simpering women with their perfumes and their fancy clothes. He had no patience for their frivolity. It was why he settled for whores in the night when the physical need inside him got too bad to ignore.

Or at least it was one reason. There were more, but he didn't deal with those reasons.

But damn her, Gwyneth of Wulfere had aroused him, and even now still aroused him, and he was even angrier with her for that.

He pivoted away, knowing it wasn't wise to turn his back on her but unable to look at her without a break to pull himself together. He took a long breath, and another.

"Why are you here?" he ground out then, forcing himself to swing back again.

She still clutched at the torn ties of her tunic. There was pride and spirit in her sun-browned, grime-streaked face. She wasn't beautiful in the delicate manner that was appreciated by the world, but there was an energy and tenacity to her expression that lent her strong features an air of sorcery that the tumbling hair framed perfectly.

The peculiarity of the so-called boy became the bewitchment of the woman. She wasn't beautiful, and yet she was beautiful, all at once.

Her mouth set in its mutinous line and she didn't answer.

"What did you come here to do?" Saints, he wanted to shake her. "Do you know what could have happened to you if any but I had discovered your true sex? Do you think there is any position for a woman in a siege camp but that of a whore?"

He clenched and unclenched his hands at his sides. He used the throbbing of his sore ribs, intensified by the physical struggle with Gwyneth, to focus his thoughts.

Control. He was famed for his control, his focus.

He watched as her eyes widened. Astonishment or fear, he couldn't tell which. Then she, too, exhibited an extraordinary control. She tipped her chin, her hands still gripping those torn ties, and stared him straight in the eyes.

"I came here," she said coolly, "to fight."

Four

He made no immediate response to her announcement. He actually walked away from her. Then she could hear him swearing, to himself, under his breath.

What now?

She'd expected arguments, more berating. She was prepared for that, accustomed to it. Then she would fight for her point of view. She would not beg him—she never begged—but she would make him see her case.

She was already preparing it, running all her reasons through her mind, organizing her thoughts—

He came back to her with a bowl of something that had been on the table, and a spoon.

It was his supper, and she realized he was giving it to her.

"Eat," he said, his hard voice gentling briefly, the way she remembered from so long ago.

It was the tone he would use when she'd fallen one last time beneath the weight of whatever load he'd placed on her that day, and he would come at last to say enough and put compresses on her aching muscles and pat her on the shoulder and relent a little on his constant effort to make her give up her dreams. It was in those moments that she'd thought she saw the real Rorke, the one beneath the cool exterior that was so very untouchable.

And yet now she wondered if she had ever seen the real Rorke, if she had ever known him at all.

She had thought they had some kind of relationship then, a strange one, but a relationship all the same. But he had left her without a word.

So what did she know of him, after all? Nothing, she had to admit.

Nothing then, nothing now.

She had thought for a strange moment that he had actually desired her. He had cut the bound wrapping away from her breasts as if he were tending his horse—with that much emotion or notice—and yet, for a heart-fluttering instant, she had thought there had been more in his eyes.

And for an even more heart-fluttering moment, there had been something inside her that had sighed and whispered, *Please*.

Oh, she was a fool! The whole thing was confusing and stupid.

The man had yet to breathe who found her sunbrowned, wild strength attractive. And amen. That was how she wanted it.

And Rorke—

He was the last man alive she'd want to notice her, anyway!

She realized he was watching her, and she looked up from the soup, the spoon half-lifted to her mouth. She focused on something she could understand. She *was* hungry. She could convince him better on a full stomach.

He was so near she could almost hear his heart-beat—or was that her own?

And there was some strange tautness—

"Eat now," he ordered, breaking the peculiar moment. "I have no time for a fainting wench. You are bother enough as it is."

"I do not faint," she said, irritated. Eleanor's chin, she hated being compared to weak, simpering saps. "I'm not like other women."

He ignored her, and she ate the soup in gulps that brought his attention back to her. She was embarrassed, then she felt stupid for being embarrassed. She did not sip her soup like a lady. She gulped like a man, and she would not stop. She slurped deliberately, and he frowned.

He brought her the cup, which turned out to be bad ale, and then walked away, giving her his rigid back. He was at the door of the tent, speaking to Ryman again, who apparently waited right outside. She could not overhear, though she tried.

She consumed the soup and ale and went over her plans in her mind. Damon was in the camp somewhere, but Rorke was not immediately taking her to him.

There was a chance—

"I thought you wanted to talk," she blurted. "I thought you wanted answers."

He shrugged. He had come to sit at the end of the table—the better to watch her?—while she supped.

"I changed my mind," he said. "I don't expect to like what you have to say." He sat back, arms crossed. "So why bother?"

Gwyneth kept her frustration under control. Making him mad wouldn't help.

She needed to make him an ally. He had been one, once, even if he hadn't ever quite admitted it. He'd admired her abilities, her enthusiasm.

"I can't go back," she said flat-out.

"You can't stay." He moved positions again, resting one hand on the table.

"I need to stay." She put the spoon down by the bowl. She reached out. She could just touch him from where she sat. The skin on the back of his hand was warm.

He flinched slightly, as if her touch were strange to him, unwanted, and yet the way his eyes locked on hers made her think otherwise.

Those confusing, mixed-up feelings came at her again and for no good reason she remembered the warmth of his fingers brushing her when he'd cut through those strips that had bound her breasts. Even now, her nipples tightened.

So strange.

And yet it also felt good in a peculiar way.

She wanted to scream. By all that was holy, this was no time to get silly, womanish feelings. She steeled herself against her strange reaction to his nearness.

Luckily, she realized he was going on in the usual stupid way men went on at women, which doused the weird-hot feelings she was experiencing.

"You need to go home. You need to act like the lady you were born to be. You need to obey your brother and guardian."

What had she expected from him? He was just an arrogant man, like all the rest.

She focused on her anger.

"You are not home," she returned, not thinking, just swiping back at him. "You do not act like the lord you were born to be. You should be home with a wife, tending your demesne, but instead you roam the countryside at will. You live your life the way you want, not the way your birth decrees. Why should I be different?"

"Because you are a woman." He moved abruptly, pushing back from the table, from her touch. He was standing now, towering over her. "Nay, a foolish girl."

She knew she had stepped across a line that was rarely crossed with Rorke. He never spoke of *her*— his beloved dead Angelette. He never spoke of his home, Valmond. He never spoke of anything, she realized, but whatever he was doing at that very moment.

And yet he was haunted, possessed, by this past of which he never spoke.

Suddenly she was even more angry than before and she couldn't control it.

"Oh, this is just fine." Her eyes were burning. She stood, unwilling to let him loom over her even though she had to tilt her head back to meet his gaze. "You are allowed to wallow in your pain, in your past, in your freedom, while I am allowed nothing. You are one to judge, one to decide what I need. You hold my life in your hands and you are making decisions about which you know nothing.

You are so smug in all your manly privileges. You are—"

He grabbed her arms. She didn't know if he was afraid she would strike out at him, or run away, or if he even realized he was holding her at all.

"Think of me what you will," he bit out. "But know this—I do not want your life in my hands. Do you think I want any woman's life in my hands— ever again?"

The last sentence came out raspy, pain sketched in every word.

That pain was Angelette. Her name hung between them, heavy.

"Then let me go. Let me disappear into the camp. Forget that you ever saw me. Forget—"

"I cannot."

She had to stop herself from begging.

"Why not? Let me live my life my way. I'm not a child, Rorke. I'm a grown woman. I know what I want. I know—"

"You know nothing!" Now he let go of her arms but only to take her face in his hands, but this time his touch was achingly tender. He leaned down into her face as he held it, as if examining her for the first time. "You are so beautiful, so young, so full of life. This is a place of death. This place is not for you."

She stood frozen, staring at him. He'd called her beautiful. This stunned her.

"You are right," he went on, his voice barely above a breath in the night. "You are a grown woman. You're a lady. You're—"

"What?" She didn't want him to stop.

She didn't know what he was going to say, only that she wanted to hear it.

One of his hands moved from her jaw, the thumb grazing along her cheek, then he dropped his hands, both of them, and stepped away.

"You have everything I have lost. Go back to it."

The sudden absence of his touch left her feeling strange. She was still upset that he'd called her beautiful.

Or was she upset?

She couldn't figure out what she was feeling, and she knew that he hadn't said what he'd started out to say.

"I want my freedom," she repeated numbly.

She didn't want to think too hard about her feelings, or his—of what he'd lost. She knew what he meant. He was reminding her that she had a family who loved her and he had no one.

But he was wrong.

"I have nothing that you don't," she continued her argument, her thoughts still unorganized, her skin still missing his touch. "I am losing my family, now, tomorrow, the next day, whenever I am forced to wed. Damon is forcing me to wed. And I will have lost them then as surely as you have lost yours to death."

He shook his head, and in the short distance that separated them, his eyes shuttered. "No," he said in a horrible voice. "No, you will not have lost them as surely."

She felt the burning behind her eyes again. He was right; she knew he was right. Her family would still be alive and she felt ashamed for her selfish words, but part of her knew that for all the truth that her family would be alive, she *wouldn't*—she would be dead inside.

Desperation filled her, but she had time yet to convince him, and she had to use that time, not give in to panic. As long as he hadn't taken her to Damon, she had time.

"Just listen," she said, striving for calm even while her pulse was leaping about oddly. "Listen to what I have to say."

"Sit down. Finish your meal."

"If I sit, if I finish my meal, will you listen?"

There was a sound at the tent opening, and he went there. She saw Ryman come inside.

"Lord Wulfere is gone from the camp," Ryman reported. He shot Gwyneth a curious look, then turned his attention straight back to his lord.

Oh, sweet Eleanor, how wrong could she have been? He had sent Ryman for Damon! And he hadn't even told her.

No doubt, he had deemed her knowledge of that fact inconsequential.

Men!

"Gone?" Rorke repeated.

"Gone. He was called home, urgent news. Some business that couldn't wait."

Urgent news. Gwyneth didn't have to wonder what that would have been. Elayna and Belle must have gotten together, realized Gwyneth was neither here nor there. They'd sent someone after Damon without delay.

Was there even one small part of her plan that was working?

"I'll need my horse," Rorke said to his soldier, "and a pack of food if you can obtain it quickly. And get word to Sorvalham. I will return as soon as possible."

The lord of Sorvalham was the one leading the siege in the king's name.

Finally, he swiveled his gaze to her where she stood, unmoving. The reason he wanted his horse hit her.

"No!" The word exploded out of her. She wasn't thinking, only reacting, as she leaned down with practiced swiftness.

The knife from her boot slipped easily into her grip. She had no idea what she was going to do with it.

She had no chance to make a plan. But what good were plans, anyway? She'd be as likely to succeed without one as with one at this point.

Even before Ryman could move, Rorke had her arm yanked behind her back, the knife thunking uselessly to the hard ground, her body pinned against his ungiving chest. Damn him, he had taught her every move she knew, so it was no wonder he could head every one of them off.

"I'm in a hurry," he said to Ryman in a deadly calm voice. "Get my horse. Forget the food."

Five

Gwyneth sat at the table, her look scathing yet docile. Rorke was not fooled. He knew her mind was busily working. Gwyneth's mind was always at work.

Her hair was unruly about her shoulders, her tunic creased, yet she gave no appearance of care. She watched as he replaced her scant possessions in her traveling sack, adding his latest acquisition— her boot knife.

He did not, of course, return the sack to her, and he would not until they arrived at Wulfere.

Rorke had not explained Gwyneth's presence, or this unexpected trip, to Ryman. His men had no need for the information. He did not use her name.

The less that was known of Gwyneth's presence in this siege camp, the less potential damage to her reputation.

He would bring none of his men on this brief journey for the same reason. Gwyneth was a young noble lady who knew nothing of the ways of the world. This escapade was folly beyond belief.

In truth, Rorke blamed himself as much as he

blamed her for it. Was it not he who had trained her, who had made her believe she could fight?

He had done it for Damon, but he would have better served his friend—and Gwyneth—if he had convinced Damon that the course they had set upon, the training of Gwyneth, was a mistake. He had tried and failed and given up, and in that he had failed his friend as well as Gwyneth. Damon had been blinded by love for his sister.

Rorke had been the one thinking clearly, and yet he had aided and abetted in the foolishness that had come to this consequence.

And he had to admit, he had been proud of her, so proud of her, that sometimes he had even thought they were doing the right thing, after all.

Seeing her now, he knew he had to have been wrong. She was independent, ungoverned as a wild creature of the woods. With that hair flung about her shoulders, she looked like something wild, too.

She was nothing that her world expected of her.

He felt the dangerous heat inside him again. Pray God, what was so wrong about her was what so appealed to him. She was strong—not just in body but in will—and he respected that quality. He didn't want to dampen it, but heaven help her, she was a danger to herself, wasn't she? He didn't want to be the one who had to decide what would become of her. But once again, fate had placed her welfare in his hands. Why?

Which of his many sins was he paying for to find himself in this situation?

He had almost forgotten how complicated she could be. Three years, and he had rarely thought of her—had rarely *let* himself think of her. Her training, despite his initial hesitance, was a good memory.

She was a good memory.

But he was focused on other memories now, and to let in something good was to let go of that focus. He couldn't do that.

Yet her life was in his hands whether he wanted it to be or not.

Ryman returned. Still Gwyneth said nothing, merely sat and watched and waited. Anger glittered in those dark eyes of hers, simmering. Rorke flung his cape over his shoulders, and grabbed the sack.

Ryman had brought back wrapped packages of food despite Rorke's words to the contrary, and a flask. Rorke placed the items in the sack.

"Yer horse is prepared, my lord."

Ryman had also brought a cloak for Gwyneth. It was rough but serviceable.

"I will not travel anywhere with you," Gwyneth said when Rorke approached her.

Rorke felt the beginnings of a headache coming on. It had been many nights since he had slept well, and there would be no rest this eve, either. Not as long as he was with Gwyneth.

But the alternative—to wait in the camp till Damon returned, or even merely to wait until dawn—was rife with peril.

He had to get Gwyneth away from this place before she found a way to escape him, to rejoin the siege, or worse, to fall into the hands of some unscrupulous soldier under the mistaken belief that he would help her.

He had an obligation to Damon, and even to Gwyneth, to get her away from this place as quickly as possible, before more harm was done.

"If you do not mount up willingly," Rorke said wearily, "I will bind you, toss you over my horse, and we will proceed that way. 'Tis your choice."

The bright, angry darkness of her eyes dimmed. He could see apprehension, and then her eyes changed again, willfulness taking over, and he couldn't tell what she would do: mount willingly or force him to toss her over the back of his horse as he had threatened.

Gwyneth, the woman, was still a shock to him. She was a mysterious stranger and a familiar friend at the same time.

Unwanted memories kept pushing upward in his mind no matter how hard he tried to reject them.

He remembered teasing her, laughing with her, fighting with her. . . .

She never gave up, never. He had a flash of recall: Gwyneth standing in the pouring rain of the outer bailey, refusing to go inside until she had hit the mark in her arrow practice.

He could have dragged her in by her scraggly wet hair, but he had respected her stubborn streak. They had stood in the rain and muck together. She would not leave, and he would not leave her.

And she had finally shot the arrow straight through the heart of the target.

"'Tis late for travel," she argued. "Why not wait for dawn's light?"

Heaven help him, she looked just as stubborn

now as she had that long-lost day in the rain. He held out the cloak to her.

"And give you that much more time to think of ways to escape me? I think not, my lady."

They picked their way over sleeping bodies in the camp. Rorke gave a low whistle and a black beast came forward, standing ready. Rorke mounted up, then leaned down, holding his hand out to her.

A young knight called Walcott knelt, cupping his hands for her. Oh sweet saints, she wanted to run.

How could she go back to Wulfere?

Damon would lock her up. She would be forced to wed Lothian.

Her brother loved her, she knew that, and in truth she adored Damon in return. But he had ever been baffled by his four hurting, orphaned sisters, and even with Belle's help, he had struggled to raise them. He wanted only what was best for her, but he was wrong in this one thing.

This had been her chance to prove it to him, but now . . .

Gwyneth looked over her shoulder. Where Ryman stood, two more men had joined him. There was no way she could escape, not here, not surrounded by Rorke's men. She looked back at Rorke. His face was impassive, yet she could see the controlled victory in his eyes. Rorke had won. Damon had won.

She had lost.

Gwyneth lifted her chin, stepped into the man's

cupped hands, and reached for Rorke's outstretched one.

They began their journey into the night. The
sounds of the camp were quickly absorbed by the
vast darkness into which they headed. Rorke apparently disdained to speak to her. He kept a
resolute air about him, his grip firm around her
waist.

She felt his breath graze her cheek when she
leaned back and his warm palm tighten against her
belly when she leaned forward.

There were things about him she had never noticed as a child, but she tried not to think of them
now. She was not prepared to give up on her cause.

But he was not prepared to listen. It seemed as if
he pretended she was not there when she tried to
persuade him of the uselessness of his endeavor.

"I will only run away again," she began. "I will go
another direction, find another siege, another
army, another battle. You can't stop me. Damon
can't stop me."

Next, "I will live under no man's rule. I would
sooner eat bugs and drink the milk of dandelions
in the middle of a secret wood all alone for the rest
of my life than be a wife. You can take me home,
but you cannot make me marry."

Then, "Can you not see that I was not born to
be a wife? I burn eggs when I boil them. I forget to
put wicks in my candles. The brewery exploded and
caught the entire outer bailey afire the time I made
beer. I near-blinded Belle when she tried to show
me how to make soap."

And, "Save yourself the humiliation of my escape. I will not let you take me back to Wulfere. Let me go now. Damon will never have to know you saw me."

Still no response.

Finally, in desperation, "Don't you understand? I cannot marry him. I do not love him, cannot possibly love him. My life will be misery. I will die inside. I will—" She stopped, realizing she was close to begging.

"Damn you," she cursed at him. "You trained me for this! You! You taught me to sweep stables, curry horses, clean armor, wield a sword and lance, shoot arrows and swing maces."

He had no response for her. His horse continued on, step by step taking her back to Wulfere and Damon and Lothian.

Gwyneth fell into angry silence in return. She focused on the dark misty land around them and, most of all, on preventing herself from crying.

Tears would do nothing but reveal to him her weakness.

She settled for shivering violently instead. She wasn't sure if she was cold, or if it was merely her body's reaction to the panic she was holding in so fiercely.

The cloak he'd thrown over her was doing nothing to stop her chills.

She heard him curse and shift, and pull a blanket from somewhere, and without stopping, toss it around her.

He muttered something about the frailty of women, something she didn't catch. She didn't know which was worse—when he was ignoring her completely, or when he was treating her like a child.

"I did not ask for your help," she pointed out between gritted teeth. "And I do not want your help."

"I do not give a damn whether you want it, my lady. You *need* it."

Arrogant!

"You are no one to talk of what I need! What do you know of me at all? You have not seen me in years. What do you care if I live or die, and how?"

"On that, you are wrong, my lady. I would have you lead a long and fruitful life. A safe life."

She made a snort of contempt but managed to suppress further bitter retort. It was clear that he saw her as weak and incapable; she was a woman, after all. She didn't have to show him her tears for him to think her soft. It had been years since he had seen her fight, and he had forgotten that she was strong.

Saints, Damon saw her every day and even he thought her weak and incapable of running her own life without a man to protect her.

Gwyneth had experienced so many squires and pages and guardsmen—especially ones who were brand new to Castle Wulfere—express astonishment when she challenged them to some competition or another.

No man ever expected her to be strong, or smart.

The night was spinning on, and as they rode into it, she began to shift her plans. She pulled his blanket close about her, feeling warmer now as her mind worked.

Escape, that was her goal, not caring what Rorke

thought of her. She had to forget about him. He would not help her.

She had to help herself. Perhaps in weakness was strength. She had to convince him that she was no longer able to run.

Then she would escape. She would not return to the siege. That would be hopeless. But she was not afraid to be on her own.

This time, she would cut her hair. She would pass as a boy with surety then.

She would find a way, a place, a battle, a home— even if it was in the woods, alone, the way Elayna's husband, Graeham, had lived in the woods, honing his warrior skills. He had hidden his identity for years while he'd trained and plotted and prepared for his future. There was no reason she could not do the same.

She *would* do the same.

All she needed was another chance.

She'd performed hard physical labor all day, but she remained nerveless, beyond exhaustion, as she waited for the right moment.

The moon had come out from behind clouds, lending a silvery magical shimmer to the night landscape. They were in a place of rolling hills, wooded and sweet-smelling with the scent of spring. The trees were not close together, but it was dense enough in this light to provide cover and confusion once they were on foot.

He might be stronger than she, but she was faster and lighter and smaller.

And she had nothing to lose.

She moved her head to casually catch a glimpse

of him. He was so close, and so unrelenting in his focus. He rode bareheaded, shunning any headpiece on this night journey, leaving his gold hair to gleam almost white in this strange light. His blue eyes were shadowed, his features near perfect.

Women had ever swooned over the lord of Valmond, but Gwyneth never recalled Rorke paying the slightest attention to them.

He had ignored them, as he ignored her now.

But for all that he appeared to ignore her, she had no doubt he was intensely aware of her every breath.

She let her eyelids drift shut, but behind them, she was wide awake. She counted in her head, letting her legs, her arms, her spine relax gently, in what she hoped would appear to be a natural course of sleep.

Finally, her head bobbed toward her chest and she swayed rather heavily to one side, forcing Rorke to command his steed to halt while he shifted to better his grip on her.

Her position was uncomfortably snug. Her upper body and head were supported in the crook of his shoulder, almost as if she were in his embrace. There was a long beat when she opened her eyes and found him staring down at her, looking at her—really looking at her as he hadn't for hours—and in that silvered darkness she felt a pang inside that almost had her pushing away from him simply to end it, to make that pang stop, but she forced herself to remain still.

She had to appear exhausted, which was made easier by the fact that she was stunned.

Damn him for being so incredibly handsome, and damn her for choosing now to have to notice. For the first time she understood why all those maids had giggled behind their hands whenever he walked by, and why they would run along the ramparts to watch him ride out of the bailey, and why they would sigh and swoon if he even said a passing good day to them.

Yes, she understood.

But she was not one of those silly girls, thank good Queen Eleanor. She was smart and tough and totally unmoved by any man.

"Rorke . . ." She spoke with deliberate weakness. "Can we not rest? I am so tired."

She let her body go even more limp, forcing him to shift again to increase his support of her.

"I worked hard all day, you know," she pointed out. "You cannot expect me to ride all night."

She turned her head into his chest, distracted by the momentary flash of concern in his eyes. He smelled of man and leather and horse.

His lightly padded hauberk was firm but soft. It actually felt good, having his arms wrapped around her so securely. She hardly ever let anyone touch her, and even then only her family, but there was something so reassuring about his strong arms that it threw her as much as his amazing eyes.

The something was . . . safety, she realized with a shock. His eyes and his arms made her feel safe.

And that was ridiculous.

There was nothing good or reassuring about Rorke, she reminded herself doggedly. And certainly nothing safe.

She had learned long ago to rely on herself, not others, and she wouldn't change now. And yet, these feelings were strange and powerful. They made her think of the past, their shared past. She had admired him, confided in him, trusted him. If only he would listen to her now. . . . If only she could explain what was in her heart. . . .

He had believed in her once, hadn't he?

And stupid or not, she had believed in him.

He had been her hero.

The valley through which they rode was filled with old oaks. The silvery moonlight turned murky here, hidden beyond the canopy of leaves.

His horse slowed, and she knew that he was responding to her plea. He dismounted, managing to swing her down with him as if she weighed no more than a sack of feathers, and she realized she didn't want him to let go of her. Maybe not ever.

Bloody boils, what was taking over her mind? Her head was buzzing; her heart was pattering.

Sweet Eleanor, save me, she prayed, because she knew, just one more time, she had to give her hero a chance.

Six

"Let me go."

Rorke still held her in his arms, but he knew that wasn't what Gwyneth meant. She was asking him to let her run away, even now, weak and worn down as she so plainly was.

Hell and damnation, did she ever give up?

"No."

She was silent in his arms for a long beat. "Please," she said at last in a tormented whisper, and he wondered what that word had cost her.

He was tormented, too.

Was he doing the right thing? He couldn't stop questioning his decision, but what other decision could he make?

"No one ever has to know that you saw me in the camp," she went on. "No one *does* know. Only you and I. It would be nothing for you to let me go—"

"There you are wrong."

She ignored him. "There is nothing left for me at Wulfere, nothing. Damon is done parading suitors through the castle. Suitors who don't want me, anyway—not the real me."

There was an ache in her voice at that.

"What man would want me as I truly am?" she

posed, though she didn't wait for a reply. "I am not biddable. I am not sweet or dainty or refined. And I do not want to be! I have driven them all away, all but this one who will not be driven. He is not a bad man."

She turned her head away from him now as she went on: "His family, all his children and his wife, died of plague. He promises to change me, turn me into a lady, to make me ride in cushioned litters and never, never will I touch a sword or bow again. He is prepared to take me on, he says, and he will not fail.

"He is an older man, rather fatherly, very patient and ready to rid me of my wild ways, and in return I am to give him many heirs to replace the ones he lost. He means well, and Damon—I think Damon is relieved, so relieved, that this kind, well-meaning man is willing to take charge, take the burden away from him—but I—"

She lifted her gaze to him again, and he saw such torture there, and openness, nothing hidden now.

"I will die if I have to marry him," she whispered.

Rorke took in her face, her wild-nymph beauty. She had done it again, brought to life that persistent pang inside him. Emotion.

He didn't want these feelings—compassion, pity, and more, more that he couldn't face.

"You will not die," he said, but he wasn't even sure he could convince himself. "It is your lot in life as a woman to obey your brother, your guardian, and eventually, your husband."

"It doesn't have to be this way. What harm is

there in letting me slip away now, before anyone even knows you found me?"

"There is plenty of harm already," he argued. "Your family misses you. They don't know where you are. You ran away. They must be sick with worry. You disappear, without so much as a good-bye—"

"And you left with a good-bye?"

He stared at her. "That had nothing to do with you." He had begun this quest of vengeance three years ago with the need to push everything else out of his mind, including Gwyneth, and now for an appalling moment, it was as if time had reeled back and he saw exactly how he had hurt her.

The knowledge was disturbing, and worked to further break down his defenses against her. But just as he felt his own defenses crumbling, he could see her own building back up.

"Gwyneth—" he began, but had no certainty how he meant to go on.

She didn't let him finish, anyway.

"Forget it." The softness was all gone from her eyes. "You did what you had to do, and I did what I had to do. It's all in the past. Just let me go now. It matters naught to you."

"It does matter." He had to touch her face now, somehow compelled. Her thick lashes lowered and she hid her gaze from him. "You were a brilliant girl, Gwyneth. You are a brilliant woman. Any man would be lucky to have you—just the way you are— spirited and strong and determined. You are *perfect* just the way you are, and I was always proud of you." He felt a surge of anger that anyone would want to change her, and yet be powerless to do anything about it.

But he could do one thing.

"I'm sorry. I should have said good-bye. I owed you that, and more, for making you aspire to be something you could never be."

Her gaze flashed back to his. "It's not true—I can do it. The Order of the Garter is considering the admission of women." She was speaking fast now, excited. "I will apply to them. I will—"

He was shaking his head, and she stopped.

"You're dreaming, Gwyneth."

Damon would never allow her to enter the Order, and without her brother's permission, she would never be admitted. It was a conundrum that had no solution.

"There are some things in life we cannot control," he said. "You must accept that."

"I will not accept it!"

"You have no choice," he said grimly. "And be sensible." He tried another tack. "Look at you—you're exhausted. Think you that a siege is a game? It is not, and you have barely discovered the work of it. You are strong, but you are not a man. A woman will never be equal to a man's task."

For the first time he saw moisture spike her thick lashes, and he felt cruel. He was stomping on her dream, and as mad as that dream was, he hated to take it from her.

He was at a loss for what else to say. He wanted to tell her again that she was a foolish idiot for the way she had run away to the siege, but the longer he spent with her, the more compassion he felt, and the more he remembered the wonderful, wild girl he had trained. The more he cared how much she was hurting.

He cupped her face in both hands now. "You are amazing. You will be amazing no matter where you are, what you are, who you are. You are everything I said, spirited, strong, determined, all those things and more—stubborn, willful, wild, frustrating, annoying—"

"Those are not compliments."

"Aren't they?"

She set her jaw. "I am not gullible. Though you must think me so."

"No." He drew her face back to him. "You want the truth, and this is it."

But he was lying. There was more truth, and it was becoming more and more difficult to ignore. He closed his eyes against it, needing not to see her, not to look into her sweet, rebellious eyes, not to think about the fate that awaited her at Castle Wulfere—the fate to which *he* was taking her.

There was a stretch of silence in which she didn't move. And then she asked him something unexpected.

"Did you mean it when you said I was beautiful?" she whispered, her voice a mere breath between them, the depth of fragility she had just revealed taking his breath away. She never showed any care for her appearance, but inside, beneath all that tough veneer, she was a woman who needed to be found beautiful by a man.

He felt the heat of her against him, and he forgot all time and place, forgot right and wrong. He opened his eyes and looked into hers, knowing only hunger and need and her lithe, taut body—torture.

Yes, yes, yes, she was so beautiful. So trusting in this moment, and he didn't want to betray that trust but he didn't, couldn't, stop when she tipped her face just that breath closer and he placed his mouth so very gently on hers and kissed her.

Seven

Rorke's kiss was a confusion of things, hard and soft, heat and cold, the possible and the impossible. His body could be massive and punishing, but she found that his lips were gentle and sweet, exerting only the lightest of pressures upon hers and yet still resulting in a powerful reaction.

She hummed, absolutely hummed, down to every last fiber of her being.

It was a new tightness, this humming, a tingling sort of tightness she had never known before, deep inside, battling for some release that was just beyond her ken. Everything—the siege camp, the forest, Castle Wulfere, the fact that he had disappointed her again—faded away to nothing in the face of it.

There was only this kiss, this incredible kiss, and his touch, his breath, his scent, and it was all more than she could bear and yet there was no stopping. It was like being drunk and wanting more wine just the same. As if she could never have enough.

Then his kiss became more insistent, as if he too were losing control, swept away on this sea of newness.

His tongue plunged, invaded, and she encouraged him, invading in return, tasting him, drowning, losing what little bit of her mind she had left—Her heart started pounding faster and she felt light-headed, and this time it was fear.

It all came rushing back with terrible lucidity—the siege camp, the forest, Castle Wulfere, the disappointment. Losing herself.

Losing her life, her hope, her dream.

"No," she gasped against his mouth, fighting the tightness, the strangeness.

What had she done?

How could she have just trusted him again like that? Right after he'd disappointed her again! It was as if the years had fallen away and they were close again and he was the man she went to with every question, every need, every passing wonder—

Back to before he had let her down so terribly.

She hadn't been thinking at all, that was the only answer. But she had to think! She was not a child now, and he was not the man she had trusted. He had not been there for her then, in the end, and he would not be there for her now.

He was not going to help her, despite his flattering words, and she was a fool to have fallen so easily for them. She had spent most of her life without praise, and she had been engulfed by the tokens of it that he had offered. Engulfed so easily, so shamelessly.

His praise had run straight to her heart, broken down her stone door. Her secret vulnerability was exposed, raw, and she hated that.

Her breaths came rapid, rough, and she was having trouble thinking straight, still. Saints, she was actually shaking.

And the only thing she had on her side right now was that he was shaking, too. As he let her go, he took a shuddering breath of his own, and he didn't speak, as if he too couldn't think.

She didn't let herself consider what it meant that her kiss might have rocked him as much as his had rocked her. She took the chance to do what she should have done before they'd gone this far, before she'd revealed so much, before she'd kissed him, before she'd felt this awful-wonderful tingling tightness. She ran.

It had happened so quickly, so effortlessly, it took Rorke several still-shaking breaths to realize she was gone. It was as if she had evaporated right in front of him. He pivoted, caught a glimpse of her—almost gone already—a shadow running through the ancient trees.

A strong, vigorous shadow, not the faint, desperate girl who had lain limp in his arms, damn her!

He leaped back onto his horse with a muttered oath, lunging after her. She could outrun him, perhaps—she had ever been fleet of foot—but she could not outrun his horse. The huge stallion darted between trees, nimble, sure, but so was Gwyneth. The path she took was haphazard, turning this way and that to elude him. The moonlight caught her here and there, lending a silvery cast to her shadowed form, then she would rush again into the darkness of low limbs and bushes.

And then she was quite simply gone.

The trick was typical of her. He should have seen it coming. She was persistent and wily. She would not give up, and she would have no compunctions.

Rorke pulled in to a clearing, his mouth dry, his heart pounding against his sore rib cage. Stillness fell about him. There was no betraying rustle of leaves, no movement, not even a squirrel or a bird.

It was as if she had never been there at all, if not for the still-hot taste of her on his lips and the still-thundering beat of his pulse and still-throbbing ache of the heart that was supposed to be dead.

Gwyneth lay on spongy ground, her face pressed into the dirt, the rest of her covered by twigs and leaves. She had snaked her body into a thicket, desperate, and was in agony from that decision now—her breasts were crushed, and a nut of some sort was between her cheek and the earth and was growing remarkably painful—but she dared not move.

She watched Rorke dismount, then walk away from his horse to examine the ground about him.

"Lady," he called out, continuing to examine the dirt, leaves, trees, brush. "You are sore pressing my patience!"

As you are sore pressing mine, she wanted to shout back at him. There was something in his voice that upset her even more, and she realized what it was— concern, sincere concern. She couldn't let herself be drawn by it. She'd already made the stupid mistake of confiding in him with honesty.

She should have told him the duke of Lothian was a horned beast who had threatened to beat her nightly.

But no, she'd had to tell Rorke the truth, lay open her heart.

Big, big mistake.

She had no doubt this was her last shot at escape. After this, he would probably do what he'd threatened to do already: bind her and throw her over the back of his horse. It would be humiliating, accompanied as it would be by the undeniable response she had made to his kiss. He would have captured her in every way, and she hated him for it in that instant.

He had made her feel, damn him. He had made her want and desire and need another person—*him*—and that was so terrifying and unforgivable. She lay there, shivering, knowing she would hold out as long as she could, which was forever.

She'd lost the cloak along the way somewhere, but she didn't care. She had no money, no weapon, no horse. But if she went home, she would have no life—at least, no life that she could bear.

Rorke stopped, closed his eyes.

Listening, listening—for her.

Could he hear her faint, panicked breathing? His head turned, slowly, toward her—

Something moved in the woods behind him, from the direction of the road, a flash of some light-colored material. The shape took form into a man, a man taking silent, measured steps toward Rorke, swinging a long-handled sledgehammer in his hand.

Shock gripped Gwyneth. She heard tales of roving bands of thieves, murdering criminals displaced by war and plague, but it was far different to experience their fury firsthand. Rorke turned, picking out the man's approach at the same time Gwyneth had seen him. Rorke pulled his dagger, but the man was already upon him.

With his free hand, Rorke grabbed the man's tangled black beard, ducking the blow. The two men rolled to the forest floor together, the man whipping the sledge again, barely missing Rorke's head. Rorke held him by the beard still, and in the beat after ducking the second blow, drove his dagger hard against the man's thick neck.

"Who the hell are you?" Rorke rasped.

"Doesn't matter who we are," said another voice. "It's what ye have in yer purse that counts, and yer fine steed and yer sword. We'll have them all, thank ye very much."

Another man stepped into the small clearing in the trees. He was burly, baldheaded, and as thickly built as his companion. He held a long, deadly dagger, and he pointed it downward, resting it against Rorke's neck.

"I suggest," he continued, "ye drop yer knife."

Rorke didn't move for a very long beat. He was on the ground, still in a death grip on the black-bearded man, who was laughing now in spite of the blood that oozed from his grazed neck.

"Drop it!" The bald man was growing impatient.

Gwyneth stared, horrified, from her prone position in the thicket. At that moment, Rorke's gaze razed straight across the forest floor—and locked on hers. She couldn't breathe for a terrible, pulsing moment. They weren't far apart, no more than a few long strides.

He removed the knife from the bearded man's neck, and tossed it down, the force of the motion causing the weapon to skid across the earth directly toward Gwyneth. She had but to reach forward, and it would be in her hands.

Rorke stared at her hard.

"Run," he said, moving his hard gaze to the man in front of him, releasing his beard. The man laughed, thinking Rorke was speaking to him, but when Rorke's gaze flashed back to Gwyneth briefly, she knew it was to her he was speaking. He'd given her his weapon, and he wanted her to flee.

He was protecting her from the thieves. The shivers she'd been experiencing turned to violent tremors. There was no way she was leaving him.

No way she *could* leave him. He'd set out on this dangerous night trek because of her.

"I've found," the bald man continued, his pate shining as the moon moved out from behind a cloud to slice down eerily into the clearing, "the best way to cut a man's throat is to plant the blade cleanly here, and simply slash."

He sounded as if he would enjoy it.

Rorke stared up at him with unflinching calm. "Is that so? How interesting. Thank you for sharing that information. Mayhap I can make use of it sometime."

The man made a snort that sounded like a cross between humor and irritation.

Gwyneth had no idea how much time she had

before one of the men made a move to follow through on their threats. She assessed the situation. She had the knife, but she could never reach the men quickly enough to make good use of it. She had to surprise them, give Rorke a chance to pull another blade.

If he had a dirk or some such secreted somewhere, in the back of his tunic or in his boot—

But she had to get that terrible sharp blade away from his throat first.

She backed, carefully but quickly, out of the thicket, her gaze scanning the ground around her. Her eyes fell on the one thing she could use—a heavy limb in the tangle of underbrush. It looked light enough to swing, but heavy enough to do some damage and long enough to give her a small buffer between herself and the two thieves.

As long as she moved swiftly.

Even as she stood, she saw the bald man yank Rorke's head back, the dagger still pressed to his neck.

"Say hello to the Devil for—"

Before he could finish his sentence, Gwyneth acted fast, praying for strength as she stood, hefting the limb up and running into the clearing at the same time.

All three men heard her coming; she made no attempt at secrecy. Grabbing their attention was her plan. The bearded man froze for a beat, and then heaved back his huge sledge over his shoulder. The bald man turned his head, relaxing his grip on Rorke. Before he could react further, Gwyneth smashed him across the side of the head with the branch.

At the same moment, Rorke moved out of the path of the whistling sledge, just barely, and sank a dirk he'd pulled so fast, Gwyneth didn't see where it came from, straight into the side of his bearded foe.

The man Gwyneth had struck roared, regained his footing, and swung his blade at Rorke, who had already picked up the sledge from the dead man's hand and used it to parry the blow. In a blur, he brought the sledge back up, knocking the man's chin so hard, he fell back like a stone, hitting the earth with a thud. But he was a man who could take pain.

He was up again, still with the dagger arcing in a savage fury.

"Don't come any closer, Gwyneth," Rorke said without looking at her, not taking his eyes off the bald man with the dagger. "Run. Now."

She had no intention of going anywhere, so she ignored him.

As the two men squared off, Rorke with the sledge and the bald man with his dagger, a movement caught Gwyneth's eye and she realized the dead man was not quite so dead.

She screamed a warning just in time for Rorke to turn, but not fast enough to prevent the bearded man from sinking a knife in Rorke's shoulder.

It was the man's last move.

Rorke slammed the sledge hard, despite the blood spraying from his own wound, against the bearded man's cheek. The other man lunged toward Rorke at the same time, but Gwyneth heaved the heavy limb again, cutting him off at the knees, tripping him.

Dropping the branch, she jumped on his back and jammed Rorke's dirk against his throat.

His astonishment alone held him immobile for the first few beats.

Rorke took in the scene with equal astonishment on his face. The bearded man behind him on the ground twitched convulsively, but he wasn't getting up again.

The man she'd jumped began to thrash, and Gwyneth realized she couldn't hold him down for long. The thought of actually sinking that knife into his throat made her feel sick. She didn't want to do it, but as she thought about the man's raw malevolence, she realized that she would, if she had to, to save her own life and Rorke's.

She could see now that blood seeped through the material of Rorke's sword arm. He was injured, badly. Yet he locked gazes fiercely with the man who had gone suddenly still beneath Gwyneth.

"Get up, move away," Rorke said to her. "You've done enough, too much."

He was angry, she realized, but not with her. He wanted this man. She could see it in his eyes. He wanted to kill this man with his bare hands, and suddenly she saw the raw power of him, but she also saw how he controlled it.

"Gwyneth, I need you to be safe," he said, repeating his order for her to move away, but it was too late.

With a roar of effort, the man moved swiftly to

hurl her off him. She rolled away, seeing nothing but the blur of his knife as he spun with her—and the blur of something else, beyond him, in the trees.

Another man.

"Rorke—" There was no chance to give Rorke her warning. She kicked the bald man in the groin, which brought a bellow of rage. His knife went flying, but she wasn't free. He was on top of her, one hand at her throat, the other pinning over her head the hand that held the dirk. She couldn't shout a word, couldn't even scream.

She realized he'd forgotten about Rorke, forgotten about whatever evil motivation had led him into this clearing.

He was angry with *her* now.

Fight, fight, she had to fight. She had to tell Rorke about the other man. She had to—

Black spots danced before her eyes. She was aware of the man's grip on her throat, of the dirk in her hand she couldn't use, the black spots coming together, Rorke's bellow of rage, and she knew Rorke was upon him.

Then the heavy weight and choking hands were gone, and she knew he'd moved to counter Rorke's attack.

She brought down the hand holding the dirk, and the man abruptly slumped to the side, off her, and she scrambled away thinking, *Oh God, Rorke killed him.*

And then she realized, no, *she* had.

Eight

Her hands shook as she slowly tore apart the sliced, bloody cloth at Rorke's shoulder. Gwyneth could barely think of what she was doing. She had to staunch the wound, fix it, somehow, only she didn't know how.

She was so damnably inadequate with wounds, blood. It was deep, and she kept thinking that it was his sword arm, though she didn't say it.

He didn't say it, either. She worked steadily at her task, knowing they had to get him bandaged and mounted. She couldn't stop thinking about the other man she'd seen in the trees.

How many men were there? They had killed two, but there could be more out there.

"Are you all right?" she whispered, worried.

"I'm fine," he said, but he was pale in the silvered light by the road.

There were no horses, no evidence of the band of thieves.

No sign of the other man Gwyneth had seen, despite her concerns. She wondered now if she'd imagined the other man, but she didn't think so and she worried about staying where they were for very long.

"For all that's holy, will you remain still?" she griped when he kept trying to stop her from fussing over his arm.

"I'm fine."

"Stop saying that!" she huffed. "You could have been killed, for the love of Eleanor! Look at this blood!" She felt dizzy.

He grabbed her with his other arm.

"Damn it, just stop already." He cocked his head. "Eleanor?"

She jutted her chin. "Eleanor of Aquitaine. Famous warrior of the Crusades. I don't suppose you'd remember her. She was a mere woman such as I. Far beneath your manly contempt."

He touched her face gently. "There is naught mere about you, Gwyneth."

"Stop it," she said from between gritted teeth. "Do not flatter me again. I was stupid once—"

"Stupid?" He arched a brow.

"Stupid," she repeated. "You flatter me, and next thing you know we're kissing instead of talking. Don't try it again. I'm not a simpering goosegirl. Your charms will not work on me."

He laughed. Laughed. She would have hit him, but it was evident he was already in a lot of pain.

"No, you are not a simpering anything, are you?" he said, and his voice was tight now, the laughter gone as pain usurped its place. "You had me going, though. I thought you were about to faint by the time we stopped—"

"I don't faint."

She pretended not to remember that she almost had fainted a minute ago over his bleeding arm.

Blood continued to ooze from beneath the bandage, which scared her. She pulled his tunic back over it. She'd slashed the side of it to get to his wounded shoulder.

"I didn't kiss you to shut you up," he said suddenly in a very low voice. "Just in case," he added, his eyes squeezing closed as she draped the last bit of material in place, "you were wondering."

Gwyneth felt her heart begin a new, dangerous pounding. She wanted to ask him why he *had* kissed her, and she wanted to know so badly, she almost believed she was bold enough to do it. But his eyes were still squeezed tight against his pain.

She touched his face, worry sharpening inside her. His skin felt like ice.

"Rorke?"

The irony struck her—she could run away now, easily. But she couldn't do it, couldn't leave him.

All desire to escape had gone.

It was Rorke who mattered now. She was afraid he wouldn't make it back to Castle Wulfere without her, afraid he would pass out long before he arrived. She couldn't bear the thought of something happening to him. She was shocked at how intense the feeling was, how the anger she'd felt toward him earlier was gone, replaced by this urgency. She had experienced so many strange feelings in the past hours with him, and this was just one more.

She couldn't explain it any more than she could explain the others.

"We need to get you to Castle Wulfere as soon as possible," she said. "We have to hurry. We have to get out of here."

"I am fine," he said yet again, but his breath was ragged, his voice hoarse. He was conscious, but barely so as they mounted up.

Together, they rode through the dark forest, and she prayed, pushing the horse as hard as she dared to get them home.

Rorke slept restlessly, almost as if between two worlds—one, where he was deep in some pit of delirious pain, both physical and mental, and another where stars shone and birds sang and there were no swords, no battles, no loss.

His family was there. And Angelette. And another figure, faceless but sweet and soft and somehow pulling him, but something told him she was part of that darker world that he dreaded, and that to find her, truly find her, he would have to battle through that seeping darkness, risking more than he'd ever dreamed of risking before.

And for the first time in his life, he wasn't sure he was strong enough for a fight.

Rorke of Valmond had been blessed with a dark talent for killing almost from the start. It had been natural. The first day he'd picked up a sword, his father had seen it when the tiny lad had held the lightweight stick sword over his head and brought it down with a crushing blow, breaking an earthen pot that had been in his way.

The lord of Valmond had been a simple man, more of the earth than of war, and he'd been almost relieved when he could send his son, at the age of six, to foster with one of the greatest knights of his day, Wilfred of Penlogan—a man who had a much better sense of understanding for his son's keen talents than did his peaceloving father who far preferred spending his days working on one of the several books of herbs he created with the monks at the nearby Millbridge Priory.

His elder son, Luke, had been similarly peaceable, a man born to run the demesne that would one day be his by right.

But Rorke had had no peaceable talents, and when he left Valmond, he hadn't looked back. He was, after all, a second son and destined to fight for whatever would be his in the end.

Fate had had another course in mind. Both of his parents, his brother, and his brother's wife and their newborn son had been taken by the cruel sweep of the dark plague that had sapped the life out of a full third of England's population at the end of the last decade.

Rorke had still been in France when he'd received the word, already numb from the death of Angelette, his betrothed, his love. The obliteration of his family in addition had been almost impossible to comprehend. Impossible to confront.

He'd gone home to Valmond. He'd found a deserted village and a dead demesne. He had not returned again, preferring instead to help Damon rebuild his demesne at Wulfere, to help Damon rebuild his life.

Rorke had no life left to rebuild. It had taken him some years to realize why he'd even survived when everyone else he loved had not.

Vengeance.

He could still hear Angelette's screams, see her blood, feel her limp body in his arms—though all of it was but the stuff of nightmares. The truth—and the guilt that crushed him—was that he had not been there to respond to Angelette's screams, to staunch her blood, to hold her body as the life passed from it.

They had planned to wed, to return to England together, meet his family, and live a dream he hadn't even known he had: a dream of love and marriage and children. It had all been a surprise to him. Rorke had never longed for home and hearth. Violence had long been his stock-in-trade. But then he had seen her, across the wide, candelit great hall of Chateau Voirelle.

Angelette had been there, visiting her sister, and Rorke had been a member of the occupying force. It was all a part of the ongoing, seesawing struggle between the French and English that had once seemed so important to Rorke.

She had danced that night, almost an other-worldly figure with her beautiful dark hair and her shimmery, pale skin. She was, indeed, the angel that her name decreed, and she had stolen his heart with one smile, one touch, one kiss.

How could they have known that she had stolen another heart, and that the evil in that heart would never allow their love to last?

In time, she had to return to her home, to Chateau Blanchefleur, and to her father, the lord of Saville. Already, she and Rorke had made plans to wed, but there would be no permission granted from her father. Saville would never allow an English knight to take the jewel of his castle. Not knowingly, anyway. And so they had schemed her escape, and ultimately, as it turned out, they had schemed her demise.

She was to sneak away dressed as a maid and wait for him in the village. The spot she chose was dangerous, but there was no stopping his sweet angel. She was in love, and he was so in love in return that he was blind to the risks, as was she.

They had planned everything—not knowing how easily it would come apart. The king had ordered Rorke's participation in a joust on the very day he was to meet Angelette. He had no choice but to accede to this request, but with his mind so distracted by thoughts of the night and how he and Angelette would ride for the Channel and love, he was stupid and careless. He was severely injured in the tournament.

There was no way to send word to Angelette at Chateau Blanchefleur—and it was too late, anyway. The only thing he could do was beg Damon to meet her for him, to send her back to Blanchefleur. But Fortune had already laid a shadow that was not to be lifted. The evil in another man's heart was already at work. Damon was waylaid, attacked, and by the time he reached Angelette, someone else had been there first.

Angelette lay near death in the village alley, brutalized. Raped. Strangled.

She could do more than whisper the words, "Help me," to Damon, who was the one, not Rorke, to take her into his arms and ride with her to the only place he could—Blanchefleur. She died, and Damon didn't see the light of day for a year.

Saville blamed him for his daughter's death, and even tortured him to seek a confession.

As soon as Rorke recovered, he spent those months of horror following Angelette's death searching for her true killer, along with their fellow comrades, Ranulf and his brother, Kenric. Finally, one of the village wardens confessed that he had seen the man who had killed Angelette. He had been afraid of Saville, well known for his maniacal fury, and had kept the secret for fear he, like Damon, would face torture and imprisonment simply for being near Angelette that night.

It had been Ranulf who had found the man and had obtained his confession.

The killer of Angelette was revealed: Wilfred of Penlogan, the same man who had fostered Rorke as well as Ranulf and Damon.

The news had been another blow. Wilfred had been more of a father to Rorke than his own had ever been, or had even wanted to be. The idea that Wilfred would have so loved Angelette himself that he would destroy her before allowing Rorke to have her was beyond grasping. And yet Wilfred had confessed, and no sooner had Damon been released than Wilfred had been executed by Saville.

Ranulf had been granted Penlogan by the king as a reward for uncovering the truth, and they had all returned home to England.

Rorke had gone on living, or at least breathing, in that shell of a life where he had believed that there was at least one true thing: that Angelette's murderer had been punished. Then had come the day he had discovered it was all a lie, the day Wilfred of Penlogan's son, Graeham, had reappeared, and that shell-life had been broken, destroyed forever.

Together with Damon, Graeham and Elayna, Rorke had discovered that it had been Father Almund, Wilfred's priest, who had secretly loved and stalked Angelette to her death, and that Ranulf himself had aided and abetted in the crime in order to seize Penlogan.

And so Rorke had learned that the man he had thought of as a father had been sent to his death under false pretenses, that Wilfred had confessed only because of his own age and frailty, knowing the torture that Damon had endured in his youth and vigor would be unendurable.

The suffocating guilt of Angelette's death had returned to Rorke in double measure, now carrying with it the responsibility for Wilfred's execution, made that much worse by the betrayal now of a brother-in-arms, Ranulf.

Father Almund had died, his body broken on the ground below the walls of Penlogan after his crime was revealed, but Ranulf's fate was less certain. His part in the murder had been uncovered, but he had fled through a secret tunnel beneath Penlogan and was chased over a cliff and into a churning, storm-tossed sea.

Others could accept Ranulf's sure death under those seemingly unsurvivable circumstances, but not Rorke. There was no body, and without a body, Rorke saw Ranulf everywhere.

Most of the time, those around Rorke certainly believed him mad.

Most of the time, Rorke agreed with them.

But from that day onward, there was never a village he passed through, a crowd in a fair or tournament, a face in a shopfront or a figure on a distant rise that he didn't think, *Was that Ranulf?*

Did he live, while Angelette and Wilfred did not? How could Rorke go on living—and not know?

Picking up his life again at Castle Wulfere had been impossible. For years he had gone without dreaming at all, numb if not dead, but now every night he heard Angelette's whispers.

Help me, help me.

And he saw the ax falling on the back of Wilfred's neck.

He couldn't punish Father Almund; he was already dead. But he could find Ranulf, who had made Father Almund's crime possible. He could avenge Wilfred's cruel execution. He had no choice.

Vengeance.

It was all he had, all he would wake to.

All except that sweet, soft figure who kept pulling him back to the dark world he had grown to despise, back to the pain and the present.

Nine

"Gwynnie, wake up."

A hand shook her shoulder, and Gwyneth jerked to awareness. Her mouth felt as if it were full of cloth, and her head pounded. She'd been plagued by headaches for days, a slowly lessening aftereffect of her struggle with the man in the forest.

But she had nothing to complain about. Rorke's condition was much worse. Fever had burned through him for days. His skin became a pasty white, and the fresh bandage on his shoulder hid what Gwyneth knew was a horrible wound. There was some question of whether he would have full movement of that arm again, but it was impossible to know until he woke.

Surely he had survived worse in battle. She had never felt so worried about anyone before in her life.

She'd insisted on being the one to change his bandages. Marigold and Belle helped, but she would shoo them away as quickly as it was done. She had seen every scar on his body now. There were many of them: long ones, thin ones, small ones, wicked ones. He had survived so much; he had to survive this, too.

She sat by his side to make sure.

Sometimes he mumbled, whispered, and she thought he would wake, but he didn't. *Angelette,* he would cry out in the night.

Angelette even began to enter her own dreams.

He loves me. He's mine. Mine, mine, mine. The sweet voice of Angelette played over and over in Gwyneth's sleep. Gwyneth had never seen Angelette, but she'd heard enough about her from others to guess what she must have looked like. And been like. Perfection basically summed it up. Angelette had possessed all the womanly virtues Gwyneth did not.

"Gwynnie," came the voice again, persistent.

"What? What is it?" The room was dim, and the shadow before her was slender and feminine and for just a second she thought it was Angelette, come straight out of her dream. "Who—"

"It's me, Lizbet."

Lizbet knelt down beside the chair where Gwyneth had fallen asleep. Gwyneth turned immediately to the cot where Rorke lay.

"He's okay. Don't worry," Lizbet said, putting her arm on Gwyneth's shoulder again, stopping her from getting up to check on him. "In fact, his fever's down. Isn't that wonderful?"

"What?" Gwyneth felt discombobulated. How long had she been sleeping?

"Belle and Marigold have been in here, seeing to him—just a little while ago. You've been sleeping for hours! Come to bed. Please."

"No."

"Gwynnie, please, I'm worried about you. You need to rest."

"You need to yell at me, you mean. You can't do that here." Gwyneth pushed Lizbet out of the way, determined to check on Rorke for herself. She placed her hand on his forehead, and was unbelievably relieved to find it was true—his fever had broken. He was sleeping more peacefully than she'd seen him sleep since their arrival. "He's going to be all right," she whispered.

Tears stung at her eyes and she brushed them away quickly in the darkness, not wanting even Lizbet to see them.

"Sweetling, I don't want to yell at you. Much. And I will do it here, if I have to." There was a trace of laughter in Lizbet's voice but also worry. "You're making us all crazy," she said softly. "First, you run away; now you sit in here day and night. What are you doing?"

"Has Lothian come?" Gwyneth asked, tense. She stared down at Rorke, unable to face her sister's concern.

She didn't know how to explain what she was feeling right now.

"Damon hasn't sent for him. Yet."

Gwyneth turned slowly. Lizbet's worried gaze met hers in the shadowed infirmary. The heavy scent of herbs filled the air around them.

"I won't marry him. I can't—"

"I know." Lizbet touched her arm. "I know. But you have to stop—stop keeping everything to yourself. Stop trying to solve everything yourself. You know, there are people who love you and worry about you and want to help you. Me, for one." Lizbet's voice cracked.

Gwyneth knew there was no one who better understood her than Lizbet, but even her closest sister couldn't share the pain she felt now. Lizbet had her birds, her falconry. And Damon hadn't taken that away from her yet. Maybe he never would. It was not so unallowable for a woman to train falcons.

Lizbet might yet live out her dreams. Gwyneth's were already shattered.

"You can't help me," Gwyneth said softly. "Everything's changing." She crossed the room, fiddled with the rows of bottled herbs on a shelf above a dinged oak table.

"Change with it." Lizbet came up behind her. "You can do anything you want to do. You are so strong."

"It doesn't matter how strong I am!" Gwyneth hissed, spinning. "It doesn't matter that I can shoot an arrow straight or heave a sword high or ride a horse fast. None of that matters."

"That's not the kind of strength I was talking about," Lizbet returned quietly. She put her arms around Gwyneth, not put off by her sister's stiffness. Gwyneth knew Lizbet saw through it to her hurting heart. "You are strong inside. No one can take that away from you."

"They can take everything else away." Gwyneth hated the powerlessness of her situation. She stepped away from Lizbet again. "Damon is furious. This is the last straw for him, I know it."

"You have to talk to him," Lizbet urged. "He's worried about you—"

"He wants to marry me off to Lothian! He wants to be rid of me."

"He wants to take care of you. He loves you."

Gwyneth felt hurt deepening. What was wrong with Lizbet? "You sound as if you're on his side."

"I'm on *your* side, Gwynnie." Lizbet stopped, stared at her sister for a long beat. "I know how you feel, sweetling. I know better than anyone. We were so alone as children. Our parents didn't abandon us, but when they died, it felt as if they had. Thank the saints we had each other, but even that was not enough. We've tried to fill that void, all of us—me with my birds, and Marigold with her art. And you with your swords and bows and—"

"I love to fight. It's who I am."

"Who you are is scared," Lizbet said insistently.

"What are you trying to say?" Gwyneth felt her whole body tingling, as if ready for something. Ready to fight. Yes, she'd used her skills to shield herself from the world's expectations of a noble girl, but not because she was afraid. She didn't want to be a lady and a wife. She certainly wasn't afraid of it!

"I'm saying you're hiding. And it's no answer. You're going to have to face Damon sometime. He hasn't sent for Lothian yet because he wants to find a way, any way, not to send for Lothian. But you can't keep using a sword to keep everyone at arm's length. You can't keep running. You have to meet him halfway, find another answer. You're not a child, Gwyneth. You're going to be wed whether you like it or not—and you can have a hand in the choice or you can force Damon to choose for you. It's time to grow up."

This from her little sister!

"What is wrong with you?" she sputtered. Lizbet had never wanted to wed any more than Gwyneth.

"Haven't you noticed how happy Elayna is now?" Lizbet said, her eyes softening. "What if she had succeeded in running away as a copyist? She wouldn't have her precious Sabrina and Sebilla, would she?" Lizbet pointed out, naming their eldest sister's twin baby daughters. "She's so content with Graeham, so—"

"Stop it!" Gwyneth turned back to the table. She couldn't bear to continue the conversation. "I'm not like Elayna. You're filling your head with stupid ideas. Not everyone is meant to have a love like Elayna and Graeham's. Don't get your hopes up. You'll just end up disappointed. Rely on yourself— you're the only one you can trust."

She saw Lizbet flinch and realized she had hurt her. But she was hurting, too, and she didn't know how to take back what she'd said without also admitting she was wrong.

And she couldn't, wouldn't, be wrong about this one thing.

There was a long silence. "I don't think we should talk about this anymore," Gwyneth said finally.

"Gwyneth . . ."

"Go away, Lizbet."

She waited for an interminable beat, but finally, she heard soft footsteps, then a door closing far across the room. The tears were falling fast. Thank God there was no one to see them.

Rorke watched Gwyneth swipe furiously at her cheeks, her silhouette a shape among the shadows. The conversation that had just played out between the two sisters echoed in his mind, almost part of the hazy, floating mist of the past days while he had laid here in the infirmary of Castle Wulfere.

He couldn't quite make sense of what he'd heard. It was out of context in a world that was out of context for him now. He only knew it was about pain, and that was a subject he knew well.

But even so, he wanted to reach out and hold her. He wanted to protect her from the pain.

But all he could do for now was close his eyes.

bundle. He couldn't remember...
...ing the room. The rest came back like
that, those weapons like a section

Ten

The next time Rorke woke, it was with the feeling that he'd endured a thousand battles with no rest in between. He couldn't recall when he'd felt so weak.

He opened his eyes, stared up at the raftered ceiling flickering with light. Candlelight. It was night. His gaze moved down stone walls, whitewashed, clean, shadows and light.

The smell of herbs.

Saints, he didn't even know where he was.

The men in the forest. Gwyneth. The camp.

It came back in vivid, lurching blows.

He sat up abruptly only to fall back with a moan he could not suppress. Pain ripped up his arm and then down to every end of his body. His brain felt seared, and he was blinded by it for a brief moment.

"Lie back, my friend," came a low voice. "I wouldn't be sitting up if I were you."

Rorke let loose with a stream of curses designed to let the owner of the voice know that his advice was quite unnecessary.

"Damn you, Damon," he said when he could breathe past the agony in his shoulder. "Damn this shoulder." He couldn't remember arriving here, but he realized he was in the infirmary at Castle Wulfere.

Gwyneth had gotten them here. Gwyneth who didn't want to be here at all had gotten him here.

She had saved his life at the sacrifice of her own.

There was more, as a dreamlike conversation came back to him in snatches. Gwyneth and some-one else, another female voice, talking about love and fear and pain—he tried to remember more, but it was like trying to hold on to mist.

He couldn't do it.

"How long—" It felt as if it could have been yes-terday, but he knew it had to have been longer.

With his good arm, he reached up and felt the scratchiness of a beard on his jaw.

"Four days." Damon scooted the stool on which he sat a bit closer, leaning over his friend. "You look better. You look like death, but you look better. I can't tell you how glad I am to see your eyes open."

Rorke felt a rumbling deep in his gut.

"I'm starving."

Damon grinned.

"Good." His face transformed when his mouth turned up in that winsome, rare smile that still gave maids pause despite his happily married status and the evil-looking scar that traversed one cheek. "You've had naught but what water and broth we could spoon down your throat these past days and nights. There were some bad moments, my friend, when I thought you might not open your eyes again."

Rorke said nothing, his mind still working to assimilate all that had happened.

"Do you know who they were?" Damon asked.

Rorke realized his friend was speaking of the men who had attacked them in the forest. "I was hoping you would. I was hoping by now—"

Damon shook his head. "Nothing. I sent men to scour the area, but nothing was found. No bodies. No sign of any other men."

Rorke closed his eyes for a long beat, suspicions he wouldn't voice swirling through him. There were times he felt as if he were not the pursuer. Times he thought that *he* was the pursued.

Had that attack in the forest been an accident?

Or was he mad, feeling the presence of ghosts that lived only in his tormented mind?

He knew how Damon would respond, so he kept the thoughts to himself.

"Thank the saints Gwyneth—she is all right, isn't she?" It hit him that he'd thought he was saving her that night, and she'd ended up saving him—using the very training he had given her so long ago. It was almost too much to contemplate. He didn't want to know what it meant. Their lives had come together suddenly, after so long, and so critically.

Damon was silent a moment. "She is. But you are another matter, my friend. You won't be able to return to the siege."

Another pause.

"Stay here," he went on suddenly. "Be my chief man-at-arms again. Or just be my friend. Damn it, Rorke, just . . . stay."

Rorke's mouth settled in a hard line and he looked away from his friend.

It was a matter of disagreement between them, this hunt for Ranulf, and had been for too long. Damon loved him like a brother, Rorke knew that, and he knew, too, that Damon had been through his own hell and had found his way out. Damon wanted the same thing for Rorke.

He just didn't understand that it was different for Rorke.

Retribution.

Rorke had much for which he had to pay. And he couldn't rest, not knowing if Ranulf yet lived. And he refused to discuss it with Damon.

"My shoulder," he said, aware of how serious the wound was without anyone telling him. This much pain could not be good.

And it was his sword arm.

"Time," Damon said. "Don't think about it now, friend. Give it time."

Rorke looked away, not able to bear the pity he saw in Damon's gaze. Only another warrior understood what it would mean if he could no longer fight.

"Tell me about Gwyneth. You said she was all right."

"She's fine, I promise. Banged up a little, but that's all. Nothing serious." Damon's face was grave. "That was some fight, and she played a part in it. Damn it all to hell, Rorke, what did we do when we trained her? What did I do?"

"You did nothing wrong," Rorke interrupted.

"I want to rail at her," Damon went on. "And I

have tried, but she only stares at me with those mutinous eyes and hides away from me. I know that she hates me, but I cannot let her join the Garter. I fear for her, Rorke. I fear for her so much. I love her. I don't know what to do."

The stool scraped again, and Damon disappeared, returning a few moments later. Quickly, a maid came in, bringing bread and soup and some very watered-down ale. Damon helped him to sit up, and Rorke nearly blacked out again. It was a long time he had to wait before he could begin to eat.

The pain was so enormous, he had to focus away from it or he could not bear it.

His mind kept returning to Gwyneth, though that was no better. He kept thinking of the strangeness of their lives coming together again now.

The warrior in him believed life was what one could see and touch, but there was a side of him that knew there were always other forces at work, that the mystery of God was the only answer that could explain how he of all men had found Gwyneth in that siege camp.

All he had wanted was to get her here, to Castle Wulfere, and leave her. She was Damon's problem, and yet that felt completely wrong.

But he had no more idea now than he had before of what else to do.

"Gwyneth was here, you know," Damon was saying quietly. "Here, by your side, almost every moment since the two of you rode into the castle bailey. I found her here, in fact, a short time ago, asleep, and carried her away. She's exhausted, though she would not admit it."

Something flickered in Rorke's mind, a misty memory, only half there, of a figure sweet and soft, with hands that brushed his forehead with cool cloths.

Gwyneth.

He couldn't eat any more of the food.

"She cannot marry this Lothian." Rorke didn't plan the words, they just sprang from his lips. Damn it all, he didn't know what he was saying, but he couldn't take the words back.

"I have no choice," Damon said. "I could lock her up here, but she could not live with that, nor a nunnery. I cannot let her join the Garter. There are no other suitors. She drove them away herself. Lothian is a good man. He will not beat her, or be cruel in any way. I have his word on that, and I trust him. Hell, Gwyneth could probably break the poor man in two. She has nothing to fear from him."

"Will he let her heave a sword? Ride a horse into the meadow at full gallop? Hunt? Swim? Shout and curse if she wants?"

These things were bothering Rorke suddenly. He couldn't stop thinking about Gwyneth begging him for her freedom. He had trained her. He had made her what she was today—totally unfit for her world.

What man understood her, would allow her the freedom she craved to survive?

"I need some peace in my life, Rorke," Damon said grimly. "I don't know what to do with her, I admit. I failed her. But I must see her safely settled, quickly, before she does something worse, runs away again. Before she ends up—"

Damon didn't finish. He didn't have to.

Rorke knew what he feared. He feared the same thing. That in seeking her freedom, Gwyneth would end up hurt, or dead.

Damn it all, he would be responsible.

And he realized how simple it all was, really. It was so obvious. A fierce feeling took him, so strongly that it almost seized his breath away.

He wondered, quite seriously, if his mind was even more deranged than the world already believed, because what had struck him now was either quite simple, or quite mad.

But he could see no choice now. He alone could save her.

Madness, of a certes. He'd never saved anyone he loved.

But saints above, if he could save Gwyneth, could he—possibly—save himself?

It was a horrible, frightening thought—and one he could not walk away from.

"Let her be wed to me," he said to Damon. "I'll let her be who she pleases. I'll let her be herself."

Eleven

Time suspended, brittle and cold, in the air of the large chamber Gwyneth had always shared with her sisters. It was Belle and Damon who were with her now, though. Lizbet and Marigold had been gone when she'd woken, which was just as well.

Gwyneth wasn't ready to speak to either of them. Especially Lizbet. She was still hurting from their argument the day before.

She didn't remember falling asleep, but she must have because when she awoke, she'd been here, carried by someone—probably Damon.

"What did you say?" Gwyneth repeated.

She barely recognized the lost voice that came out of her mouth. She stood there, in the rubble of her dreams, longing only to keep her pride.

"He has offered to marry you." Damon crossed the room to her, took both of Gwyneth's ice-cold hands into his as he continued. "He wants you to be his wife. And I have accepted."

Of course, he had accepted for her. She wanted to pound her fists on his arrogant male chest, but she was in too much shock.

"No," she breathed, mind reeling. She pulled her hands away, pivoted. The thick glass of the tall arched windows shone in with bright morning sun that hurt her eyes. She blinked, horrified at the moisture that pooled over, spilling. "He can't have said that. He's mad. He's feverish."

"He's well. Weak, but well." Belle closed the space separating them, touched her shoulder softly.

It would be so easy to lean into her warm, soft arms. Belle was like a mother to Gwyneth and her sisters, sometimes even like another sister.

Sometimes just a friend. But always, she was someone they could trust.

But Gwyneth didn't feel as if she could trust anyone now.

"I want to be a knight. I want to join the Garter." Even as she spoke, Gwyneth heard the futility of her desires.

"Sweetling, it's not going to happen," Belle said gently. "The Garter will never accept you without Damon's permission."

"But Rorke—why would he—" She turned back to Belle. She couldn't look at Damon. She was too angry with him.

Her sister-in-law's lovely face was drawn with concern, and Gwyneth hated to see all the worry around her. Lizbet was worried. Damon was worried. Belle was worried. Belle should be playing with her children, Ryen and Venetia, not fretting over Gwyneth's future.

Her whole family was upended over this situation. She was fighting with everyone.

Was *she* the one who was wrong, after all?

Guilt rammed hard into her chest, but what could she do? How could she give up?

This new twist, Rorke's proposal, only made her more miserable.

"What is this now, pity?" she demanded. "Why would he do this?"

"I don't know," Belle admitted. "But he wants to help you. He cares about you, he always has."

"He loves Angelette," Gwyneth blurted. She couldn't believe she'd said that.

She sounded—horrors!—jealous! Of a dead woman!

Over a man she basically detested!

If she detested him . . .

"Angelette is dead," Damon said. He was staring at her queerly.

"Oh, Gwynnie." Belle walked toward her again.

"No." Gwyneth turned away, moved across the room, but it didn't matter. It was too late. She'd said something irreversibly stupid.

It had just bubbled up out of nowhere.

"You have feelings for him." Belle's soft, gentle voice followed her across the room. "I know you always worshiped him, anyone could see it. Anyone except maybe the two of you. But you are not a child now, Gwyneth, and he—"

"Well, it's not as if I'm in love with him!" Gwyneth cried, spinning back to face her brother and sister-in-law. "You've all gone mad, that's what. I can't believe Rorke wants to marry me. You think I actually could have feelings for him. You—" She pointed accusingly at Damon. "You apparently think I'm an idiot, incapable of managing my own life."

"I don't think you're an idiot," Damon replied, looking stumped. "I think you're a woman."

Belle cast him a warning glare.

Gwyneth hated it when her brother looked as if he didn't know what to do. It made her feel sorry for him, and that was a mistake. He was ruining her life. She could *not* feel sorry for him.

"What about Lothian?" she said, changing the subject slightly.

"You would rather wed Lothian?" Damon asked.

Gwyneth blew out a frustrated breath. "No!"

"It's one or the other," he said.

Belle stepped in. "Rorke has asked for your hand. If you want to know why, you should ask him."

She reached out, tenderly lifted a lock of hair from Gwyneth's neck, skimmed her shoulder above the line of the plain tunic she was wearing.

Belle went on, "You have a decision to make, sweetling. This may not be the choice you wanted, but it's the only choice you're going to get."

They left her alone to think, but in the end, there was no decision. It was either Rorke or Lothian.

She could run away again, of course. That was always an option.

Considering the idea, she tiptoed to her chamber door and opened it.

Two soldiers stared back at her.

She shut the door with a bang. She was a prisoner in her own castle.

And there was only one way out.

* * *

He was asleep, or she had thought he was, when she arrived in the infirmary. His skin was still pale beneath the tan of the sun. His wound was bandaged freshly again and he was breathing evenly.

She sat down on the stool by his side.

He opened his eyes, and she noticed again how very bright the blue was in those enigmatic depths. Like the heart of a flame. Her heart pitter-pattered. Bad, very bad.

"Hello," she said.

He stared at her for a long beat.

She had to break the moment. "Why?"

Her question needed no elaboration.

"Why not?" he said at last.

"If you were not in pain already, I would hit you," she said, exasperated and angry and only too happy to find an outlet. "Do not answer my question with a question!"

He smiled, actually smiled, one of those amazing and unusual moments that made her breath choke in her throat. She experienced the sinking fear that Belle was right, that she had feelings for him, after all, more than as a mentor and hero, and that she had been so thickheaded that she hadn't known what everyone else around her had known forever.

But she couldn't afford to accept those feelings, especially now.

"I care about you," he said quietly.

"You care about your horse."

"I can give you your freedom," he added.

"And what," she asked, "can I give you?"

He looked away. "Nothing."

Silence stretched.

Finally, he went on. "Mayhap you can do something with Valmond, make it whatever you want, found your own order of lady knights. I don't care. You don't have to give me anything." He looked back at her again. "I don't expect you to be anything but what you are."

She blinked.

"What do you mean by that?"

"I mean, you don't have to wear stuffy gowns and host feasts and tend flowers. You don't have to play the lady of the castle for me. I don't expect you to act like a lady."

She huffed. "I can act like a lady."

What did he think she was, a wild pig from the woods? She thought about the night in his tent at the siege camp and how she'd slurped her meal.

Oh, sweet lady Eleanor. He probably did think she was a wild pig from the woods.

It's time to grow up. Lizbet's advice came back to her.

He glowered at her. "I'm just telling you that you don't have to do anything you don't want to do, and that's a promise."

She glowered back, annoyed with him and herself and life in general. She was confused about everything, and he was just making it worse.

Didn't he remember kissing her? Why wasn't he kissing her now? Even Lothian had kissed her when he'd proposed, albeit on the back of her hand.

She shook herself. What was she thinking?

Did she want Rorke to kiss her?

Of course she didn't. And yet her skin prickled and her heart pounded and—

"We are friends, you and I," Rorke continued. "Old friends. You don't want a husband. I don't want a wife. We're a pair."

Friends. "Right. Friends."

Rorke leaned back, pain washing the vestiges of his energy away. It had been worse than he'd expected. God's breath, he wanted her. In spite of how much trouble she was, he could think of nothing but her lips, her eyes, her nose—

Oh, God.

He remembered touching her, holding her, kissing her, and how warm and sweet she had tasted and he wanted to taste her again—

No. He couldn't do that to her. He was going to protect her, save her, take care of her. He was not going to take advantage of her.

He'd made her a promise, and he was going to keep it.

It was a week before Rorke was strong enough for the ceremony. Looking at him in the chapel, Gwyneth saw it would be difficult for anyone who didn't know about the attack to realize anything had ever been wrong with him at all.

He stood at the altar, tall, powerful, though beneath that fine gold tunic, she knew he was in pain.

She walked toward him on trembling feet. There was a feast afterward, but it was all a blur to Gwyneth. They left immediately afterward. His men had been sent for from the siege camp.

Damon had ridden back to Manvel for a few days, long enough to see the lord of Manvel's defense crumble in the face of the siege army's greater strength, and then had returned posthaste to see his sister wed.

The intervening period had been difficult for Gwyneth. She was out of sorts with her sisters, and herself. She couldn't get along with anyone, and she was sure they were all glad she was leaving.

They set off for Valmond in the cold of a spring rain. In the darkness of the heavy evening, she had her first glimpse of her new home. She had ridden her own horse, and Rorke kept pace with her, his expression one of taut control. She knew every jostling step was throbbing pain to him, but he never mentioned it.

The wind had made a mess of the simple braid in which she'd confined her wild hair, and her cloak was soaked. But it was the chill inside that scared her. Every heartbeat that took them away from Wulfere also seemed to take her away from the Rorke she knew.

"We are here, my lady," Rorke said, his voice cool, impersonal. Not cruel, just . . . detached.

She couldn't read him, couldn't guess what he felt now looking at his home again. She knew he hadn't been here, spent any time here, in many years.

Birdsong scattered around them in the evening mist, and she realized that was all there was, birdsong. No people to greet them. No villeins coming from the shuttered cottages of the village as they rode by, no servants rushing down the road from the shadowed mass that was the castle.

Against the pewter sky rose turrets and towers, fanciful crenellations and arched windows. No moat, but a gate, a heavy one. A closed gate.

It creaked wide, opened by unseen hands.

"Where is everyone?" she asked as they rode into a deserted bailey.

Rorke dismounted, then lent a hand to her, his good arm. She saw how he winced at the movement, but knew he would reject any attempt to fuss over his injury.

"There is no everyone," Rorke answered finally. "There are a few servants, yes, and you will soon meet them. But other than that . . . they are all dead."

The wind chose that moment to blow through the open gate and into the bailey, whipping her hair into her face and sending a shiver to her bones. She lifted her gaze to the circular keep straight ahead.

At the very highest window, she saw a movement, a face. Watching.

Then the face was gone, and she wasn't sure if it had been real or her imagination. It had been a long, long day and she was tired, and Rorke's careful distance only added an element of emotional fatigue to the situation. So much had changed in her life so fast. She knew she hadn't taken it all in yet, and she tried to put her uneasiness down to that fact.

"Welcome to Valmond," he said, his voice almost

that of a stranger to her, something different about it now, something she couldn't put her finger on.

As she stared at his harsh profile against the eeriness of his home, she wasn't sure what it was that she so feared—this place, or this husband whom she didn't really know at all.

Twelve

Within, the keep was no more welcoming than without. The hall was dark, lit only by the slanting moonglow cast through the slitted windows near the top of the hall. On the floor, there was no fresh herb-strewn straw; instead there were gnawed bones and moldy bits of nameless scraps. Wall sconces were unlit, shrouded in cobwebs. The few servants at Valmond had not been expecting their lord, and certainly not a bride, but when she met them, Gwyneth had to wonder if their greeting would have been any different if they had.

They huddled together, staring at Rorke with expressions of dread or awe or shock, Gwyneth wasn't sure which.

"I've brought you a new mistress," Rorke finally said. "This is Lady Gwyneth of Wulfere.

Gwyneth's confusion mounted as she watched their faces sway from their lord to her with the same impenetrable, stunned expressions.

Burnet, the steward, finally broke free of the huddled group. "Welcome home, milord," he said without the least bit of welcome in his tone.

Nobody spoke to her.

The steward's wife's name was Hertha, though Gwyneth learned that only in passing.

"Light the fire," Rorke ordered, glancing about at the quivering mass of servants as if he didn't notice anything amiss in their behavior. "Lay a meal, whatever is at hand, for we have traveled long and are hungry." He barked another series of orders. Gwyneth gathered that he was instructing them about which rooms to prepare.

He strode across the stone floor then, toward a dusty table near one of the hall's two huge hearths. Gwyneth trailed after him, reluctant to surrender the familiar comfort of his broad shoulders no matter how cold his eyes and voice.

Hertha had disappeared briefly, now reappearing with candles that offered flickering light. A young girl, maybe ten at most, carried ale and tankards, and a lad followed with sliced brown bread and cheese and a bowl of what looked like apples and nuts. Burnet was at work building a fire in the hearth with the help of one of Rorke's men. The illumination their efforts yielded did nothing to erase the chill of the hall—but rather further revealed its crumbling state. Gwyneth was more shocked with every passing moment. She'd heard stories about Valmond, but she had not expected this shattered, mournful ruin.

"Shall I— Is it all right— Would you let me take yer things to yer room, m-m-milady?" the young girl asked Gwyneth. She curtsied clumsily, gazing up at Gwyneth. The girl's face was thin, soulful, but she had huge eyes that betrayed curiosity. Her energy appealed to Gwyneth. It was almost as if the girl were the only thing alive in this desolate place. And she was certainly the only servant who had deigned to speak directly to her.

"Thank you," Gwyneth said, trying to sound more confident than she felt. She was the lady of Valmond now, as impossible as that seemed. The people of this castle were her people now and she was their lady. If they were afraid of her, and she was afraid of them, nothing would get accomplished here. She was determined to press ahead. "What's your name?"

The girl bit her lip. "Magwyn," she said, her voice soft but somehow eager just the same. "I'm but a kitchen maid, milady, but I would be proud to aid ye in any way I can." She curtsied again. Then she glanced back over her shoulder at Hertha. Her look was almost guilty, Gwyneth thought. It was as if she thought she'd get in trouble for speaking to her.

"Would you like to be my maid?" Gwyneth asked. She was not in dire need of a maid's assistance, but the shy friendliness of the girl's eyes drew her.

Magwyn gasped, bringing her gaze around. It seemed she forgot to be fearful now. "A lady's maid?" Her eyes popped. She looked back at Hertha again.

Hertha, tall and bony shouldered, nodded sternly to the girl, then turned without a word. Gwyneth had the idea that she was not in charge here at all, and would never be. This was Hertha's castle.

The girl sprang into action, followed by one of Rorke's men. Walcott, Gwyneth recalled his name.

Ryman and the other men were already gathering round the long, dusty table, draining tankards of the ale and devouring the fruit, cheese and bread that had been set out. The servants had disappeared with her trunk and her cloak, almost as if into the woodwork of the paneling that lined the lower level of the high stone walls.

Rorke watched her with eyes so mysterious and wrenching that she felt her heart pinch with an almost violent pain. What was she doing here? What was Rorke thinking? He was so withdrawn.

Miles and years away from France, she had to wonder if he was thinking that the woman he'd dreamed of bringing home to Valmond as his wife was not her but Angelette. Did that explain his eerie manner as they had neared his home, or was there something else?

"Sit, my lady," he said finally, and held out a chair for her. "Eat."

She wasn't the least bit hungry, but she sat. He placed cheese and bread in front of her, and she toyed with the food. Normally, she possessed a hearty appetite, but the dark castle dampened it. She was used to the bright, airy spaces of Castle Wulfere. Even here at the table, with her back to the warm fire, she was chilled to the bone.

"How long," she said abruptly, placing the cut apple back on the pewter bowl he'd shoved before her, untasted, "has Valmond been like this?"

"Like what?"

She stared at him. "Falling apart." Was this not obvious? "Surely it was not like this when you were growing up. Where is everyone? What happened to the village, the castle? How could you let Valmond fall into such complete disrepair?"

The knights at the end of the table had stopped their drinking and were watching, waiting.

"Valmond is what you see, Lady," Rorke replied grimly.

That was no answer. "It's . . . filthy," she pointed out.

"Then have it cleaned if it bothers you."

"It doesn't bother you? This is not even my home—" She caught herself, realizing it *was* her home now.

"It's not my home, either, Lady."

She gaped at him. "You were born here."

"It was never supposed to be mine."

"Nor mine." She was baffled by him. What was going on here? Valmond was a strange place, and Rorke was even stranger, as if merely arriving here had changed him in some incomprehensible way.

"Then we have something in common," he said.

He wasn't even looking at her now. She felt a wave of melancholy. What was happening? She didn't know what she'd expected of this marriage, but it wasn't this. She was terrified, but determined not to show it. She was made of sterner stuff than that.

"Tell me about Valmond," she persisted. "Tell me what it was like in better days."

"The past is over. I prefer not to discuss it."

"But I would like to discuss it."

The knights at the end of the table got up in unison.

"And I think," she went on resolutely, "that if you

exert yourself just a tiny bit, you could be pleasant long enough for me to eat this meal."

"And then," she kept going in spite of the fact that the man beside her, shrouded in the flickering shadow and light, had seemed to turn to ice, "you can lock me up in whatever tower room you're having prepared for me. I'll go back to Castle Wulfere first thing in the morning and we can forget this whole thing."

The knights had disappeared now as completely as the servants.

"But in the meantime, I'm not going to sit here while you alternately glower at me and ignore me," she finished.

"They will not have prepared your chamber yet," he said.

She noticed that he referred to it as *her* chamber, not theirs.

"Your hair is still wet. You will stay here and get dry. I won't have you getting ill."

Damn him, he made no response to her remark about returning to Castle Wulfere.

"You know, I'm not hungry," she said suddenly, and pushed back from the table.

"Then you will sit by the fire and have a drink." He filled a mug. She could smell it as he poured from the jug. It wasn't the ale he and the men had been drinking. It smelled heavy and sweet. Mead.

He pulled one of the huge chairs to the fire, and she was surprised when he drew a second one after it. So surprised that she sat down, after all. He sat beside her.

"I'm not used to making conversation," he said as he handed her the mug. "In fact, I avoid it."

"I never would have dreamed."

She could see him bite his lip, and she realized he was trying not to smile.

"Most people are smart enough to leave me alone," was all he replied.

She took the mug, careful not to touch him but unnerved by the nearness of him just the same. "Tell me about Valmond," she tried again, not giving up.

"It's a castle." He moved away from her with unflattering haste, as if he, too, was being careful not to touch her.

"I mean, what was it like before?" Before it had fallen into a depressing shambles was what she didn't add.

"It was built in the eleven hundreds. It has a checkered history," he explained. "It started out as an abbey, in fact. It was added on to at various times."

"How long did it belong to the Church?" She sipped the mead and sat back to listen.

"Not long. Maybe twenty years. Then a fortress was needed to fight uprisings on the Welsh border, and the abbey was moved away and the castle completely altered. You can barely see remnants of the monks' cells in the east wing, but the walls were mostly knocked out and the chambers enlarged, at least on the upper floors, though the reconstruction was never completed. There were a series of construction accidents and my father abandoned the work."

"There's a monastery across the river now—Mill-bridge Priory," he went on. "The abbey was moved away completely. They say—" He stopped, looked at her with a playful light flashing in his dark blue eyes. "They say the ghosts of jealous monks haunt the east wing. But I wouldn't go looking for them; most of that part of the castle is in such disrepair, it's dangerous. Behave yourself, Lady, and I won't have to lock you up."

She wasn't entirely certain he was joking about that last bit. She sipped her mead.

"There, is that enough conversation for you, Lady Valmond?"

She blinked at his use of her new formal title.

"What about your family?" she asked, pulling herself together.

"What about them? They're dead, every one of them."

Any amusement, any light, was gone from his eyes now. It was the wrong question, but she wanted answers just the same.

"I'm sorry."

He got up, put his own tankard back on the table. "Don't be. It's not your fault. They've been gone for nigh on eight years. I've gotten over it."

She rose, too, and followed him to the table. She put down her mug. "You haven't gotten over it if you've been avoiding this place ever since."

Rorke turned, and his cool gaze told her he wasn't pleased. She had worn out her welcome with this conversation, but she didn't want to give up.

"Don't start trying to figure me out, Lady," he

warned her. "You will not like what you find if you
do."

She swallowed thickly. "Don't try to scare me,"
she said. "I'm not afraid of you. I refuse to be afraid
of you. Everyone else here may be"—she waved her
arms around at the empty hall—"but I am not. I
know you."

"You know nothing about me."

She thought about the time they'd been hunting
during one of their training sessions. She'd been
bitten by an injured hound she'd tried to help. In
the clamor, their horses had run away and he had
carried her all the way to Castle Wulfere in his
arms, whispering words of comfort to her all the
way.

"I know that you are good and kind," she said
quietly. She reached out and touched his arm without thinking. He felt solid and strong. There was
something reassuring suddenly about the realness
of him in this unearthly desolate hall. "I know that
you are courageous and honorable and loyal."

"Do not make me out to be a hero, Lady," he said
stiffly and jerked back from her touch. "You will
be disappointed." He turned, giving her his back.

The fire glowed red around his silhouette. He
was so close but so very far.

A shape moved in the shadows across the hall.
Hertha moved into the light.

"Your chamber is ready, Lady," Rorke said without looking at her. "Go to bed. Sleep."

Thirteen

Gwyneth followed Hertha's bone-thin form through the shadowy warren of passageways that seemed to make up Valmond Castle. She thought of Rorke's explanation of how the castle had been changed throughout the centuries, supposing it must explain the complicated layout.

"Our family has served the lords of Valmond since the early twelve hundreds," Hertha replied when questioned. She explained that she and Burnet were second cousins, so when she spoke of their family, it was the same one. "My Burnet is the steward, but I'm the one who carries the keys. He can be forgetful now that he's getting up in years."

Hertha looked at least as old as Burnet.

"You are very loyal to have stayed on," Gwyneth said conversationally. "It must be difficult these days."

Hertha sheltered the tallow flame she carried as they began to ascend a curving staircase into a tower. Everywhere, there were shuttered windows and cramped arrow loops filled with cobwebs. Drafts seemed to come up out of nowhere, and every time the flame wavered, Gwyneth held her breath for fear it would go out and she would be left alone in the darkness with this old woman.

There was a weird keening noise that she knew must come from wind whistling through some crack in the castle's mortar somewhere, and yet she found herself thinking of the monks Rorke had mentioned.

Angry monks haunting Valmond. Silly, of course.

"You must miss the family," Gwyneth tried again.

"Everyone's dead now," Hertha said. "All dead."

"It's very tragic. You must be happy now that Lord Valmond has returned."

Hertha stopped short and turned to face her, her bony face white, almost ghostly, from her position above her on the stairs.

"There is nothing here to be happy about these days," the steward's wife said. "There's too much sadness now. Let me give ye a mite bit of warning," she said in a lower voice, "Valmond is a castle that treasures its solitude. Ye don't want to go disturbing it."

"Excuse me?" Chills swept up Gwyneth's back, tingling at the nape of her neck. She spoke of the castle as if it had a life of its own.

Hertha continued up the tower stairs.

"Wait!" Gwyneth followed, afraid even more of being left in the darkness alone than she was of being left in the darkness with Hertha.

They reached the top of the stairs and Hertha threw open a massive oaken door. Gwyneth stepped inside after her.

"I have no idea how we got here."

"Don't get any ideas about exploring on yer

own," Hertha intoned abruptly. "Ye wouldn't want to get lost in this old place."

"If I don't show up to break my fast in the morning, send a search party," Gwyneth joked.

"I'll send someone to fetch ye down," Hertha said. "Safer that way." And she shut the door.

Gwyneth stared at the closed door, almost afraid to turn and face the chamber. Her imagination was going wild, she thought to herself. She half-expected to see a crazed ghost-monk when she turned, but all that met her shocked gaze was the girl Magwyn, standing by the bed holding her silver hairbrush.

"Shall I brush yer hair, milady?" Magwyn asked shyly.

The room surprised Gwyneth. The sconces on the walls were lit, and the floor was evidently freshly swept. Herbs had been found somewhere and strewn amongst new straw to lend a springlike scent to the air.

Crackling tongues of fire licked a huge yew log in the fireplace. A basin of steaming water rested on a table near the bed, a linen towel draped beside it. A four-poster bed took up most of the space in the room, its wine red curtains drawn back to reveal plump pillows and thick blankets.

Her belongings were piled in the corner, though Magwyn had managed to withdraw a gossamer-silk chemise that was part of the trousseau Belle had rushed into production during the week leading up to the wedding. The nightgown was meant for a wedding night.

But Rorke had made it abundantly plain he did

not intend to join her. *Go to bed,* he had ordered. *Sleep.* Those were not the words of a man intent on making good on his marital rights.

"Milady?" came the small voice again, and she looked back at Magwyn.

The little girl looked so hopelessly eager.

"How old are you?" Gwyneth asked.

"Nine."

Even younger than Gwyneth had guessed. "Where are your parents?" The girl seemed far too young to be set to work in the castle.

"Dead, milady. They died in the plague. The others—the other villagers, I mean, sent me here. I was hardly more than a wee babe. They couldn't take care of me and so—"

"Mistress Hertha took care of you?"

The girl shrugged with frail shoulders, her big eyes solemn and suddenly seeming too old for her tender years. "She's not like my mum or anything," she said.

"Are there many still in the village?" she asked, thinking how deserted it had appeared when they'd ridden through it, but the girl had spoken as if some might have remained.

"Not many," Magwyn said. "They mostly went into the woods, milady. But they're still out there."

They mostly went into the woods? Gwyneth was more baffled than ever.

"But the village—"

"They're afraid, Lady," Magwyn said. "Of the curse," she added plainly as if the point were so obvious she shouldn't need to make it.

"Curse?" Gwyneth wanted to press the girl for

more information about this curse, but it suddenly struck her that Magwyn looked tired. She let it go. For now. "Are you the only help Hertha has in the castle?" she asked.

She'd seen few enough servants when they'd arrived. A few boys, and some men who evidently guarded the gates and the wallwalks to whatever extent Valmond was guarded. And Hertha and Burnet. She hadn't seen any other maids.

"Yes, milady. 'Tis just me."

No wonder the castle was filthy.

"You help in the kitchens?" she prodded.

"And the stables. And with whatever is needed. We made candles today. Started first thing this morning."

Gwyneth sighed. She was tired, and all she'd done all day was sit on a horse. This child had been doing real work.

"I don't know how to be a lady's maid," Magwyn said, perking up again. It was clear she was thrilled to be Gwyneth's personal maid. "Will ye teach me?"

"The first thing I want you to do is sleep," Gwyneth said sternly. "Tomorrow, we will talk about being a lady's maid." Maybe by then, she'd figure out how to teach her to be a lady's maid. Either that, or she'd suggest she be her page. She knew more about that.

She just managed not to laugh at that thought. Really, it wasn't funny. Magwyn probably knew more about being a lady's maid than Gwyneth knew about being a lady.

Magwyn looked confused, but when Gwyneth explained that she hadn't done anything wrong or displeased her, the girl took the blanket Gwyneth gave her from the bed and curled up in the connecting anteroom. She was asleep before Gwyneth shut the door.

Gwyneth stood in the middle of the room feeling lost for several moments. Then fighting the continued waves of loneliness that struck her now, she jerked off the fine blue gown in which she'd been wed and pulled on the featherlight fairylike chemise Magwyn had laid out on the bed.

Tired yet restless, she padded toward the tall, narrow windows. They were covered in impenetrable glass. She unlatched one and pulled it open.

Cold air and spatters of rain struck her immediately. She hugged her arms around her body and closed her eyes, breathing in the unfamiliar scent of Valmond, piney-sweet and thick and mysterious.

Wind swept her hair from her face, and she leaned into it, wanting, needing, craving to find fear swept away as well.

What would her life be like here? What did Rorke want from her—if anything?

Did he want a chatelaine for his castle? A wife in name only? Or a friend who could also be a lover, even if not a love?

Or would he only, ever, always, see a child?

She opened her eyes, shivering, and slammed shut the window. She wished like never before that she could talk to Lizbet. She hated that they had parted so badly. Lizbet had wished her well, even kissed her cheek, but Gwyneth had been still upset, even as she'd left home. She hadn't kissed her back. She'd been angry with Lizbet—for what?

Making her face the truth that she'd been childish and stupid to run away and join a siege?

Gwyneth didn't know how she felt about anything anymore. She didn't even understand herself, much less the man she'd wed.

He had made it clear he did not intend to make this a true marriage—in sooth, it was evident it had not even occurred to him. He preferred the ephemeral memory of his beloved Angelette. He might treat her with respect, even kindness, but it was the ghost of Angelette who held his haunted heart.

She sat on the edge of the bed, picked up the mirror that sat beside the comb and brush on the nearby table, and stared intently into her own reflection.

Her face looked white, her eyes huge and dark, her lips pale. She was striking, with her dark, dark hair and darker eyes—but no great beauty.

She was not a woman who cast sorcerous spells upon men, making them forget all else.

"What did you expect, pudding head?" She laid aside the mirror, then bathed her face and body with cool water from the basin. She blew out the candles in the sconces. The room remained warm with firelight.

She laid down and closed her eyes, tried to relax.

Her entire body ached from the journey. Sleep eluded her. She realized she was listening for Rorke, as if he would come to her. But all she heard was the pop of the fire and the occasional morbid-sounding wind creaking through the castle walls. She hated that she was scared of this place, scared of the people in it. Too scared to sleep or eat or even think straight.

Damn Rorke for bringing her to this godforsaken place and stuffing her in this room like so much baggage to be stored.

She sat bolt upright in the bed. What if he left her here? Alone?

He'd said nothing of giving up his endless quest for Ranulf. Nothing at all.

The prospect of endless years stretching out before her, alone and lonely in this dank, dark castle pressed down on her suffocatingly.

Her heart pounded hard against her rib cage. What did she want from him? What did he want from her? He had kissed her once and—sweet Eleanor, she had liked it. She had more than liked it.

Why should there not be more kisses?

More—

She felt her nipples tighten beneath the gossamer material of her chemise. And she felt a surge in her belly that was even more dangerous than desire. It was determination.

She was awkward and clumsy and completely lacking in womanly sophistication, but she was his wife. And she was a fighter. This was some new kind of battle, and she wasn't quite sure what she was fighting, but she knew she could not fight anything in this room all alone.

Rorke climbed the tower stairs, every weary tread adding to the heavy load of memories that crushed

him here in his old home. At every turn, there were
ghostly remnants of his father's calm presence, his
mother's warm laughter, his brother's solid com-
panionship.

He ached from the remembrances, and he ached
for Gwyneth—in his heart and other regions of his
body that were better left unexamined.

Were things not bad enough?

He reached the corridor outside the chamber.
A fierce urgency rocked him, drove him to reach
for the iron handle, push it down and in. . . . He
stopped, crushed by guilt. What was he doing?

Would she even want him? And was it worse if the
answer turned out to be yes?

She was an innocent, despite her bold ways.

And he—

He had been cold and cruel to her. He'd tram-
pled on her dreams and rushed her into a marriage
that would likely make her miserable. She deserved
better than a man with no heart and a broken
home. He'd thought to help her, but maybe it had
only been selfishness all along, his own stupid need
to save her when he couldn't even save himself.
What the hell had he thought he was doing?

He wanted to get drunk, and he wished to God
that he had not made it a decision a long time ago
to watch how much ale he consumed—knowing
how easily he could kill himself with drink, and unwilling to go in such an undignified way. Better to
slit his own throat with his sword, but perhaps he
was too much of a coward to do that, either.

Damn Gwyneth for shaking him from the almost
easy numbness in which he had lived for so long.

And damn him for not being able to control it. He had made a solemn decision to leave her alone, and yet his baser urges were already betraying him into something they would both regret and they had been wed less than a day.

He was supposed to be protecting her.

And the person she needed protecting from the most . . . was him.

He turned away, fighting to control the stinging in his blood, thinking of her virtue and his brutality, knowing shame and hunger and the fear that this was his new nightmare.

Fourteen

Gwyneth was glad she'd pulled on her cloak, damp though it remained, before she left her chamber. The castle was absolutely frigid. She could see her breath as she held the candle out before her and examined her choices at the bottom of the tower.

A mazelike selection of corridors fanned out around her. Which one? She took a deep breath, made a selection, and moved forward—to do what, she wasn't sure.

She walked for what seemed like forever, first down one corridor, then another. She was absolutely certain it hadn't taken this long to get to her room from the great hall when she'd been with Hertha.

Where was she?

She finally stopped and struggled for bearings. She listened for the sound of a human voice, but there was nothing but the keening noise of the wind outside and the smell of dust and damp.

And yet as she stood there, she heard a sound. A footstep? A voice? A figment of her imagination? She walked toward it, the candle she'd carried from her room flickering.

Pushing shakily at the loose locks that fell out of the braid and about her face, her hair's wild tendencies exacerbated by the dank, humid condition of Valmond, she wished she had never left her room. The floor was uneven, and her feet were bare and cold on the stones.

She almost tripped when steps appeared suddenly, two of them, and she descended into a lower level of the same corridor. It was another place where the architecture was mashed together haphazardly.

There were more doors here, and some of them were open.

She heard the sound again, then realized it was just the wind. Must have been the wind all along.

"Hello?" she tried, just in case.

There was no reply.

She pushed at one of the doors, held her candle out and looked inside. The room was tiny, and empty. She pushed open more doors and found the same layout and realized she was in the east wing.

The old monastic cell block.

There was another sound, and she whirled, not knowing what she expected to see. Rorke, Hertha, Burnet—

A ghostly monk?

Not that she believed in ghosts.

Her fingers shook and the candlelight fluttered.

She squeezed her eyes shut for a brief moment, berating herself. She was not going to be stupid about this. There was nothing to be afraid of inside Valmond.

Maybe. Probably.

The light of the candle spilled onto the stones, and something dark moved—she gasped, then collapsed back against the ice-cold stone of the corridor wall.

"Well done, Gwyneth, you idiot," she whispered, "you're being stalked by a mouse."

She shook her head to clear the remainder of panic, squeezing her eyes shut for a moment. She opened them, ready to forge back the way she'd come—

There was something—or someone—a visage, straight ahead of her in the corridor, ghostly, indistinguishable as male or female, lost in shadows but with eyes that shone clear and bright in the murky dark.

"Go away, Lady" came the ghost breath in the thick stillness. *"Go away."*

Oh sweet Eleanor of Aquitaine. She felt as if all the bones had simply disintegrated from her body.

She backed up, stumbled, dropped the candleholder. Immediately, she was thrown into pitch-blackness.

Then she felt a breath of air, and the sound of something slamming shut. The door! She reached for it, felt its solid strength, tore at the iron latch, but nothing happened. She banged and shouted and then was utterly still, listening. Nothing. Not a sound. Not even that of a mouse. Blood rushed in her ears.

She was trapped inside a monk's cell.

* * *

Gwyneth woke to the crackling of a warm fire. She rolled over, snuggling into the pillowy comfort of the bed, clinging to the seductive solace of sleep even as she stretched and sighed into wakefulness. A soft hand touched her brow—

"Rorke?" she whispered and opened her eyes.

Magwyn's thin, elvish face peered down at her. "Good morning, milady. I made yer fire and brought yer tea. I'm here to dress ye and comb yer hair and—oh, anything ye like!"

Gwyneth blinked, startled for a moment, unable to place where she was and who this sweet child was speaking to her, then it all came back. Valmond. Rorke.

What wild dream had made her think he would be here beside her?

She had had dreams, though. Snippets of fantasy-like images washed through her mind. A man's arms holding her, touching her, caressing her . . .

Oh, dear saints, she was going mad.

She turned her head, took in the vast expanse of empty bed, turned back to where Magwyn perched on the other side of her, on the edge of the mattress, swinging her legs over the side beneath her plain brown kirtle.

The events of the night before came back to her. Lost, in Valmond. The endless corridors, the monks' cells. The ghost eyes and ghost voice . . . She'd finally fallen asleep, in the blackness of the tiny, empty cell, to awake at dawn and find the door standing wide open.

Had it ever been closed? Had she simply lost her bearings inside the cold, black cell and sought a wall rather than a door? It made no sense, but was it more impossible than that she had been shut in one of those cells? Her imagination had been carried away by the stories of the monks.

She'd wandered back, through the corridors, finally finding her own room. She'd fallen dead asleep then, exhausted from her wanderings.

Now, in the full light of day, the entire episode seemed idiotic. Had she really heard a voice? She could put it all down to panic.

"I've taken out all yer gowns, milady, and if ye'd like to choose one, I'll help ye dress. I found yer ribbons and combs—and oh, would ye teach me to fix yer hair? Please, milady?"

Magwyn sounded so eager, she hated to point out that she hadn't the slightest idea how to fix hair. She'd always tied hers back in a braid or left it loose, and never had she had the patience to let Fayette and Belle twist and twine it into elaborate styles the way they always wanted.

"Magwyn, do you believe in ghosts?"

The little girl stared at her.

Gwyneth shook herself. "I'm sorry, never mind." She shook herself. "I went out of my room last night, tried to find the great hall and got lost. I ended up in the east wing—"

"Ye shouldn't go there, milady. 'Tis dangerous."

"I got locked inside a monk's cell. I couldn't get out."

"Those rooms don't have locks, milady."

Gwyneth stared at her. Right. Those rooms didn't have locks. And there were no such things as ghosts. And the only creature she'd really come across last night had been a mouse.

She had to get a grip on her imagination. And her dreams.

Looking around the chamber, focusing her attention on something else with deliberate care, she realized how much larger and brighter it was than she'd realized. There were tall windows with glazed glass, and the morning sun beamed through them.

The tall windows—and the normalcy of the dawn—drew her.

Throwing her legs over the side of the bed, dressed only in the gossamer chemise, she padded across the floor to the windows and threw one open. The air outside was thick and damp.

The courtyard below was empty, but beyond, in the outer bailey, she saw men on the wallwalks and at the great gatehouse. Even farther off, in the tiny, seemingly deserted village, she saw smoke rising from the center chimney holes of a few thatched cottages.

A small figure—a child—ran along a muddy path by a streambank, and ducks walked in a straight line on the opposite side. Day sparkled with dewlights over meadows and fields, some farmed, many fallow. It was, in many ways, an ordinary scene. She could almost imagine she was at Castle Wulfere.

A boy appeared on the hall steps below carrying a pail of something and hurried toward a building tucked against the inner bailey wall.

A walled cluster of neatly laid-out roofs was visible in the distance, across a narrow river. There was an orchard and a pond outside the wall, and a curved road leading between it and the castle, crossing a bridge with what appeared to be an abandoned mill. It had to be the monastery Rorke had mentioned. There was a lone figure in the orchard, pushing a cart of some sort.

There was life here at Valmond, sparse at it was. At one time, it must have been a bustling place, and now this was all that remained. Gwyneth's gaze skimmed the line of trees where a thick and endless forest began.

Magwyn had said most of the villagers had fled there, into the woods. Why?

And why had Rorke so abandoned this home he had never expected to inherit?

"Milady?"

She looked back at Magwyn. Behind the girl she noticed the piles of clothes that had been, very carefully, taken out of her bags. The clothing was all new, packed by Belle, sewn in a rush by Wulfere's expert seamstresses: colorful bliauts, undergarments, shoes, even ribbons and combs Gwyneth knew had mostly come from her own mother's things that Belle had saved for all of them over the years.

Magwyn had laid out each new garment along the top of the trunk and even on the chairs by the fire. Shoes waited in neat rows on the floor. Fillets and brushes were lined up on the dressing table.

None of her favorite comfort clothes, her boyish gear, had come with her to Valmond. In the daze of the past week, she had let Belle take over the packing of her things.

"What would ye like to do first, milady? Would ye

like to dress, or would ye like to drink yer tea?"
Magwyn nodded to the cup on the table.

Gwyneth sipped the hot, sweet drink, then suc-
cumbed to dressing in a tawny gold cotehardie that
the little girl picked out. Together, they managed
to twist her hair in two braids, one arranged over
each ear with gold combs.

The effect when she looked in the mirror was unfamiliar.

"Ye're so pretty, milady!" Magwyn clapped her
hands together proudly.

Valmond seemed just as complicated and im-
mense as it had the night before as, thankfully,
Magwyn accompanied her through the twisted
maze to the great hall. Unfortunately, after she
reached it, Magwyn seemed to melt away. She saw
Burnet at the far end of the hall carrying what appeared to be some sort of pots and tongs.

A table was still set up by the hearth, which was
unlit, and a couple of men-at-arms were breaking
their fast. She thought for a moment about joining
them, but saw them staring at her and their look
was not welcoming.

A boy flashed by from the corner of her vision
headed toward the door, busy about something she
couldn't even imagine.

Gwyneth followed him, walked out to the steps,
breathed in the fresh air again, and studied the
empty bailey. A soldier appeared from inside, stuffing an end of bread in his hand and wiping his lips.

"Er, excuse me, milady," he said from an overfull
mouth, sidestepping around her as he continued
quickly on his way.

"Oh, wait," Gwyneth said.

The man stopped, turned to look up at her from the bottom of the steps, still chewing. He wasn't any of the men she'd seen with Rorke in the camp, so she supposed he was one of the guards that maintained the watch at Valmond Castle.

"Could you tell me—" she started, then broke off.

Could he tell her what?

What to do, how to act, where to go? She strove for an air of confidence she didn't feel.

"Could you tell me where I might find Lord Valmond?"

The soldier swallowed, frowned.

"Lord Valmond?" He wiped at his mouth again with the back of his hand. "Why, he's gone, milady. Rode out first thing this morning."

Fifteen

The kitchen was deserted. Hertha was nowhere to be seen, though a cheerful fire flickered in the wall-size hearth. Gwyneth helped herself to a fresh piece of one of the sliced cardamom cakes she found cooling on a rack set on the large table in the middle of the kitchen. She'd found the place by following the wonderful smell.

She sat down on a stool near the fire and held her cold booted feet toward the hearth. She missed Castle Wulfere with breathtaking sharpness. She missed the open feel of it, the green hills, the happy village, and cheery servants. She missed her sisters, her family.

Was this to be her life, left alone while Rorke continued his mad mission of vengeance, endlessly seeking a man who'd died years ago?

Even now, still wounded, he couldn't wait to set out again. He was no use with his sword arm the way it was.

She worried about him, but she was also angry. How dare he leave her in this place alone!

It was not the first time he had left her, and again without saying good-bye.

She put down the cardamom cake and closed

her eyes, fighting off a feeling of overwhelming loneliness.

At a noise across the kitchen, she opened her eyes to find Burnet entering from the garden door. He was so tall, he had to duck his head as he passed under the low stone lintel. He was carrying an overflowing basket of vegetables.

He stopped when he spotted her, and she felt a weird, uncomfortable feeling, which was foolish because he was old and for saints' sake, he was the steward. What did she think he was going to do, hurt her? But she thought about the voice in the east wing.

Go away, Lady. Go away.

She refused to believe she'd really heard those words in the night. She didn't want to think any of that was real.

She'd gotten lost and spooked, that was all.

"Burnet," she said, forcing assurance into her voice. "I would like it if you would escort me around the castle this morning. I was exploring last night, you see, and I have to admit I got lost. I found myself in the area of the monks' cells—"

"That's a bad idea, Lady."

"That part of the castle is closed." Hertha appeared in the door behind her husband. She slipped around him to move into the room. She carried another basket, also overflowing with carrots and leeks that looked fresh-pulled from the garden.

"It wasn't closed last night," Gwyneth pointed out. "I was just curious—"

"Best be more careful, Lady Valmond," Hertha

said with a worried frown. This morning, her tone was soft, soothing, nothing like the ominous warning of the night before. "I'm sorry that Burnet's quite busy today, though, milady. He cannot escort ye anywhere this morn."

Hertha plopped her basket on the floor by the hearth, scattering bits of moist dirt that fell off the carrots and leeks.

"Go, husband," she said without turning around to look at Burnet again. "Go on about yer business. We've all got our work to be doing."

Burnet stood there for a moment. He shook his head, his pale, gaunt face seeming to almost cave in on itself.

"What business?" he said in a strange voice. "There is no use."

"There's always use!" Hertha said sternly. "Ye must be gone now."

Burnet's angular shoulders dropped and he shuffled away. Gwyneth watched the baffling interplay between the two.

"Ye'll have to excuse Burnet, milady," Hertha said after he was gone. "He's not well these days. His humors are out of balance, and his mind is not what it was."

"I'm sorry." Gwyneth bit her lip, not sure what to say about that. "Would you mind explaining . . ." She went back to the previous topic. "Why is that part of the castle closed?"

"Lord Valmond closed it. Only Lord Valmond can open it—and he will not. He *should* not. Those old corridors are dangerous. This castle is so huge; there's no way Burnet and I can keep up with it with as little help as we have. There are sections that are in poor repair. 'Tis no place for ye to be wandering."

"I was actually locked in one of the monk's cells for a time," Gwyneth went on, standing. "I even thought I saw someone right before . . . a face, a voice. Almost like a ghost—"

"Do ye believe in ghosts, milady?"

"Do you?" Gwyneth couldn't resist returning.

Hertha moved past her. She smelled of vanilla and herbs and clean laundry.

"I don't give a thought to such things, milady. I'm just thinking of yer welfare. It'd be best for ye to keep to yer rooms."

"But I'm just wondering—if that part of the castle is dangerous, why not repair it? And what's this about a curse? Rorke—Lord Valmond—mentioned an old tale about ghosts in the east wing, but this morning Magwyn said something about a curse."

"How odd," Hertha said in reply. "I don't know anything about a curse, Lady."

She patted Gwyneth on the arm; but if she meant to be reassuring, she'd failed. Gwyneth couldn't rid herself of the idea that things weren't right here, and the fact that the housekeeper didn't want to talk about it only bothered her more.

Hertha had turned her back on Gwyneth and was packing up the cardamom cakes in baskets she took from a shelf below the table.

"Last night," Gwyneth said suddenly, "you said something about Valmond treasuring its solitude, and that I shouldn't disturb it. What did you mean?"

Hertha gave her a blank look. "Did I say that?" she said vaguely. "That was just my way of explaining about the castle being shut up in parts and all."

Gwyneth wasn't so sure about that. "Who are those baskets for?" she asked finally.

"Villagers."

"Villagers?"

"Lord Valmond requires it. I make packs every week. Breads, vegetables, sometimes meat or fish. Whatever we have."

Rorke had not quite abandoned his people, after all, Gwyneth thought, surprised though not sure that she should be. He was a good man, she couldn't help believing, no matter how stern and distant he could also be.

"Who takes the baskets to them?"

"One of the lads. Or a soldier. Or Burnet. Whoever's available."

"I'm available," Gwyneth said. "Unless, of course, there's something I could do here to help you—"

"Heavens, no." Hertha laughed comfortably. "I'll see that a soldier fetches the baskets for ye. They're rather heavy and—"

"No, no, I can get them myself," Gwyneth argued. "I'm quite strong."

Hertha looked at her strangely, but Gwyneth didn't wait for permission. She didn't need the housekeeper's permission for anything, she reminded herself. She was the lady of the castle now, whether Hertha liked it or not. She made a mental note to ask for a set of chatelaine's keys later. And she would get one of the soldiers to show her around Valmond.

Maybe she could recruit some women from the village to help her clean out the hall and maybe even the east wing and the towers. She'd ride over to the monastery one day soon and make the acquaintance of the prior. She knew that Valmond must get a lot of their supplies from them considering the working farms and gardens at Valmond were quite scarce. As lady of Valmond, surely it was her duty to meet the prior.

Suddenly she was full of ideas, things to do, people to see.

Busy, busy, busy, that was what she needed to be. It would take her mind off the strangeness of Valmond.

And damn Rorke, he didn't expect her to do any of it, and so perversely, she would. She wanted to do the complete opposite of anything he expected. She didn't want to examine all of her motives. She was angry, and that was enough.

And she missed him, and that was worse.

"I'd like to go over the household accounts later," she added. "Please let Burnet know. I'll meet him in his office this afternoon."

For a moment, she thought Hertha looked as if she'd like to give Gwyneth twenty reasons she shouldn't do any of the things she was planning, but then she nodded her head and said: "As you wish, milady, of course. This is yer home now, and ye're the lady."

But as she took a basket under each arm in the warm kitchen, something in the old woman's gaze didn't feel right and Gwyneth shivered in the warm kitchen.

* * *

The morning mist was all but gone as Gwyneth made her brisk way down the narrow cart path that wound from the castle to the village. Despite the fact that she didn't need or want a soldier to carry the goods down for her, she noticed just the same that her movements were observed by those manning the gates. When she looked back over her shoulder halfway down, she saw that a guard was trailing her.

She wondered if Rorke had left orders for them to watch her, for fear she would run away. She found the situation irritating and determined to ignore the soldier.

Magwyn kept pace by her side. She'd found Magwyn in the hall and had recruited her to come with her. The maid seemed excited to be wanted and chattered as they set off, though she grew quiet as they came into the village.

Wattel and daub huts sat in a forlorn fashion, some clearly abandoned though smoke still rose from the roofs of others. The gusts of wind that had cleared the mist and driven away the rain blew around them eerily.

There was no sign now of ducks or children. Gwyneth saw that there was a field of graves between the village and the woods. A field of graves to remind her that there was little left of what this place must have once been. She imagined a thriving community of people and animals such as the village that lay below Wulfere filled with dogs and sheep, chickens and children.

Here, there was only a kitten.

She knelt, put down the heavy baskets to pick up the little cat that twined about her ankles, crying. Its tiny furry body felt soft and warm in her hands, and thank the saints, alive. The most alive thing she'd touched since she'd arrived.

The kitty purred, and she held it against her cheek, loving the feel of her.

Carrying the cat, she looked around, seeing she'd stopped in the center of the small village. There was a pretty vine-encrusted well, rocks arranged like benches circling it. A well-worn wooden bucket sat to one side.

She glanced back at the castle, saw how its stones gleamed white now in the streaming sun, almost as if formed by the very clouds brushing the sky above it. In this moment, Valmond looked radiant, and yet remote and stark, as well.

Now, she cast her gaze again about the village, thinking she had to be bold. Go straight up and knock on doors. She noted the cottages that appeared vacant. One hut's door flapped sadly in the breeze.

But from another, she heard a child's muffled cry. And from another, the moo of a cow.

From the corner of her eye, she detected movement. The cat sprang from her arms, its thin, sharp claws cutting into her hands as it jumped to the ground and ran toward the small, hollow-eyed girl who materialized in the cracked opening of a doorway. A woman came up behind the child, sliding her arm protectively around her daughter.

"Poppy," the girl cooed, and pushed away from

her mother. Her eyes suddenly became bright as she reached for the cat.

The kitten leaped into her arms and she straightened, holding the pet close to the dirty woolen kirtle that scant reached her calves, clearly outgrown.

Gwyneth stood deathly still, afraid to move right away for fear she'd scare away the child or the mother. It was a good thing she'd brought Magwyn, she realized, when the maid said, "'Tis our new lady, Lily. Isn't she beautiful? She let me be her maid. I fixed her hair! I'm a lady's maid!" Magwyn beamed.

Two, three, five, ten, more villagers appeared out of doors and around corners of huts. Most were children. Gwyneth saw few boys, and no men. Many of those families with menfolk, she guessed, must be ones that had been able to leave after the plague years when the castle had been abandoned. The widows and children had stayed on, eking out a miserable living here with their ducks and their gardens and the charity of their absent lord. What few men or older boys still lived here would already be in the fields.

"Is she real?" a small girl asked, peering from behind her mother's ragged skirt.

"Don't be a dunce, Kirie," Lily, the girl with the cat, chided, her tart voice showing she had little patience with nonsense. "Of course she's real." But behind the tart voice, Gwyneth detected a flicker of anxiety. Still, Lily was a bold one, and the little girl walked toward her and touched her arm—a soft, quick poke. Then she looked back at her friend. "See?"

Her mother gasped even as Gwyneth laughed.

"Don't ye be so disrespectful, Lily-girl." The woman managed an awkward curtsy. "Milady."

She tugged on her daughter, pushing her down into an even more awkward curtsy.

As Gwyneth watched, others crowded around, bending their knees in deference, and she realized, a bit of apprehension.

"Please, there is no need." Gwyneth touched the woman's shoulder and then Lily's dirt-smeared cheek. "Do not bend your knee to me. I'm here to be of service to you, not the other way around. Here, I've brought baskets." She indicated the overflowing packages she'd set on the ground near the well.

"I'm here to help you," she repeated because she didn't know what else to say. "I don't know what you need," she went on blindly. "So maybe you can tell me. I have sweet cakes," she added with a bit of desperation when nobody moved.

She reached into the nearest basket and held one out. It was the little girl Lily who pushed away from her mother and was the first to take one. Quickly, Gwyneth found herself and Magwyn handing out cakes faster than they could take them out of the baskets.

From that small start, she spent the next several days making a series of clumsy attempts to gain their trust with something besides cakes. She'd gone over the household account books with Burnet, dizzied by the pages of parchments filled with numbers and goods and prices.

All she came away with was the notion that Rorke was quite rich. Valmond was the family stronghold and was crumbling, but he was owed allegiance by a number of vassals with wealthy estates who were happy to pay their liege lord his due in return for the protection he and his men gave in return should they ever be in need of it.

And while she avoided taking off into parts unknown in the castle, she had made headway in examining all that the main keep held in store. She brought the villagers cloth she found in the sewing rooms, spices from the storerooms, even a slate and bits of chalk from the old schoolroom.

The villagers met her attempts at charity with polite acceptance, murmured gratitude. But to her dismay, they still seemed wary. They resisted coming to the castle when she suggested some of the women could help her clean out the hall.

She would see that Burnet paid them, of course. But that didn't seem to be the issue preventing them from coming with her.

"Valmond will be like it used to be," she said. "Clean and bright. Happy."

The villagers looked at each other and down at their feet. Anywhere but at her.

"What is it?" she demanded finally.

"It be cursed, Lady," one women said.

Gwyneth couldn't get any further explanation. "There are soldiers everywhere," she said. "No ghosts. No curses. Really."

She tried everything to convince them. Finally,

she said, "I'm not scared of anything. You know why?"

They stared at her.

"I'm a knight," she said, and nodded when they gaped. "Really. I've been to a siege." She'd have to elaborate on that one since she hadn't been at a siege for long, but she knew enough stories.

The eyes of the little girls popped while the women glanced at each other, confused.

"I'll show you." Gwyneth picked up a nearby stick that looked handy. It was long, with a sturdy end she could use as a hilt.

They were in the center of the village again, and she stepped away from the well where the children and women sat watching her, and went to work.

"Basic sword attacks consist of cuts, thrusts and swipes," she started. First, she demonstrated the killing blow of the cut, then a pass and thrust. She tossed the stick sword to the first girl to stand. It was Lily. "Come on," she encouraged the little girl. "No, no, keep your center low," she chided her as the girl attempted to recreate Gwyneth's movements. "Your head shouldn't bob up and down. You should be able to keep a mug of water on your head, if you had one, and not lose it."

The other girls scrambled for sticks. The afternoon passed so quickly, that when the sun started to go down, Gwyneth was shocked. She'd even gotten the mothers to join them.

Eventually, they gave up the stick swords completely and Gwyneth got serious and demonstrated a few simple self-defense skills that Rorke had taught her long ago: basic wrestling moves and some surprisingly powerful kicks that he'd insisted would stand her in good stead if she were ever without a weapon and in danger. They practiced until the children fell over with exhaustion.

She didn't know if it was because they believed her when she told them again that the castle wasn't cursed, or if it was simply that they'd finally decided they liked her, but when she asked them again to come to the castle, this time they said yes.

And as she walked back to the castle under the greenish-silver cast of a coming rain, there was a feeling in her heart that she couldn't name. She only knew that the feeling was right and that it wasn't just anger driving her anymore.

It took Rorke six days to realize he wasn't going to stop thinking about her. He was in the tiny hamlet of Redmund, where he and his men had tracked a lead about a man in a holding cell. The man was dead by the time they got there, and the stench of the lockup nearly knocked them all down. It wasn't Ranulf.

It hadn't been a good lead to begin with, but Rorke followed every one he found, good or bad or indifferent. They already had their next one. There was always another one.

It had started within days of Ranulf's disappearance. A fisherman had come to Penlogan, claiming to have rescued a broken man from the sea. The tale had led nowhere, of course. None of them ever led anywhere, but into a nightmare with no end.

The trail was endless as they tracked every crip-

pled stranger, soldier, beggar, criminal who
sounded, on the surface, so much like Ranulf. The
process of developing leads, following rumors,
combing villages and even cities, had been honed
over the years.

But on this trip he felt different. His hands felt
empty, restless, even when they held his horse's
reins, and there was a hot spark inside him that
wouldn't burn out. It was dangerous, hungry. It was
his bride, damn her wild heart.

No matter how far he rode, how long and how
hard, he couldn't stop thinking about her. And
damning his own cowardice for leaving without saying good-bye.

He begged a bit of parchment and ink from the
reeve in Redmund, and then he paid him double
to find someone to take his letter to Valmond.

And then he prayed he hadn't made yet one
more huge mistake.

Sixteen

"This, my dear lady, is what is known as a square physic garden, or what we like to call the herbularius," Prior Bruin said as he led Gwyneth or a tour of the religious enclave.

She had spent the entire previous day sweeping out dirty rushes and scrubbing down cobwebs in the great hall with the village women. One of the children had tripped and scraped a knee. She'd bandaged it up, and thought about Rorke's terrible injury and how inadequate she had felt then. It had struck her keenly that she was unprepared to be Valmond's lady in ways more important than her lack of fashion sense.

What if someone were really hurt, seriously? Belle, most often with Marigold at her side, tended the people of Castle Wulfere, including the villeins. Elayna performed a like role at Penlogan. Along with eschewing music-making and hairstyling and candle-dipping lessons, Gwyneth had avoided learning anything about herbs and medicine. Generally, she'd forsworn anything that was part of the lady lessons her brother was constantly attempting to drive down her throat.

She'd been eager to visit Millbridge Priory, and

she'd taken the incident with the little girl's scraped knee as a reminder that she should not delay. And so she'd left her new friends—for that was how she thought of them—behind carrying in fresh rushes and strewing flower blossoms picked from the high meadow to introduce herself to the prior and, hopefully, avail herself of an opportunity to learn from his apothecary.

"We have three main gardens," Prior Bruin went on. "There is our orchard, with fruit and blossom trees planted amidst the brothers' graves. The kitchen garden, near the toolshed, and of course not far from the priory kitchen itself. And this, the herbularius. We keep it here, near the house of the physician and the bloodletting room."

Gwyneth shuddered. She was going to have to get over her revulsion about blood, she chided herself, if she was to take care of castlefolk who were injured. Still, she avoided glancing in the direction of the bloodletting room.

"Here we have sixteen beds." The monk went down the list of herbs: cumin, fennel, mint, lovage, sage, and on and on. Gwyneth couldn't keep track of them in her mind after the first few.

They came to a workshop, the enclosure hedged and well trimmed. The place emitted an aromatic fragrance that was almost heady, it was so strong.

She had just barely gotten used to Prior Bruin when he introduced her to Brother Arnulph as they entered the workshop. Prior Bruin was the most incredibly frail creature she'd ever met and she was shocked that he could even walk. He carried a cane to assist him, and he waved her off

when she tried to help him over a few uneven flag-
stones as they'd made their way through the priory
to the gardens.

She'd heard a bit about him from the villagers,
who seemed in awe of him.

"He spent one Christmas night in the snow with
nothing but a hairshirt and his prayers," Melia,
Lily's mother, had told Gwyneth. "He will go down
as a saint someday, mark my words."

Brother Arnulph, on the other hand, was as powerful looking as any warrior. He had massive
shoulders beneath his robes, and hands that looked
like hams.

"Brother Arnulph spent many years in service to
the Crown before taking the cowl," Prior Bruin explained. "It was among the king's physicians that he
learned his skills."

Another man was at work at a rear table trans-
ferring a pot of dried herbs into small bottles and
capping them. He was tall and thin, and when he
turned, Gwyneth thought for a moment that she
was staring at Burnet until she realized that of
course this man was much younger. His eyes were
hollow and evasive, and they flared darkly as he
nodded his greeting.

Prior Bruin introduced him as one of their lay
brothers, Godric.

Just then, another brother hurried into the workshop, begging their pardon, but the prior was
needed to supervise a dispute over a translation between two brothers in the scriptorium, which was
looking a bit "ugly" according to the harried-look-
ing brother who had come to fetch him.

It was not the first interruption. The prior appeared to be a busy man despite the small numbers of monks laboring in the monastery. He had told her upon her arrival that they now hosted as many lay brothers as committed monks and barely met the apostolic number of twelve in their chapter house. The plague, he had said sadly, had hit their tiny enclave as hard as it had hit the village and nearby castle.

Still, despite his full schedule, he had been enthusiastic about her desire to learn more about the healing arts and herbs.

"Brother Arnulph will be your guide," Prior Bruin said, "and we will meet later in my office. I have some books to send back with you, my lady."

He nodded to the other monk.

Brother Arnulph gave her a rather reluctant look, she thought, but he opened a sack of something that filled the air with sudden sweetness. "Here," he said, nodding to the sack. "Put your hands in there."

Gwyneth plunged her hands wrist-deep into the sack. "Lavender? Such a great harvest of it! What do you do with it?" She knew Belle had made perfumes from it, but had also used it for other things in the infirmary mysterious to Gwyneth.

"It's useful for numerous disorders," Arnulph noted. "It can be used to treat cuts, bites, stings, and such, but can also be made into a soothing tonic for tension and insomnia. A sprig," he added, "placed behind the ear cures headaches."

He took the sack away, closing it back up, and went on for some time demonstrating various ways the sweet-smelling herb could be prepared for medicinal purposes.

Eventually, having given her the great bag of it to take back to Valmond, he took her out into the open herbularius and finished his lesson over the bed of lavender itself, and he dug up a small plant, urging her to take it with her to start her own physic garden.

Gwyneth thanked him and Arnulph nodded, gazing off beyond her. She watched his stern profile, wondering what sort of warrior became a monk. She would have liked to ask him, but she didn't feel quite comfortable with him.

She had the distinct impression he didn't approve of the tutelage Prior Bruin had pressed on him.

A brother appeared from across the garden, calling to him from the bloodletting house, then gesturing as if there were some urgent matter.

"If you will wait here, my lady," Brother Arnulph said. "I will escort you to the prior's office anon."

Gwyneth wandered aimlessly, looking back over the beds as she passed them, trying to remember which herb was grown where. The second time she passed the workshop, she put her head inside, noticed that the lay brother, Godric, was still there, tending to his mysterious bottles.

"Hello," she said.

Godric turned, nodded, then turned back. *Not very friendly*, she thought, but she had questions. She decided to ask them.

"You remind me of someone," she said, walking into the workshop. The door was nothing but an arched opening, really. There wasn't a proper door. "Are you kin to Hertha and Burnet of Valmond?"

"They are my parents," he said.

She felt a finger of something on the back of her neck, and she didn't know why.

"Brother Godric—"

The young lay brother turned. "Please, Lady, you mustn't come in here."

"Why?" She smiled. "Are you doing something secret?"

He frowned. "Of course not."

"Then I would like to come in."

He shrugged and went back to his work.

"You must know something of Valmond if you come from there," she said carefully. "What do you think of the notion that it's cursed?"

"'Tisn't a notion, Lady."

A cold chill ran down Gwyneth's back that didn't have anything to do with the temperature in the workshop. "Are you saying it's true?"

He turned around suddenly. His hollow eyes flared.

"Do you know why the king took that abbey away from the monks two hundred years ago?" he asked her.

She waited.

"They took in travelers, as their order instructed them," he went on. "But travelers didn't leave."

"What happened to them?" She felt her heart starting to pound.

"They killed them. They took their gold and jewels, whatever they had, and they murdered them for it. They had convinced themselves it was their holy duty to take from the rich and give to God. They were certain they would be made saints some day for their charity. It was a madness, of course, and the treasure they'd built up was the beginning of the wealth of the lords of Valmond. That's why they're angry and jealous to this day. That was their treasure, theirs! And they want it back!"

"That was a long time ago," she pointed out. "They're all dead. What does that have to do with the here and now?"

"More than you want to know, Lady."

She frowned. She wasn't going to be scared by his weird, enigmatic words.

"Maybe I do want to know," she persisted. "What then? Will you tell me?"

He took hold of her arm suddenly. "Don't be curious, Lady. Don't ask questions."

She swallowed, wanting to shake off his arm, but his grip was very tight.

"I went into the east wing, to the old monks' cells, myself," she said, playing up the story that even she didn't quite believe. "Someone was there—and it wasn't a ghost. But it was someone who wanted to scare me, not kill me. They shut me in one of the monk's cells."

Godric started to speak, then stopped abruptly, his face changing instantly into a blank mask.

Gwyneth turned, and saw Brother Arnulph approaching through the open doorway. If he'd heard anything of what they'd been discussing, she couldn't tell from his stern face.

"Prior Bruin is ready for you now."

* * *

The prior's office was quiet and dark, lined from floor to ceiling with huge bound manuscripts. Gwyneth had never seen so many books in her life, but she was still thinking about the lay brother, Godric, and his strange story.

"How did your first lesson go?" the prior inquired. He nodded as Brother Arnulph entered with a tray of steaming tea in mugs. He handed one to her. "It's lavender tea," he explained. "I'm certain Brother Arnulph gave you quite a lesson about this sweet herb today, did he not? He is quite wise in the way of plants."

Gwyneth sipped the tea. It burned her tongue.

"He had much to say, yes." She almost confided in Prior Bruin the whole bizarre mess of what Godric had told her, but she didn't want to make a bad impression. It all seemed too silly for words.

"How are you settling in at Valmond?" the prior was asking.

She focused on his gentle face. "Not easily," she admitted. "It's been long neglected."

"Yes, it has," the prior agreed. "Too long. It is good that the lord is returning. You will be starting a family soon, I suppose, and the place will be filled up with merriment, with children, the way it once was."

"Yes," Gwyneth said. "I suppose . . ." And it struck her that she had just agreed that she wanted to have a family with Rorke.

She wasn't ready for the full implications of that thought.

"You mentioned you had some books for me," she prodded. She drank down the tea and stood. The prior fumbled to his feet, almost collapsing. She reached across his polished, dark wood desk to lend balance.

"I'm just fine, but thank you for your help, Lady," he said, smiling again. "Here you go." He picked several manuscripts from a shelf and handed them to her. "These are heavy," he warned.

"I'm strong," Gwyneth said, smiling back at him.

"That you are, my lady." He walked with her from the office, through the open cloister and down the flagstone path to the priory gate. "You won't let any of the nonsense get to you, will you, Lady?" he asked as they reached the gate.

The brother who acted as porter swung it open mutely. The soldier who had accompanied her from Rorke's castle waited for her outside with her horse.

"No," she said, wishing now that she had actually gone ahead and confided her fears to the prior. It was obvious he knew all about the ghost stories already. Maybe he knew that Godric had a habit of saying crazy things.

"Good," he said, and he patted her arm and shut the gate. She could hear his cane tap-tapping as he went away down the flagstone path into the cloister.

She started to mount up, then looked back one more time and saw a face in the iron grid of the gate. A face with hollow, burning eyes.

"Go away, Lady," she heard a whispered voice that was eerily familiar. It was the voice she'd heard in

the night when she was lost in the east wing of Valmond. *"Go away."*

She blinked, and the face was gone and she wasn't sure it had even happened. She glanced at the soldier.

"Did you hear that?" she said.

He frowned. "Hear what, milady?"

She shook her head. Was *she* the one going mad? She was letting herself be spooked . . . again.

But as she rode back to Valmond, she was trembling.

Seventeen

"Lady Valmond?"

Gwyneth looked up from the sheet of parchment where she had begun making notes. She placed her quill on the table where she sat by the tall windows in her chamber and smiled at the little girl peering round the door.

It was Lily, the bold village girl who had captured her attention right from the start.

"Come in, come in." Gwyneth noticed the ink on her fingers and frowned. "Oh . . . blow it," she said, remembering the child's presence in time to keep herself from cursing more strongly.

She looked around for a handkerchief and didn't see one, but before she could so much as move, Lily cried, "I'll get you one, milady!" and ran back out.

As always, Lily's enthusiasm was impossible to stop; it was the very trait that had attracted Gwyneth to the child. Also, there was the small fact that Lily reminded Gwyneth of herself. Eager, quick, strong, driven . . . and sometimes a little sad.

Like Gwyneth, Lily had lost her father, and like Gwyneth, Lily had immediately taken to the idea of learning to fight once it was introduced to her.

Gwyneth could see in the little girl her own early need to cover up her fears with physical prowess. Watching Lily practice swords that first day in the village center had made Gwyneth all the more determined to help these women and children in any way she could. And in so doing, she knew already she reaped so much more in return than she could ever give to them.

She was quickly becoming attached to them like a new family. After they'd swept out the hall and cleaned the cobwebs from the keep the first day, she'd enticed the widows to make their homes in fresh-scrubbed sleeping chambers in the tops of the towers. She'd set up a schoolroom for the children and a sewing solar for their mothers.

She'd discovered that Melia could read and write and even knew a bit of Latin, her own father having once worked as a clerk at Valmond, so she had put Melia in charge of the children, who were mostly surprisingly tractable to Gwyneth's mind, who had only herself and her sisters with whom to compare them.

She found jobs for them all. Spinning, candle-making, soap-making, sweeping, sewing, baking, laundering.

It was as if the castle had awoken from a long, dark sleep.

The days blended together, and it was a quite a warm, cheerful, unremarkable little circle they had become.

Except for the sword lessons and the bow and arrow practice and the wrestling exercises Gwyneth led. The women, too long without a man's protection, were eager to learn, and Gwyneth had so much fun teaching them, she scarcely noticed the guards' strange looks and the not-so-quiet comments they made when she blew into the practice room with her troupe. In the same way, she ignored the comments Hertha made under her breath when the children raced through the great hall, laughing and dancing on their way to their chores.

After all, was she not following Rorke's orders? *Mayhap you can do something with Valmond, make it whatever you want, found your own order of lady knights.*

Ha, well, maybe she would.

Her days filled with purpose and meaning, and for the first time in her life, she didn't want to be someone else.

She wanted to be exactly who she was, Gwyneth of Valmond.

The only dark spot in her days was the deep, secret part of her that missed Rorke. She was angry at him, and angry at herself for wishing he was here, for feeling as if nothing were complete without him.

That incompleteness made her vulnerable, and she was scared.

Magwyn had been delighted as she by the sudden filling of the hall, almost as delighted as she was to be Gwyneth's maid. Gwyneth couldn't resist her each morning as she pulled out a a new gown from the dozens packed by Belle.

"Ooh," Magwyn would sigh. "Ahh." Every morning, just the same, her excitement never diminishing.

Gwyneth would watch in the silvered mirror over

the dressing table as the tiny girl's unexpectedly talented hands worked magic in her hair, twisting braids and twining ribbons. There had been makeup in the bags, too. Rouge and kohl and powders and creams.

Magwyn took so much joy in the hairdressing and clothing, the powdering and perfuming, that Gwyneth hadn't the heart to stop her. She gazed, fascinated, at the woman she faced in the mirror each day.

A stranger she wanted to become and to know.

Her hair this day was yet another of Magwyn's curious creations: two plaits, one rolled round at each side of her face, with a shining silver fillet on her head to hold them in place. She wore a gorgeous cotehardie laced up the front with a low neck and tight sleeves, and a narrow belt to accentuate her hips.

What would Rorke think if he could see her now?

What if he had remained all this time at Valmond?

What if he had kissed her again, and even shared her bed?

Would he have resisted her, and would she have resisted him?

What if he was not obsessed with chasing Ranulf?

What if he was not still in love with the ghost of Angelette?

What if, what if, what if.

The questions went round in her head, and she made certain to fill her days with things to do and people to see.

And yet in odd moments, she would feel the incompleteness so strongly that it was like a gaping hole in her soul.

Rorke.

She shook her head, wishing away the thought of him. He had left her, cut his losses. True, they'd never agreed to a real marriage, but the seeming ease with which he'd given up on her stung.

"Milady? Milady?"

Gwyneth blinked, realizing Lily was back with a handkerchief.

"Thank you." She wiped off her hands, leaving stained fingertips but at least none of the liquid that would have ruined her lovely gown.

She picked up the cup of sweet, warm mead Hertha had brought her earlier, along with a slice of honey cake, and took a sip. The mead had grown cold and bitter while she'd been otherwise occupied. She set the cup back down and focused on Lily, brows raised, waiting for the little girl to speak.

"Milady." Lily tipped up and down on her toes in the way she did often, her child's energy always just barely under control. "We are done with the day's lessons and my mother wishes to know if you would like us to work on the new tapestry, or to see if Mistress Hertha could use our help in the kitchen. My mother also says that the kitchen garden wants weeding. Or if you do not wish us to do those things, we can do something else. Whatever milady desires. Or we may play, but only if you say we must."

Lily said the last bit in a rush, with her eyes lighting, and Gwyneth bit back a laugh.

Just then, she saw that Melia had come up behind Lily. The woman looked embarrassed, but before she could speak, Gwyneth forestalled her.

"Oh, my, I think you must play," she told Lily very seriously. "I insist." She cast a glance up at Melia. "Would you like to sit down?"

Melia looked even more embarrassed. "Shoo," she said to her daughter, and Lily ran out. "Milady, I apologize for—"

"No, you must not," Gwyneth interrupted. "I didn't bring you all here to work your fingers to the bone every moment of every day. There is time to work, and time to play. You are doing a wonderful job with the children. I appreciate all that you do."

Melia looked at her feet.

"Thank you, milady.

Gwyneth stared at the bent head, wondering what to do next. At Castle Wulfere, she had always had an easy relationship with the servants in the castle and the villeins in the village and the craftspeople in the baileys. Belle had encouraged a family atmosphere that transcended status.

"Melia." Gwyneth fingered the parchment upon which she'd been jotting notes. "Do you remember when they used to hold Midsummer's Eve feasts at Valmond?"

"Oh, yes!" Melia's head jerked up and her eyes were as bright as Lily's had been a few moments before. "I recall them quite well. It is, in sooth, why I came to see ye after Mistress Hertha said you had mentioned it to her. I was hoping ye might let us help. It would be a good lesson for the children and—"

"Oh, that's wonderful! Sit," Gwyneth said again,

patting the other chair that was pulled up to the small table. This time, Melia took her up on her invitation. "I have no experience in planning a festival at all. You're a godsend."

Melia blushed. "Nay, 'tis ye that is that, milady," she argued. "I never would have believed we could be happy and safe here, considering—" She stopped, frowned.

"Considering what?" Gwyneth pressed. "You don't still believe in curses, do you? There is no such thing, you know."

She made her voice very confident, but there was a little part of her that was uncertain. She had not forgotten the voice that had ordered her away; real or not, it haunted her.

And so did the occasional strange incident that she couldn't explain or even quite believe. Things seemed to go missing—like the complete disappearance of the book of herbs given her by Prior Bruin. And the lavender plants from the priory that she'd planted the day she'd brought them back only to find them entirely dead, shriveled as if poisoned, the very next morn. And the bright green bliaut that had been found torn apart on the hall steps one morning.

Mayhap she had not put the book where she thought and it would yet turn up, and mayhap she had planted the lavender incorrectly and killed it herself. Maybe even the slashed gown could be explained. She had been fighting a losing battle keeping the destructive hounds from wandering the keep at will.

But the incidents bothered her because she

didn't quite think her excuses were true, and the idea that someone did not want her at Valmond wouldn't entirely go away.

How much could she put down to overactive imagination? Sometimes she woke in the night with that voice in her head. *Go away.*

And she would almost feel as if that voice had been right there in the room beside her, and she would stay up the rest of the night, sick to her stomach with a fear she hated to acknowledge.

Then dawn would break, and she would feel safe again, at least for another day. But sometimes, lately, the sick gnawing would come back during the day, when she least expected.

Like now. She'd skipped the noonday table because her stomach had been so ill. Even now, she feared she couldn't hold down the cake Hertha had left.

The nightmare had been particularly vivid last night. She'd been locked in the monk's cell, and all around her were the voices, soft but frightening.

She'd woken, cold, to a dead hearth and a chamber door just barely cracked open.

It had been completely shut when she'd gone to bed. Or so she had thought.

"There is nothing to fear at Valmond," Gwyneth assured Melia, or perhaps herself.

She'd asked Magwyn about the open door, and the maid had insisted it had been closed, but she'd looked frightened, as if afraid *she* might be in trouble, so Gwyneth had dropped the questioning. She'd gone about her day—another visit to Brother Arnulph and the physic garden for more lavender and lessons—and then had come here, to the table by the tall windows to work on her festival plans.

"I fear nothing when I'm with ye, milady," Melia countered.

"All right, then." Gwyneth determined to change the subject. "We must have it all: Saint John's bread, destiny cakes, crowns and boughs, a mumming play. We must have a mumming play—I was thinking a play of Saint George."

"I was hoping you would say that." Melia exchanged a happy look with Gwyneth. "That was always my favorite part of the festival."

"Perfect! You can help me plan it out. We need to write down roles. We'll have something for all the children. And we've got to get to work on costumes, and make menus. We've less than a fortnight to prepare. For the first time in my life, I'm looking forward to something that involves cooking and sewing. I can't believe it!"

At that, Melia laughed, for they all knew by now that Gwyneth possessed any number of extraordinary skills—and a rather odd lack of ordinary ones.

"Shall we start by inspecting the trunks in the solar, milady?" Melia suggested. "There are reams of material there, and perhaps there is something that will be sufficient to make a dragon costume. The sewing will take the most time—that, and staging the play with the children. We must choose a Saint George and teach him to slay a dragon."

"You're right. Let's start with the costume, then we'll assemble the children. And I am so glad that you know how to make a dragon costume, for I do not." Gwyneth stood up, too fast perhaps.

She could hear Melia speaking, saying, "Ah, milady, but ye know how to slay a dragon with a sword!"

A rush of lightheadedness took Gwyneth as pain seared her belly.

"Oh, milady, are ye ill?"

One hand gripping her middle as she sank down again, Gwyneth lifted the other to her forehead. She felt hot suddenly, though the fireplace was all the way across the room and the chamber itself was quite cool. Her mouth was dry.

She felt Melia's gentle arm on her shoulder.

"I'm all right," Gwyneth said, forcing strength back into her voice. She was absolutely never ill, had the constitution of an ox, Damon was wont to say.

She took a deep breath, then another, willing the tight pain in her stomach to ease.

"I'm not getting enough sleep lately. My humors are out of balance."

"Milady, are ye certain it's not something else?"

Gwyneth glanced at the young woman, puzzled.

"Mayhap ye're with child, milady."

"Oh, no, Melia, you don't understand." Gwyneth choked back a bitter laugh.

No, of course Melia didn't understand.

"But milady, of course that is what it must be!" Melia sounded excited. "What else?"

Gwyneth stared at her, middle-of-the-night anxiety building in her belly again, making it hard to breathe.

What else?

* * *

The days that followed passed in strange layers of pleasantness mixed with apprehension. There was much to do to prepare a feast, and for Gwyneth it was a novel experience to be in charge. She oversaw every detail, no matter how minute, from the endless testing of the precise combination of ginger, anise and basil that would go into the cuckoo-foot ale to the weaving of the birch wreaths and the sewing of the dragon costume.

She left the preparations only once, to make her weekly visit to the priory to learn more from Brother Arnulph, returning this time with rosemary, fennel and mint for the new physic garden she was determined to nurture. But between mumming play practice and crown-weaving, there had been little time for gardening—or anything else.

But she hadn't forgotten about Brother Godric, even though she hadn't seen him during either of her last visits. She felt as if she saw him every time she caught Burnet watching her strangely from beneath his shuttered lids as he shuffled across the hall.

Even Hertha, with her usually benevolent smile, made her uneasy. She could not forget they were Godric's parents, nor the queer way he had spoken to her in the workshop.

"A terrible dragon has been menacing a kingdom!" Valora's voice rang out, interrupting Gwyneth's thoughts as another round of mumming play practice—their fourth run-through this afternoon—commenced. The girl was the eldest of the children and had therefore been designated the narrator.

"Only one way to placate the dreaded worm has been found: to feed it the fat cattle and sheep and geese of the land," Valora continued. "But when these are gone, the dragon turns to the people of the kingdom, to its tender and sweet young damsels. Even the king must offer up his own child, his darling princess."

Gwyneth nodded approvingly, and Valora's rosy cheeks grew brighter. Now, Gwyneth turned to Thacker, the young boy designated as king, and stared long and hard at him, then waved her hand at him when he didn't move. Above them, the sky rumbled with the threat of summer rain.

Queen Eleanor's bones. They were going to get wet. It had been her idea to take their practice to the high meadow beyond Valmond. The idea had seemed good at the time. Even with the happy sounds of children and work filling the once-deserted hall, there was still something of gloom about the place that she found hard to shake off beneath its roof.

It was so much easier to dismiss her fears beneath the open sky where she felt strong and healthy and free. She loved the spongy grass under her feet and the far-off sounds of sheep's bells tinkling and birds flapping their wings overhead. The children's laughter was sweet and easy, seeming to rise up around her like the breeze.

She could forget the queer looks of the castle guards, and the mysterious words of Brother Godric.

And she could forget that sometimes, inexplicably, she felt sick.

Thacker stood unmoving for too long, until Lily smacked him on the back of the head.

"Ow!" He stumbled forward.

"Woe is me," she hissed. "Woe is my daughter. Woe is all this awful slaughter."

Thacker repeated the words as Lily, the natural Saint George despite her female status, jumped before him brandishing her stick sword.

A splat of rain struck Gwyneth's cheek.

"Fly away, good knight," Kirie, the princess, sang out. "Save yourself, and your might."

Magwyn, Tulia and Ardin managed even without the costume that their mothers were busily stitching to present themselves with their dragon roars as they ran with linked hands in a circle around the players.

"I think 'tis ourselves we must save!" Gwyneth announced. "To the castle, children—ere we are all soaked!"

As they ran, several of the older children picked up the younger. Gwyneth took Lily up, and they raced across the sodden meadow, tramping through the tall grasses and summer blossoms with their gowns sticking to their legs and the rain pounding down all around.

They burst into the muddy bailey, laughing helplessly as they struggled to catch their breath, beyond any thought of remaining dry at this point.

"Ho, sir knight, have you courage?" Hadria shouted, sitting atop Valora's shoulders, and before Gwyneth knew it, Hadria and Valora with Tulia atop Thacker, were engaged in muddy mock combat. Thacker and Valora, as the lower portion of the pairs, played the steeds while Tulia and Hadria fought to unbalance each other and win.

Valora stumbled, and she and Hadria slipped into the muddy mess of the bailey.

"We are the champions!" Thacker and Tulia cried gleefully, mopping wet hair out of their faces.

Gwyneth had already set Lily down, but she couldn't possibly miss the girl's bright-eyed interest in the game.

"Come on," Gwyneth said, suggesting what she knew the little girl, despite her eagerness, never would have dared. "We're already wet, already muddy. Get back on my shoulders. We'll show them who the champions are."

"Oh, milady!" Lily barely seemed to hold herself back from leaping onto Gwyneth's back, as if she couldn't quite believe she meant her invitation.

"Come on," Gwyneth said again, and Lily didn't have to be asked another time. Gwyneth held tight to the girl's lower legs and together they circled Tulia and Thacker, teasing, darting, taking them off-guard and almost toppling them several times.

"Champions, ha," chided Lily.

They circled back toward the keep steps, though Gwyneth took care to keep their game at a distance. Any falls would be on soft mud, not on wood or stone. The children around them cheered and laughed at every near-spill.

Thacker, at first shy of taking on his lady, had forgotten his initial hesitance and he, too, danced around, calling out advice and encouragement to Tulia.

The rain still lanced down over them, but they paid it no heed.

"We're coming for you, milady," Thacker warned. "Hold tight, Tulia!" This would be no push or shove, but a full-out assault.

He rammed Gwyneth's shoulder, and together, she and Lily rammed him back—and they both fell at the very same moment.

"Tie!" shouted Valora.

Lily scrambled up and so did Tulia. Gwyneth and Thacker went at it again. She would have held firm this time, she was certain.

Only the door to the keep beyond Thacker crashed open and her gaze caught the blur of movement, then focused in on a pair of vivid blue eyes as thunderous as the sky above them.

Then she hit the ground in a spray of muddy water.

Eighteen

Gwyneth swallowed a trace of panic, stunned at the unexpected sight of Rorke. He looked the same as ever—stiff and formal, his mouth flattened in a grim line, the mature lines of his face that she could have drawn from memory.

But he looked different, too.

His eyes were red-rimmed and dark, as if he hadn't slept since their last meeting. There was an air of desperation to sharpen his expression. His hair was unkempt, his clothing stained from travel, as if he had ridden hard and long.

He was a savage stranger, and yet something within her longed to reach out to him. She did not dare.

Then she remembered herself and her position, sprawled in mud, her clothing soaked in muck. All her visions of Rorke returning to find her arrayed in her newly feminine splendor shattered around her.

She remembered a time not so long ago that she had purposely rolled in mud and presented herself at a feast thusly to cast off the interest of a passing suitor.

Oh, how the Fates were paying her back.

The rain had lightened to a drizzle though the sky above loomed no less gray. She scrambled halfway up, then he was moving down the hall steps to snatch her arm, pulling her the rest of the way to her feet.

He let go of her as if he had accidentally laid hold of a leper. She wanted to disappear.

The children seemed to do just that. They had receded, quietly, soundlessly. All but Lily, and even she hung back in mute fear of this smoldering-eyed lord.

Gwyneth saw now the movement in the stables across the bailey, the men and boys and the light through the open doorway. She had been too full of their childish fun to notice anything different, and the rain had washed away the signs of their horses' trampling on the bailey grounds.

She put a hand to her soaked chest, struggling to steady her breathing. Rorke's gaze followed the movement of her hand, and sealed there upon her, and looking down, she only then realized how the thin material of her summer-weight gown exposed every curve.

Now that they had ceased their play, the chill of the rain-laden air, or perhaps the shock of seeing Rorke, had her nipples pressing against the fabric in visible buds. A sheen of mud covered her such that one could scarcely tell where fabric ended and skin began.

She looked for all the world like a tavern whore in a mud wrestling match.

He jerked his angry gaze from her chest.

"Hie thee to the keep," he growled at the wide-eyed children who had yet to take their awed gazes off him.

Lily jumped before Gwyneth suddenly as if she would protect her lady against this harsh knight.

"I'm not leaving our lady!" Lily cried at him.

Rorke scowled at the girl and muttered something under his breath, then said with controlled evenness, "I will not harm her, child. Do as I say for I am the lord of this castle!"

"Lord Valmond?" Lily breathed, and her awed eyes grew even rounder.

"Go, Lily," Gwyneth said quietly, and this time the little girl heeded the admonishment. The little girl's protectiveness touched her, but this was not the time for it.

They were alone in the bailey now, she and her savage husband. She grew colder simply looking into his eyes. Then, without warning, he reached out and took hold of her with both hands on her upper arms. The rain continued to drip-drip upon them, though slowing all the time, and yet he paid it no heed.

"What in the name of all that is holy do you think you are you doing, Lady?" he rasped hoarsely.

She swallowed thickly again and raised her chin, shaking back the drenched tangles of hair that fell across her cheeks. They were close now, and her breasts felt his warmth as their bodies touched.

"I am doing," she said willfully, "whatever I wish, as you ordered me."

"I surely did not order you to wallow in the mud like a pig. Had I intended thus, I would have left you in a sty instead of a keep."

She hid her hurt behind a mask of scorn. "I was playing with the children, my lord. But I suppose you wouldn't understand that, of course, because I doubt you have ever played a day in your life, even as a child." She would have shaken off his grim hold, but she knew better than to think she could. "What brings you to Valmond, my lord? Shelter? Provisions? Or merely the urge to rail at me once more?"

"This is my home, and I will return to it when I will," he replied. "Is this how my wife will greet me? You knew I was coming. I sent you a letter."

Letter? She didn't know what he was talking about. "I received no letter, my lord." She dug her heels in, angrier all the time. "But no doubt in your mind I should ever be prepared for your imminent return. Silly me. From this day forth I will array myself in finery and sit at the high table from dawn to dusk in anticipation of your arrival."

"That would be preferable to your wallowing in mud in my castle bailey, Lady," he grated back at her. "Look at you!" His gaze raked her again, and his jaw flexed with some effort at control that she realized a breath before he did was doomed to fail. "Look at you," he repeated in a soft rasp. "Saints damn you, for I do not want to look at you, Gwyneth."

"Then don't look if I offend you."

"I can't stop—"

His eyes were tortured, aching. She could feel the sinewy might of him, the taut intensity, and then it wasn't fear clogging her lungs but awareness. Devastating, tingling awareness.

"I can't stop this," he whispered now, and then his mouth slashed across hers, the pressure of his tongue opening her lips to him and igniting a shiver that went through her entire body.

She opened to him immediately; no one could say he ever forced her. He hesitated just long enough to give her a chance to push him away, and then he filled her mouth, licking, tasting, brushing his tongue over her teeth, tracing the line of her mouth, as if it had all been held back too long. He plundered inside yet again with a ferocity that was as much despair as passion. She was chilled and burning all at once, and then she felt as much as heard him groan against her mouth.

He tore his lips from hers abruptly and she stared at him, wobbling, almost lightheaded—for lack of air or lack of him, she wasn't certain. He had sent her to a place where there were no thoughts, only feelings and a restless need.

This kiss was what she had been craving. This kiss and this man filled the hole inside her, and the comprehension was overwhelming. She had to think. She wanted him! Holy women warriors, she wanted a man. There was no more denying it. And she wanted *this* man. Would she run away from these feelings—again—or would she do something about it?

She was scared.

She bit her lip, suddenly realizing that she might cry—and desperate to keep it from happening. She marshaled her strength.

"You may be my husband, but I am not yours to use as you will." She shoved at his chest, knowing she didn't have long. She had to get away. "You will not be a stranger and my lover at your whim. I may be wallowing in mud, my dark and brooding lord of Valmond, but at least I am not wallowing in my own selfish misery, doing everything I can to make everyone around me equally as miserable. That, I leave to you."

She could feel her eyes filling with moisture, but Rorke's flinch told her she'd struck well and deep. She seized the opportunity to shake loose of his hold.

Lifting her chin a notch higher, she added: "Welcome home, my lord. I have worked hard to restore your hall. I hope it pleases you even if I do not."

And then to her absolute horror, the tears spilled onto her cheeks.

"Gwyneth." He looked drawn and harsh, pale beneath the sun-dark of his skin. "I never said—"

"No, you never did," she cut it off. "You never said a lot of things. Like, good-bye. Again."

She pushed past him, running up the stone steps of the hall, through the open doors, and past the gaping stares of his men.

Rorke stood at the door of Gwyneth's chamber and pounded on it yet again. Damn bars and bolts, he knew she was in there. He was still again, waiting for a response, but heard nothing. Of course not. She was probably sitting there polishing her sword, waiting for him to leave again so she could go back to . . .

I am doing whatever I wish, as you ordered me.

He hadn't ordered her to drive him mad.

But that wasn't her fault; it was his own. His anger had deflated as quickly as the great oak door of the hall had slapped shut behind Gwyneth—if not before.

In sooth, he didn't know what he'd been feeling out there.

Seeing her wrestling in the mud with the children had kindled emotions, but he knew if there was any good reason for the ire he'd expressed it was not that she displeased him but rather that she pleased him too much.

Watching her flashing eyes, unfastened hair falling wildly, gown clinging to her mud-slick breasts, he'd filled with a powerful passion, a desperate starvation, a tender agony. He couldn't bear it.

His body wanted what he'd denied for so long: her. But he could lose his mind with her, and that terrified him. When he kissed her, she made him think he could be whole again.

He couldn't risk the peril of her, and yet he couldn't resist her, either—and that was wrong, not just for his own sake but for hers. It wasn't her crime that his heart was ruined, and she shouldn't be paying the price. And yet she was.

Those tears had killed him, even more so because they were tears she would never have wanted him to see.

But even so, he'd stood for a damnable time in the courtyard, in the chill of the air, damp even as the rain dissipated, putting off going within to do what he knew he must, wondering what had happened to his comfortably bland life, the one in which he was focused and had no thought but to ride and ride and ride—

He'd forgotten all about his lost, blackened heart. And he'd forgotten all about Valmond, and his people. Now Gwyneth was bringing it all back to life—his home, his people, and even his creaking, hurting heart—and he hated her for it. He wanted to be left alone, and she wouldn't let it happen, which was blatantly obvious when he finally did go within.

The hall was, in fact, full of people! People who stared at him with awe and trepidation. Conversations lurched to a halt wherever he passed, their gazes searing his back.

His keep was like a foreign land. But it was not, it was his, and she was his, too.

And she would not bar him from any chamber in it. Especially when he owed her an apology.

There was something inside him that was going to swallow him whole if he didn't make it.

And then—then, he would ride away again.

"Open this door, Lady, or I will break it down!" he thundered.

And he verily would have if at that very moment he hadn't heard the iron bolt slide from its bracket. The face of a pale girl appeared in the cracked opening.

"Milord—" she started, but he didn't give her time to finish, pushing the door wide and moving past her and into the chamber. The room was empty but for a tub by the fire. The air carried the heavy scent of honeysuckle, and the windows swathed the room in the gray light of the rainy dusk.

"I was bathing, my lord husband, and if it is all the same to you, I did not want company," Gwyneth said from behind him.

Rorke slowly turned. She stood there, motionless, the cheerless cast of the light behind her softened by the glow of firelight flickering within the chamber and lending a misty, golden quality to her. She looked otherworldly in that instant—angelic, or fairylike.

This was his first true look at her since he'd returned, and he was spellbound.

She was more slender than he remembered, but hardly thin. She was too strong to ever be called skinny. Her breasts swelled against the embroidered bodice of her red bliaut as if they might yet burst from the confines. Above the line of the bosom, her bare skin was flushed and dewy, fresh from the bath. Her hair tumbled freely, still wet but combed, dark and shining.

Her cheeks were pink, her lips as rose-hued as her gown, her eyes hidden even as they gazed squarely back at him. There was something different about her, and he couldn't put his finger on it. She was strong, boyish Gwyneth, and she was another person entirely at the same time.

"Magwyn, you may go," she said quietly to the girl still hovering in the doorway.

The girl scampered out as if only too glad to go, and Rorke, without turning, reached back and shoved the door shut.

"Did you forget something?" Gwyneth asked, still

watching him with those secret eyes that told him nothing of her thoughts. "Was there something else you wanted to shout at me about before you leave again?"

She crossed her arms. "Maybe you'd like to bellow at me for bringing the women and children up from the village?" she went on, clearly just warming up. "Or for teaching letters to the villeins? Or how about the Midsummer's Eve festival? Maybe you could thunder at me for not gaining your permission before planning such an event?"

He stared at her, surprised and yet not surprised. What had he expected?

Surely it was a joke that he had thought he could tuck away Gwyneth of Wulfere in his old, crumbling family home and not expect her to turn it upside down.

And equally mad that he'd thought she wouldn't upend his life and his heart just as well.

"Or, I know, you will for certes want to rebuke me for teaching the women to heave swords," she added.

She was teaching the women to heave swords? He drove a hand through his hair and prayed for patience to deal with her.

"I'm not here to rebuke you."

She didn't move, just stood there glaring at him, and suddenly he saw the hurt burning through her eyes. Then she spun away.

He closed the space between them, took her shoulders in his hands and turned her around. He wanted to banish that hurt, but—how?

"Are you going to kiss me again?" she demanded,

her dark eyes shiny. She was looking at him as if she wanted him to react.

"No, I'm not going to kiss you," he said with every ounce of will in his body for oh, how he would have liked to do just that. He dropped his hands from the temptation of her and stood back.

"Why not?" She jutted her chin at him.

Were the saints laughing at him? Or was she?

He was a fool and a half to have come in here. The less he was around Gwyneth, the better, because when he looked at her, he thought maybe he *could* kiss her again.

Could even take her to bed, then go on his way with no regrets, no recriminations, no pain—for him or for her.

But none of that was true. Sleeping with Gwyneth, even kissing her again, would only make things so much worse. There was no redemption for him, only doom.

He took his hands from her, and they shook with the need to touch her again. His desire for her grew thicker, deeper, more powerful all the time.

"I'm sorry," she said abruptly. "You don't have to answer that."

She drew a nervous hand through her bath-damp hair.

"Gwyneth—"

"I don't know what I was thinking—" She started to walk away.

"No." He stopped her. "Don't apologize for anything. I came here because I'm the one who owes an apology to you."

"Then you've made it." She shrugged. "You know what? I've got things to do." She pushed past him.

How had this conversation gone so ill? He found his senses before she was completely out of the room. He took hold of her from behind.

"Let go of me," she demanded, fighting him with all her considerable strength, but he was stronger. "Damn you, Rorke, stop! You don't want to have this conversation with me, trust me. I don't want to have this conversation!"

"No. No, I'm not going to stop," he said gruffly against her hair. He won, she ceased her struggle, but her body remained tense beneath his hold. "I do want to have this conversation. I wasn't rejecting you just now, don't you understand that?" He gritted his jaw. "God, no, I know you can't understand that." He turned her in his arms. "You just shocked me, that's all."

"No. That's not all." She shook her head. "There's more, a lot more. But let's just leave it alone."

"What do you want?" he asked, his voice low, imploring. He would give almost anything to take the hurt from her eyes.

He was totally unprepared for what she said next.

"I want you to kiss me again." The words came out in a stark rush, and for a frozen heartbeat afterward, he was convinced she was as shocked by them as he.

"That would be a mistake." It was the first thing that came out of his mouth, and immediately he regretted it. Saints in hell, he was no master of words, and she was killing him here. Did she have any idea how much he wanted to pick her up and

take her to that huge bed only steps away from
them and do exactly as she'd asked—and more?

But she'd cast her glance away from him, hiding,
and he had no idea what she was thinking now. He
pulled her chin up and she jerked in shuddering
breath.

"I'm sorry. God, that was stupid," she said. "It's
just that I have these feelings, inside. I've never felt
this way before." She stopped, clearly confused.

"What feelings? Tell me." He had to know. He
had to torture himself.

"Tight. Hot. Yearning. Terrible and wonderful."
Her words came out soft, each one killing him.

His own body became tight, yearning, hot. She
was describing physical desire that she could not
even comprehend in her innocence. God save him.
She desired him. That made everything so much
worse.

"Gwyneth—"

"Forget I said anything," she interrupted tensely,
the confusion disappearing behind the brittleness
he hated. "Go away again—forget about me. You're
good at that. I am not your problem."

The strangeness he'd seen in her before took her
over, masking her expression. He didn't like the
mask. He preferred her honesty, her impulsivity—
even when that part of her took him off-balance,
like now.

She was his wife, dammit. She *was* his problem.
What if he left and she took out these new—feelings—with another man? What did she mean, she
wasn't his problem? He felt an uncomfortable

twinge, and was shocked to realize it was posses-
siveness.

Why hadn't he ever thought about the possibility
that she would not be satisfied to remain an eternal
virgin? He had been so busy convincing himself she
was a child that he'd forgotten she was a woman.

"Good-bye," she repeated.

But for the first time, he didn't want to leave.

Nineteen

It was sometime past midnight when Gwyneth knew she would not get a wink of sleep, and rose. The flames burned low in the grate, and it was cold. She stoked the fire with the extra wood left behind for the night by Magwyn but remained restless. Throwing on her mantle, she climbed the tower stairs and walked out onto the battlements. The figure of a guard pacing out his watch was a distant shape on the wallwalk.

Below lay the shadowed muddiness of the bailey and above, the shimmering sky. The thick clouds and rain had passed away, leaving a clear night with stars so bright, she could almost believe that she could reach out and touch them.

The moon hung low and round, magical.

She leaned against the cold, damp stone crenellation, closed her eyes, and wished—for what, she did not know. Courage, perhaps.

A sound, like the heavy creak of a great door, broke through the thick quiet. She opened her eyes to see a shape move out of the shadows in the bailey, coming away from beneath her where the keep steps lay and into the moonlight. A brace of hounds lifted their heads curiously as the shape passed but made no sound or movement. She recognized the man immediately as Rorke, as must the guards on watch because none challenged him. There was no knight as tall or broad-shouldered as he.

His stride was purposeful, grim. There was something about the way he walked that said so much about who he was as a man, and she watched him, captivated against her will.

So he was awake, too. Perhaps he was still poor-humored from their clashes earlier, or perhaps it was something else. She couldn't look at him now without feeling a shivery reminder of that delicious and dangerous desire that had so betrayed her when he'd kissed her.

She was embarrassed, and she didn't like being embarrassed.

She'd lost her head, acted like a goosegirl, kissing him back of all things! Crying! She'd even, saints forbid, had the audacity to demand he either be her lover or a stranger. And what was worse, he'd chosen neither one!

Things couldn't possibly get worse than that, but somehow they had. Her tongue had further escaped her.

No, I'm not going to kiss you.

Why not?

Of all the fool-mouthed things to say! What had made her say that? But of course she knew the answer.

She tried so hard not to care. Their marriage was a sham, a horrible joke. And yet the terrifying truth was that she did care. She wanted him. She loved him.

It was sheer stupidity. She could never have him, and yet she was forced to face the truth she'd been hiding from herself—possibly, for years. She could deny it no longer. She craved his touch, his kiss, his very breath upon her cheek. She wanted another kiss.

Nay—millions of kisses.

But she knew Rorke's kisses were not freely given. They came unwilling, out of some black torment inside him. There was a very good chance that it was not even her, Gwyneth, whom he kissed in those mad moments. Rorke couldn't forget Angelette, the grief of her loss ever clouding his mind. Were his kisses meant for Angelette? And if so, then as soon as he snapped back to reality, he pushed Gwyneth, the poor stand-in, away.

It was the only thing that made sense. She allowed herself no other delusion.

But the truth was, she would kiss him all over again even knowing it. Look how easily her heart, mind, lips were carried away every time she found herself in his presence. She had never been good at keeping her thoughts to herself. And all she could think about was kissing him.

No doubt about it, she was in trouble.

She watched as he stopped now in the middle of the bailey, slowly turned, and stared up at the keep toward her position between the crenellations. She remained frozen in the shadows, and yet somehow she knew that he saw her, or merely sensed her, even though his expression remained inscrutable in the pale moon's glow.

For a very long moment, it was as if time suspended on a taut thread, and then he turned away again, engulfed by the inky shadows and whatever purpose led him out on this night. She slipped away to the tower stairs.

But not to sleep.

He saddled his stallion on his own. No stableboys were awake, but he didn't mind. His horse was well trained and stood obediently, awaiting his master. Rorke led the animal into the bailey, unable to resist looking up again to see if she was still there, his reluctant, troublesome, bewitching lady-bride. But there was no sign of her. She'd gone, back to her chamber and her bed, where she belonged.

Her spell lingered.

If he had any sense at all, he'd lock her in that tower and never let her go. He'd be safer that way, and so would she.

Damn her and her bold, bedazzling eyes, her rash, challenging mouth, and especially her proud, tender heart. Damn her shockingly luscious body, and damn him for not being able to ignore her.

He didn't want to think about her, about her fearless innocence that could almost make him believe in virtue and goodness again. He didn't want to think about kissing her, about satiating that desire of hers, or about looking up in the moonlight and seeing her staring down at him, as if she were as awake and as tortured with need as he. He didn't want to know that.

It would only make everything so much more difficult.

He passed outside the walls of Valmond, and at his signal, his horse began to canter. He headed across the high grounds beyond the castle, away from the village and woods. In the moon-splattered night, the way was clear, the land glimmering like a sea of tall, fragrant grasses. He passed over it with the strange feeling of a ghost flying over the land, lost and not belonging.

Only the lingering ache in his wounded and not completely recovered shoulder reminded him that he was alive.

He rode until dawn, away from the sweet promise of her arms and her body, away from Valmond, away from himself.

But there was no escape.

The morning was fine and bright, in stark contrast to the thunderous afternoon of the day before. The priory gardens glimmered softly with the dew as she followed the soft lines of the turf walks alongside Brother Arnulph.

"This is one of our busiest times in the gardens," the warrior-monk stiffly informed her as if he wished she would not bother him but was too polite and obedient to his prior to come right out and say so. "There is more than enough for one man to do, but there is only one man to spare for it these days."

Again, she had not seen Brother Godric on this visit. There had been no sign of him since the first time she had come to the priory. Another monk had been stationed in the workshop, busily hanging up herbs to dry and tending bubbling concoctions over a fire.

"Now come," Brother Arnulph prodded when Gwyneth hesitated near the doorway of the workshop, staring at the unfamiliar man working there. "I'll show you what there is to show, and you are welcome to take whatever cuttings can be safely carried with you."

"Thank you. I fear my tutelage is an imposition on your time. Perhaps if there was some other among you who could teach me, it would be a relief to your schedule. I have not seen Brother Godric—"

"I do not seek to evade my duty, my lady," Brother Arnulph interrupted her. "I do not complain of whatever is required of me." He increased his pace, and she hurried to keep up with him. They passed a fountain in the middle of the garden, and then the low outbuilding that she knew was the bloodletting room.

"What occupies Brother Godric that he is not available to assist you in the garden?" she asked as she kept pace with the monk. She did, and didn't, want to see the strange lay brother. She didn't know if she would have the nerve to ask him if she had truly heard him whispering, *Go away*, that day at the gate.

In any case, the question of it at the very least kept her mind off Rorke for a short time. She hadn't seen him since the midnight locking of their gazes from battlements to bailey. She'd woken to discover he and his men still at the castle, though busily occupied at the gate tower where Rorke appeared to be engaged in the planning of needed repairs to the inner mechanics of the portcullis.

She had ridden out, accompanied by one of the men, pointedly not issuing a good-bye to her lord husband as she passed him. Unfortunately, she doubted he appreciated the symbolism, or even took the time to notice.

Brother Arnulph's face was rigid in profile. He didn't look at her as he responded to her last question about Brother Godric.

"He remains in the bloodletting room."

"The bloodletting room? Is there something wrong with him? Is he ill?"

Brother Arnulph did look at her now, and his tone was impatient. "We are all bled about six times a year. 'Tis a way of relieving the build up of bad humors in the body. Afterward, the brother being treated will enjoy a sojourn of recovery, receiving nourishment and relaxing walks in the solitude of the private garden."

He made a sharp wave of his hand, and she realized the vined tunnel to the side of the bloodletting room must lead into that private garden. In the shadowy recess of the trellis, she could see that there was an iron gate and that it was locked with a chain.

She had a mind to ask him if she could peek in to that hidden garden and wish Brother Godric well on his recovery, but suddenly, Brother Arnulph knelt down as if they had arrived at their destination and began to expound quite volubly upon the nurture and uses of fennel. He was full of hints and tips for its use as a reliever of stomach ailments, especially for babies, and most curiously, as a facial pack to remove wrinkles.

"Ah, I will have to keep that in mind," Gwyneth murmured, thinking to make a joke of it, but put off by Brother Arnulph's consistent seriousness.

"We chew the seeds on fasting days to ward off hunger," he ended. "Now, it is almost time for High Mass, and the prior has instructed me to make sure that you visit with him before taking your leave. If you will wait here, my lady, I will see if he is ready. You may complete your cuttings as you wish."

She nodded, surveying the plantings she had already taken. There was little enough time for gardening at Valmond as of yet, though she expected to have more leisure to devote to her new physic garden there as soon as the Midsummer's Eve festival was over.

Still considering what to add to her basket, she jolted at a sound behind her. She turned, transfixed on the viney tunnel.

Run, Lady. Go home. Return to Castle Wulfere where you belong. Delay not! Run away now.

Those words sounded in her mind, but they were not in her imagination. They were real.

Basket in hand, she strode across the turf paths, careful only not to tromp on any plants, not stopping until she was enclosed in the shadowy passageway where she halted to allow her eyes to adjust to the dimness created by the foliage-dense covering.

At the end of the tunnel-like passage, Brother Godric stood on the other side of the locked gate. Even in the dimness, she could see he was thin and pale, his skin almost ethereal-looking. His eyes were huge and dark and very intense.

"Are you ill?" she asked in spite of what Brother Arnulph had told her about the routine bloodletting. Brother Godric didn't look as if he were being nourished and pampered into recovery. He looked as if he were dying. "Brother Godric?"

"Go away," he said again.

"Why?"

"Come closer," he beckoned her. "Come closer and I'll tell you—"

"Lady Valmond?" she heard behind her.

She wheeled to find the tall, dark figure of Brother Arnulph stalking toward her down the viney tunnel.

"You have no business here, my lady. This is a place of quiet recovery and reflection. You will obey our rules, or—"

He stopped short, took a deep breath at the same time that he gripped her arm and began to guide her firmly out of the passageway. She glanced behind her and saw that Brother Godric was gone, disappeared, as if he had never existed at all.

"I'm sorry," she said as they emerged into the open garden again. "I didn't mean to break any rules—"

Brother Arnulph dropped his hard grip on her arm, and bowed stiffly. "I'm sorry for my reaction, Lady. I did not wish to distress you, but it is true that Brother Godric is ill, much as it pains me to confess it."

"Ill, how? What's wrong with him?"

Brother Arnulph shook his head. "'Tis his mind,

my lady. He is not right in his mind. It is perhaps not safe for you to be near him. We fear, truth be known, that he is mad, Lady. It was your own well-being that roused me so, but I didn't mean to rail at you in such an offensive manner. I trust you will forgive me."

Gwyneth swallowed, shocked. She thought about Hertha and Burnet. Did madness run in their family? There were times Hertha had seemed . . . strange. And Burnet—he *always* seemed strange. He was ever walking about alone, muttering, avoiding her and watching her all at once.

Did they know about Godric's condition? She thought back to the first time she had visited the priory and had met Godric. He had been busy in the workshop, his demeanor normal if not for the dire warnings. What had happened since then? Did the prior and Brother Arnulph know about the things Godric had said to her?

But these were questions she couldn't resolve on her own. She nodded. "Of course. I understand."

"Then please, come with me now. Prior Bruin awaits."

Without further discussion, he escorted her to Prior Bruin's office, though she was surprised that when they arrived, he took her through to the rear and out into a private walled garden she hadn't realized existed. She found Prior Bruin there, trimming off dead roses.

"It is a task I keep jealously to myself," he explained with a twinkle in his eyes after she joined him. "I take a sinful pride in my roses, my lady, but worse, I do not repent for I enjoy it too much."

Gwyneth had to laugh at that genuine comment, finding that with each visit the awesome, fragile prior became more human to her, which made him only that much more inspiring. His health was clearly frail, and yet he had a strength of will that made her think he could do anything.

She set down her basket, and he gestured her to a seat at a small stone table. The seat was cushioned and comfortable. She set the basket on the ground. A young lay brother arrived with flagons of the sweet herbal tea Prior Bruin favored. The prior took his own seat and they enjoyed their refreshment in the warmth of the summer morning. Her mind constantly went back to Brother Godric, though, and the small conversation they made about the upcoming Midsummer's Eve feast was little distraction.

"My lady, I fear you are sore plagued by worries this day," Prior Bruin said at last, and Gwyneth blinked, realizing she had been staring off at the moss-covered wall of the garden for a long time without saying anything.

"I'm sorry—" she began, but he stopped her with a gentle pat on the back of her hand.

"I am not offended, my lady," he soothed. "I am only concerned."

"It's Brother Godric," she burst out. "I—" She didn't know what to say, how to explain all the jumble of fears and fancies that had filled her mind since she'd arrived at Valmond. She fiddled with the carved base of the drained mug she still held. "He said strange things to me the first time I came here. He told me about a curse—"

"My dear lady—"

"He isn't the only one," Gwyneth rushed on. "The village women, they spoke of a curse, too. And the first night I was at Valmond—" She didn't know how to put the spookiness that had emanated from Hertha's words that night. It was all too thin and unreal to hold up under the light of a bright morning.

"Lady Valmond." Prior Bruin was patting her hand again. "Do not bestir yourself on account of these wild stories. They are naught but fevered imaginings of a fevered mind."

"Was the tale about the abbey and the murders true?"

The prior's aged, kindly face drew in sorrowful lines. "Yes, my lady. It saddens me to confess, that is true. But that was a long time ago. There is nothing but lunacy to the tale of the curse. When the great plague doomed so many here at the priory and at Valmond—and across all England—there were those who saw in every death a curse. When the lord of Valmond, along with his heir and his wife and child, perished, some claimed it was the hand of that curse. The monks taking back Valmond's treasure from the grave. But that is not possible, my lady. Fear not."

Gwyneth felt foolish. Of course it was nonsense. "I shouldn't have mentioned it." She was allowing herself to get ridiculously worked up. Her stomach was tied in a knot from it.

She took her leave soon afterward. The prior walked her to the gate despite his fragile bearing, as always. She saw nothing of Rorke. The midday meal was laid on the great tables in the hall. The children were eagerly supping, and she sat with them but could eat nothing. Her stomach hurt, and she couldn't stop thinking about Godric.

Why was the lay brother so bent on warning her away from Valmond?

She went into the kitchen to seek Hertha, but she wasn't there. Burnet wasn't in his office. He was, in sooth, rarely in his office. She had no idea how he occupied his time, but he was always occupied elsewhere.

What would she have asked them, anyway?

Was Hertha as mad as Godric? And what about Burnet?

Gwyneth straightened her spine, shook off the mire of thoughts. She was worrying herself sick. She scarcely made it to her room before the tight spiral of pain in her stomach overcame her.

She didn't know how long she rested. She slept, and the pain in her belly unwound by the time she woke. The afternoon was near past when she woke, feeling wrung out from the bout of sickness. She was able to eat some of the bread she found waiting for her on the table by her bed, and even drink the cool tea.

Determined, she sought out what had always made her feel strong.

Gripping the sword now, she cleared her mind, closed her eyes, focused inward on the strength upon which she had ever relied. The practice sword—heavier than her usual weapon—was held in her right hand, outstretched downward. She visualized her imaginary partner.

Opening her eyes, she stepped out on her left foot and parried.

"Opponent runs past on the right," she whispered, even that sounding loud in the empty guardroom. Late-day sunbeams striped the stone floor from the small, high windows.

She brought her sword over her head, pivoting, following her nonexistent foe.

"Second opponent enters from the left." She pivoted and passed forward, making a cut at the new adversary. Her sword whipped air. She pushed at a damp lock that fell from the simple braid with which she'd bound her hair.

The gown she wore now was her plainest, one fit for physical practice not fashion. She was not trying to impress anyone here but herself.

This was her element. Her mind, jumbled with too many worries and emotions, was clear here, focused. The stress and uncertainties surrounding her life at Valmond fell away completely, if only for a few blessed moments.

Even time spent with the children, rehearsing the Saint George drama they would perform in only a few more nights, could not take her mind off her troubles as utterly as this false combat. Her skill and prowess with a blade had always been her comfort and her shield.

She passed forward again, struck out again, then balancing on her right foot, thrust her other foot in a high kick.

"Ha!" she whispered, her fantasy foe defeated.

"But what about the first opponent, Gwynnie? Don't forget him." She pivoted in time to receive the next fictitious attack, defending herself with a powerful horizontal swipe. The muscles in her shoulders strained, but she held the sword steady.

She delivered another series of passes, pivots, thrusting and parrying with her nonexistent partner, ending with a crushing two-handed cut. "Cleaved in twain, he dies," she finished.

After a moment, she lifted her chin and swung the sword in a great arc over her head once, then twice, and lowered it to her side.

It was at that very moment that she heard the applause.

Twenty

Today there was no rich red bliaut that made her lips look like lush, ripe cherries, nor any innocently tempting mud-plastered kirtle that revealed every other attribute he'd never wanted to know she had. Both of those Gwyneths were, in many ways, strangers to Rorke.

The woman he found in the guardroom now was the one most familiar to him.

Gwyneth the warrior, the fighter. A sword in her hands, a fire in her eyes as she faced him.

The splendor of the late afternoon rained over her, touching off shimmers in her hair. She looked like an angel. A strong, dauntless angel, tall and curvaceous and sensual even without the womanly accoutrements she had surprised him with last night.

She didn't need them.

The feeling in his heart belied its death. Why did his chest hurt when he looked at her if his heart was long ago laid in a grave?

"You fight well, my lady." He straightened, moving from his position leaning in the doorway to the guardroom where he had watched her for too long. The beauty of her movements had captivated him.

What a woman he had wed—wild and free and strong, brighter than all the rushlights burning around them combined.

Had he actually believed he could hide her away at Valmond and forget her?

He was a fool, in too many ways to count.

"I had a good teacher," she said, her eyes carefully shielding her every secret.

He came within a few paces of her and stopped, not sure what he'd do if he got too close. Kiss her, perhaps, as she'd dared.

Or worse, quench the desire in both of them right here on the stone guardroom floor.

"And I had a good student. Sent by God to torment me for my transgressions, I suspect," he added.

"Not God. Maybe it's the ghosts of the jealous monks," she countered, turning. "The curse of Valmond. There is a curse, you know."

He shook his head. "Surely you have not become superstitious, Gwyneth. You were always practical, if a bit on the unexpected side."

"Maybe I've changed."

He prayed for strength. *Yes, God, she'd changed.*

The dying light caressed her face, though he noticed that her skin, usually sun-warmed in a way that was utterly unfashionable for a lady, seemed pale beneath her tan, and the bones on her cheeks were more prominent.

She had lost weight since she had come to Valmond. Was she unhappy here?

The prospect troubled him. He'd wed her and brought her to Valmond to save her, protect her, offer the only kind of freedom she could hope to own.

And yet he'd withheld more than he'd given—out of his own selfish misery, as she'd called it. Was there any way he could make her happy without destroying what was left of himself?

The thought was as haunting as her huge darkling eyes that surrounded him every time he looked at her.

To change the path of his thoughts, he said, "What do you know of this curse?"

"'Tis not I who knows anything," she said. "The villagers are the ones who fear its mysteries. I can get nothing out of them; they fear even to speak of it freely. The villagers are not all gone, you know. They have simply fled into the woods. The ones who remained in the village were, for the most part, the old or those who had no husbands with whom to build new lives. It was these women and their children I brought to the castle.

"Slowly," she went on, "some of those who have fled have been returning to the village. They're curious, but hesitant. I was hoping the Midsummer's Eve festival would bring them out, and that maybe—"

"What, that one night—of song, of dance, of games—would dispell their grief?" he interrupted her, amazed at her innocent expectations. "For there is no curse here, only grief."

"Mayhap it would be a start." She lifted her chin. "It is not impossible. You may have given up on Valmond, but I have not."

"You don't know what you're talking about."

"Neither do you," she responded heatedly. "You choose not to make this your home, but it is mine now—whether I chose it or not. As long as I am here, I will do what I think is right."

As long as she was here. He didn't like her words. He didn't want to lose her.

Suddenly, fiercely, he knew that.

But he knew that he didn't even begin to deserve to keep her.

"I believe you will do whatever you think is right," he said quietly. "I believe that without a doubt. But what if you are wrong?"

What if *he* was wrong? What if he followed his feelings with the same impulsive faith that she did?

Oh, how she tempted him to live with the kind of faith and hope that he had long ago given up.

He took a deep breath, and it sounded oddly shaky in the empty guardroom stillness.

"Just remember that not all problems can be fixed," he added after a moment. "Not all people can be fixed."

Was he warning himself, or her?

She lifted her chin, pugnacious as ever. "Maybe you're the one who's wrong," she pointed out. "Did that ever cross your mind, oh lord of gloom and doom and disaster?"

Without giving him time to respond, she made a disgusted sound.

"Of course not. But lucky for you, I'm here to burst your arrogant bubble. You don't know everything. You're wrong—about a lot of things. Don't feel bad—most men are. Wrong, that is."

"Really?"

"Really."

"That's why I'm founding my own order of lady knights. We'll run the world, solve all the problems. Clearly, men can't handle the job."

"A woman will never—"

"—be equal to a man's task," she finished for him. "Ha." She turned, surprising him by reaching up to the weapon-filled stone wall. She replaced the heavy practice broadsword in her hand and took down not one, but two, lighter, narrower blades.

She strode to him and shoved one at his chest. He caught it in his left fist.

"What are we doing?" he asked.

"Fighting."

"We were already doing that," he teased.

"I like this way better."

She switched her sword to her left hand.

"I'll fight lefthanded to even the field. I know you're not fully recovered in your sword arm."

She was right; his sword arm had not yet regained its former might.

"You don't have to do that," he said, his soldier's pride kicking in.

She shook her head. Her eyes twinkled. Dazzled. "When I mop the floor with you," she said, "I want it to be fair."

He wanted to look away from her, even walk away, but he couldn't. She was starkly beautiful in her plain gown, tangled hair shoved back behind her ears, skin glowing in the syrupy glow of the guardroom. He was absolutely captivated.

And he didn't know whether he wanted to win or lose.

He felt something inside yield itself to her with a sharp, stabbing pang.

She seemed to have gone to another world, concentrating now, as he had taught her. He could see her steadying, focusing, taking deep, even breaths and plotting her strategy.

He had taught her too well, and she was focused and he was not.

She faced him for a long moment, her position one of readiness. He waited for her.

This was her game.

Passing forward, she started with a bold swipe. He evaded, and she passed him again, aiming a cut at his shoulder with careful skill. Even with dulled tips for practice, swordplay was never completely safe.

He pivoted, passed her, and made an answering cut that she parried deftly. Thrusts, parries, cuts, evasions—she was too good and he was too experienced, even without his usual focus, to make it easy.

Her eyes burned into him, alight with her own dark fire. Her hair snapped and danced around her shoulders. She was intense and serene at the same time.

She was fairy queen and warrior spirit.

Saints, she was so lovely, and he wanted her so terribly much.

He realized what he had yielded with that sharp pang before. It was the drive inside that had centered him, that always seemed so important for years. It was breaking apart.

Vengeance, vengeance, vengeance.

Why did his quest seem so empty now, when it was the only thing that had filled him for so long?

Instead, he felt starved for her, and he had fought it, was still fighting it, even as they waged this other, physical and mental battle.

He would lose this battle, too, if he wasn't careful.

She made a diagonal swipe, which he evaded. He countered with a cut to her hip. She parried, but he had her, his blade pressing hard on hers.

"Yield, Lady," he whispered tautly.

She met his look. He kept the pressure on her blade, binding her.

"You taught me better," she breathed back.

"I always beat you. I was the master, remember. You were the pupil."

"I'm not the pupil anymore. But I see you are still a patronizing man."

He laughed, and he saw her eyes drop to his mouth as if she were fascinated by him, unwilling, captured as he was by her. Then her gaze snapped back to his and for that one pulsebeat, he was absolutely lost, swallowed up in her disastrous temptation.

Mistake.

She pushed up with her sword, sending his weapon flying.

"Now," she said sweetly, dulled sword tip at his throat, *"you* will yield."

Rorke didn't move a muscle, not finished taking in the sight of his wickedly capable wife in her triumph. Amazing, he felt no regret at losing.

Yet the words still came with difficulty from his lips.

"I yield, ladywife."

She smiled, smug and beautiful. Fairy warrior. "'Tis about time," she said, and replaced her blade in its place on the wall.

What made him say it? He'd never know. "Demand your prize," he dared her.

The idea had come to her without forethought. There had been no planning. She had not suspected that Rorke would come upon her at practice in the guardroom, or that she would challenge him and win.

She was proud of winning, but not so vain as to grasp that his wounded shoulder had played a large part. Even fighting with his left arm, she could see the flinches of pain in his eyes at certain movements.

It bothered her, knowing that he continued in pain, and she worried that he clearly gave no ground to the weakness. He still rode out on his treacherous quest.

That he was yet at Valmond was a mystery.

A strange set of emotions warred inside her, and just as she had not planned anything else that had happened this afternoon, she had no plan for what would happen next.

She put on her new battle gear—a vibrant gold cotehardie over a light, simple kirtle, and woven ribbons in her plaited hair. She allowed Magwyn to rouge her lips and powder her cheeks.

It made the girl happy.

Silly, that she couldn't quite admit that it made *her* happy, Gwyneth thought. Just as she'd ever hidden from her brother that his order that she stop cutting her hair like a boy's had grown on her in more ways than one, she also found it baffling still to accept that she liked her new femininity, that it didn't have to take away from her strength.

Even harder to confess was how much she wanted Rorke to notice.

He'd seemed to ignore her new look last night when he'd come to their chamber for their brief, uncomfortable conversation. But then, he was good at ignoring her, except when she wanted him to, she thought with a bitter laugh. She'd wanted him to ignore her at the siege of Manvel.

How different would her life be now if he had.

She'd come to the disturbing conclusion that her life had turned out exactly as it was meant to turn out, that somehow, some way, for some reason, she was exactly where she was supposed to be. Which left her with only one question: Why?

Why was she meant to be at Valmond?

What was she supposed to do—heal the castle, its people? Rorke? *Not all problems can be fixed. Not all people can be fixed.*

Rorke was right, she knew that. But she also knew she had to try, anyway. She was headstrong. Or mad. But she had never played it safe in her life, and she couldn't play it safe now. Every time he had kissed her, she had come to that dangerous line between them and she had run away from it. But she was not a coward. There would be no more running. She had always pursued what she wanted, and now she wanted Rorke.

She could not let him ignore her tonight. She had requested a supper basket from the kitchen.

"Follow me," she had told him with no further explanation. "And ask no questions for you have not the right. Do not forget that you lost to me." She enjoyed rubbing it in.

He had watched her with amusement and complied without argument.

They strode in silence now, the evening sun an orange globe in a horizon of unearthly sapphire. Gwyneth couldn't remember ever seeing a sky quite that deep a blue before. The gold of summer rye fields in the distance gilded the landscape. She headed toward the river, a shimmery ribbon in the apple green earth on either side. Stands of leaf-laden trees ran along the banks.

Farther off, the walls of the priory stood quiet and meek.

She shook off a shuddery feeling as the image of Brother Godric in the private garden entered her mind.

Looking back, she saw Valmond rising above them now, dwarfing everything else in the landscape. The pale stones shone gold against the sun, as if something burned up out of the shadows that cloaked the rest of it.

Rorke walked behind her, carrying the basket and rolled blanket. He stopped, looking back as she did.

The evening air was comfortably warm, but she shivered suddenly with a sensation of being spied upon. It was absurd. There was no one about that she could see except the guards pacing out their watch along the ramparts.

Yet she found herself looking around, nervous, edgy.

It was not a new feeling. Since she had come to Valmond, she had felt on numerous occasions as if she were being watched. But she didn't want to think about those ephemeral premonitions tonight.

Rorke glanced at her with a serious intensity she knew matched her own. For a heartbeat in time, she couldn't look away. Her stomach danced with flies, and still they stared.

He looked away first.

Gwyneth blinked, startled at how easily he affected her.

She continued on to the riverbank. Food was about the furthest thing from her mind, but it was something to keep her hands busy. He spread the blanket, and she knelt to unload the basket of its minced beef pasties and hard cheese and honey bread. There was a flagon of ruby red wine and two engraved pewter goblets.

The monastery rested on the rolling distance through the trees, and in the opposite direction loomed Valmond. The river was gentle here, lowering into a bend, pooling deep, surrounded by mossy rocks and the shade of heavy-leaved oaks.

He didn't seem any more hungry than she. He sat with his back against a large tree trunk, eyes closed. Perhaps it was as well. She found his eyes to be the most unnerving aspect of him, and it gave her a chance to observe him. Sometimes she forgot that he was so much older than she; the grim bracket of lines around his eyes and mouth reminded her.

His lips were well shaped, narrow yet sensuous. His nose was perfect. It annoyed her that he could be so stunningly beautiful, the angles of his face elegant and aristocratic. Effortlessly handsome. His blond hair touched the neck of his maroon tunic.

She didn't want to look at his body, but there was no resisting. He was but a man: two arms, two legs, a nose, a mouth—and yet her heart stumbled, her breath caught, and again she wanted to kiss him, taste his mouth, breathe his breath, touch his face . . . she wanted—

Him.

His eyes were open, she realized. He was watching her watching him.

"You're staring at me," he said.

"No, I'm not," she lied. "I was just . . . thinking."

"About what?"

She wasn't ready. Or maybe she was a coward, after all. *Don't play it safe, don't play it safe, don't—*

"About"—she looked away from him, her gaze captured by the silvery ribbon of water beyond the bank—"going swimming," she said suddenly, daring to glance back at him. "And you don't get to ask the questions, my lord. Need I remind you of your loss?"

He ignored her. "Swimming?"

She shrugged gamely. "I love to swim. You know that." She'd had a habit of sneaking out to the river below Castle Wulfere with the village children to swim when she was supposed to be engaged in embroidery or brewing or some other such undesirable task.

"You love to swim when you're avoiding something," he pointed out. There was something rough, reckless even, in his eyes tonight.

"I'm not avoiding anything." *Liar!* Oh, how difficult it was to be a woman. She wanted to be Tucker again, a boy in a siege camp. But it was not possible. She was Gwyneth, Lady of Valmond, picnicking by a river with a man she wanted to seduce.

She was here, at the dangerous line again.

Even he knew she was lying. "That's the second lie you've told me since we got here," he pointed out.

She squeezed her eyes shut, gathering her courage, wondering why joining a siege at Manvel had seemed easier than being honest with her husband. But she knew—at Manvel, she'd only risked her life. Here, she risked her heart.

There was a movement on the blanket, and she felt his nearness as he leaned toward her.

"What is the truth, Lady?" came his low, hard-gentle voice. "I would know your thoughts. I would know—"

She lifted her lashes to meet his gaze head-on. "Me? Would you truly know me, Rorke? We have known each other for so long, and yet still we are strangers, are we not?"

She hesitated, trying to frame the words for something that had only been felt, not voiced, up to now.

"I do want you to know me," she said at last. "I

want you to see me." *Don't play it safe.* "I want . . . you." There, she had said it—again—and this time she would not back away from it, not downplay it, not pretend it was about anything but her heart.

She would risk it all, true to herself no matter how it turned out.

He frowned, clearly puzzled. "But of course I see you."

"No," she said, in too deep to back out now—and glad for it. Relieved. Stronger. "As a woman. I am a woman, you know. I'm not a child."

She rose, stripped off the overgarment of her cotehardie, leaving only the lightweight gown beneath. Oh, sweet Eleanor, she prayed. Help. She was no seductress, only a woman who was in love with a man.

"Do you think I don't know that?" There was a catch in his voice.

As he gazed at her, she saw the awareness in his eyes that matched her own. Crackling. Alive. Anticipation that was like a living, breathing creature.

"Then kiss me," she said.

Twenty-one

Rorke was aware of the physical tension in his body like he hadn't been aware in years. Did she know what she was doing to him?

Gwyneth's eyes were so damn wide and serious.

"Kiss me," she said, and this time it was not a question but an order.

His gaze flickered to her mouth. Her blunt demand surprised him, but he responded with equal honesty. "I want to."

"Then do." She lifted her mouth the scant breath it took to trace the distance separating them. He was close to her, could almost feel her heart beating in the tense air between them, as if a taut string connected their two pounding chests.

Her eyelids fluttered shut as he cradled her face in his hands, and he lowered his own eyes, dizzy with pleasure unsought but no less deeply desired. Sweetly, delicately, he kissed those closed lids of hers.

He groaned, tugging her closer, needing her closer, passion exploding inside him that he knew, once unleashed would be impossible to check.

Alarms sprang into his mind. *He was supposed to protect her. He was supposed to take care of her.*

But as he filled his arms with her softness, he felt the passion taking control and his kisses moved to her nose, her cheeks, her forehead, ever avoiding her mouth. Her lips. Hell and heaven awaited him there. If he kissed her mouth, now, he would be lost. And he couldn't afford to be lost.

Or would he be found?

Truth or lies, he couldn't tell the difference.

He opened his eyes to stare down at her, his gaze seized by her ripe, lush mouth. *Don't kiss her; don't kiss her.*

Just one touch. Just a breath of a kiss, a caress, a taste.

"Don't be afraid," she whispered, and lifted her huge eyes to his.

"You're telling me not to be afraid," he said incredulously. "You're the one who should be afraid."

"Of you, my lord? Oh, no." She searched his gaze—for what, he wasn't sure. But whatever had been her purpose, she seemed satisfied. She leaned forward—and this time he had no choice, she kissed him, took deliberate possession of his mouth.

She made no bones about wanting him—and God knew he wanted her. He could feel every thundering beat of his pulse down to his toes. He wanted her. And she was making it very clear that she wanted him.

"See me," she breathed against his mouth. "See me." And she pushed away from him, her hand on his chest, and then she stepped back. He watched, transfixed, as she reached for the simple ties that bound the bodice of her undergown.

With a shrug, she let it pool down to her feet and she stood nymphlike before him, cloaked in naught but the shadows of the trees, the rest of the world far away. The rhythm of his heart filled his ears.

All he could do was stare. Sweet heaven, she was beautiful. Slender and strong, standing straight and proud before him.

His chest tightened with each breath he took.

"I see you," he said raggedly.

Sparks flared in the rich depths of her dark eyes. "Then come and get me." And she took a step back, pivoted, and made a shallow dive into the pooling bend of the shaded river.

He heard a splash, and a gasp as she came up that told him the water was cold. He stared at her as she rose in the water, naked, and he swiped a desperate arm over his forehead.

He was hot. Very hot. Sweating.

Moisture was bending on his temples, running down his ears.

Come and get her?

What would happen if he did? Suppose he gave in to this madness, this passion, this need and desire and—something more, something deep, that he wasn't quite ready to confront.

But his feet were moving on their own volition, not waiting for his head to give permission. Moving toward her even as she came toward him, her body pale, luminous, wet. And close.

Her eyes, like pools themselves, met his. She stood waist-deep, nothing but the long ribbons of her hair covering her breasts.

His body wanted what she was offering, and the heat of the need was weighing him down. Was she mad, or was it just him? The repercussions of this would change everything, in ways he couldn't calculate in his current, dire state.

But there was no more question, no more wondering. No matter what came of this moment, he was going to go forward with it. He was going to make love to her. He couldn't *not* make love to her. He had a river, a wife, and a hard, pressing heat that overrode all equivocation.

He stripped down to the hard, pressing heat in question and dove into the river after her.

The sky above loomed velvet blue as the last shimmers of golden sun through the trees slipped away. The pool of the river's bend was a paradise apart from the rest of the world, or at least it seemed in that moment. There was no Valmond, no priory, no ghost voices or mysterious servants. Nothing but Rorke, rising in the water before her, his body tensile and powerful.

Sharply aware of him, Gwyneth sucked in a breath. She'd asked for this moment—no backing out.

There was no sound in the river pool but their breathing, and then he slipped his arms around her, gathered her close, and kissed her deeply, covetously, as if he wanted her more than anything else in the world, and that was how she felt about him.

His mouth left hers, and then his hands were parting the damp hair over her breasts. His gaze was a seeking of permission, she realized, and smiled tremulously. Permission granted.

She felt the hard, gentle pressure of his hands cupping her breasts. Her nipples, already taut, tightened and strained against his touch. She let out a breath of sheer surprise at the thrill of his caress. He filled his hands with her and she moaned her need, afraid he would stop. She felt his body responding against her, the rigid core of him pressing against her abdomen.

Curious, she reached between them and touched that hot core and he responded by tangling one hand into her hair, crushing her to him as he seized her mouth in a kiss of such need, she almost cried from her own helplessness and her realization, suddenly, of his. He was as lost, as overcome, as she.

Then, without breaking the kiss, he scooped her into his arms and waded resolutely to shore, lowered her to the blanket-covered spongy ground. They were both wet, both cold and hot at once. Both amazingly, frantically needy.

He covered her with his large body, took her into his arms and away to another place where there was no time or space or thought, only this craving that they shared. This was Rorke's body pressed against hers, Rorke's mouth on her breasts, Rorke's hands sliding down her belly to her untouched places—and making them untouched no longer. He buried his face in her, kissing her, tasting her, exploring. He sucked her nipples, pulling, torturing her until she writhed and begged him—but not to stop. To continue. But his tongue slipped down between her mounded, tormented globes to her stomach, and then lower, his fingers brushing her soft womanhood, parting the heated folds there, rubbing, enticing, and oh saints, slipping inside.

She'd had no idea, no thought of such intimacy. She clutched at his hair and cried out his name in soft, pleading whispers that were nearly sobs. Her entire body ached and ached. And it didn't stop, only built, as his fingers began to move in her slick heat, sinking into the ache, feeding it.

Beneath his relentless hands, she writhed, arched, cried out. A wave of shudders took her, shocking her.

"Rorke, Rorke, what are you doing to me?" she whispered hoarsely.

Dipping his head to kiss her mouth again, he said against her lips, "I'm seeing you, Gwyneth. I'm seeing you. And you are so lovely. So precious. So mine."

His words sent her spiraling back into the dark, seduced world where nothing mattered but his touch and the sweet, insistent craving that he fed. His mouth, rough and tender, assaulted her breasts again while his knowing fingers repeated the torment of before.

"You like this," he said huskily, his endlessly blue eyes anchoring her in the shadows of trees and evening and their aloneness here in this river glade of their own separate world.

"I love this," she said. "I love—" *You*, she would have ended if his mouth had not swept hers, carrying her away beyond thought, beyond words.

She reached between them for his arousal, encircling him with her hands. He rocked against her touch, the sound he made both anguish and desire. He felt huge to her touch, and she had no idea how he could fit inside her, but instead of feeling fear, she felt excitement. She wanted to find out. She felt wild and hungry and ready.

Moving against him, she arched into his hard length, sliding her hands around his back to let him know that she couldn't wait, wouldn't wait, any longer.

He shifted and reached between them, easing her center apart, carefully lowering just the tip of him inside her. The pressure of him against her, stretching her, pushing against her boundaries, was amazing.

"I don't want to hurt you," he said. "If you want me to stop—"

How could he think she would want him to stop? She was delirious with the desire for him to go on.

"No," she breathed. "No. Please do anything *but* stop." And he kissed her, consumed her, and she gripped him tighter, shamelessly begging him with her body so that he gave in to what they both wanted. He plunged inside with one sure stroke.

Crying out against his mouth, she stiffened more from awed surprise than pain. The burn of his entrance was ephemeral, gone before it registered, leaving only the sweet sensation.

She couldn't catch her breath. She was aware only of holding on to him, afraid to let go, afraid to be lost in this vast sea of pleasure alone. The experience was meant to be shared—with him and only him. It was fate and truth and everything that her heart had ever led her to believe about him.

"Hold on to me," he whispered against her ear, and she knew that he, too, didn't want to be alone. This was more than physical, it was emotional.

He held her and whispered things she barely heard, and they moved together, cheek pressed against cheek, belly to belly, his body guiding her into the steady rhythm, his heart beating strong with hers.

Then white fire fell over her, taking her, and she was aware of something taking him, too, and his arms tightened convulsively around her, bringing her even nearer as if he feared losing her in this moment. She surrendered to him and the storm, overwhelmed, and then gasping, spent, as he drove in hard one last time. He filled her, possessed, and she was aware only of thinking that the world could end right now and she wouldn't care.

Then his lips were on hers again. Kisses. Many of them. Worshipful, as if she were a sacred object to him.

With a sigh, she opened her eyes and gazed up at him. He shifted slightly, taking his weight off her, so careful of her as he tugged the blanket around them, wrapping them against the deepening night.

She was exactly where she wanted to be. He was her lover. Her love.

Time lost meaning for awhile. In Rorke's arms, she felt protected and safe and warm as still he kissed her and whispered to her.

"You think I *don't* see you—see everything about you—your hair, your breasts, your nose, your eyes, your lips?" He kissed each spot as he spoke. "You think I haven't noticed?"

She blinked back the moisture that sprang to her eyes.

He rose above her, his eyes shining down through the cloak of dusk. "I don't know whether to tell you exactly how very beautiful and perfect and desirable you are, or to scold you for not knowing it already."

A lump filled her throat. "Last night—"

"Last night I could scarcely speak or breathe when I saw you," he told her. "Think you it was any different at the siege of Manvel? When your hair came tumbling down your back, and I ripped away those bindings—think you that was nothing to me, that I didn't notice you were a woman?"

"Did you think I didn't notice you were a man?" she countered. "But you asked me to marry you—and you called us friends."

"I wanted to protect you."

"From what? From whom?"

Rorke closed his eyes briefly. "From me."

He rolled away from her, suddenly, and she didn't feel warm and safe and protected anymore. He took his tunic and pulled it on. She sat up, pulling the blanket around her now-shivering body. Without him, she was cold. Her wet hair tangled around her shoulders.

"Don't you dare," she said softly, but with all the iron in her will. "Don't you dare walk away from me now." She jerked to her feet, clumsily twisted in the blanket but determined. With one fist, she clutched the blanket and with the other she pounded his chest.

She was crying, and she didn't care if he saw.

"Lizbet accused me of hiding behind my sword," she yelled at him. "And mayhap she was right. I know that I am afraid—of my feelings for you, because they make me vulnerable. They make me exposed. So don't think I can't recognize what you're doing. If you are too afraid to feel anything for me, then tell me that. Just don't walk away without saying good-bye. Not again. Not after . . . this."

"I'm not afraid of feeling anything for you." He took her by the shoulders and his gaze through the darkness was raw. "And I don't want you to be afraid. I don't want to hurt you."

His words were sweet but not enough.

"Then what are you afraid of?" she demanded, and what he said next surprised her.

"I'm afraid of losing you."

Twenty-two

"How could that happen? How could you lose me? Don't you . . . trust me?"

Her last question all but killed him. He couldn't let her think it was her fault, and she was not going to let him go without an explanation. She was so damn persistent, always. And she deserved the truth.

She deserved so much that he couldn't let her go on thinking another moment that he didn't feel anything for her. If anything, he was afraid of feeling *too much* for her. His words had emerged, ripped from the most secret depths of his damaged heart where he'd kept them sheltered for longer than even he knew.

Much longer than he'd ever wanted her to know.

Here, in the dark, under the trees, he had been more honest with her than he'd been with himself.

"Gwyneth—" He gazed down into her soul-deep eyes. She'd had enough pain in her own life without being burdened with his. But he knew that he'd added to her pain. Her reminder of the words Lizbet had spoken to her brought back that day he'd listened, half-awake, to the argument she'd had with her sister.

The gist of it came tumbling into his mind now. Gwyneth had compensated for her parents' loss by taking up the sword, defending not just her physical self but her heart as well.

She had grown up feeling unloved, and perhaps unlovable.

Had he added to her hurt? He had abandoned her, more than once, though he hadn't intended it as such.

He had been wrapped up in his own selfish agony, then and now.

"I could lose you in a thousand ways," he said roughly, reaching out to wipe away the teardrops that traced her cheeks. "The worst of which would be through my own negligence. Nothing matters more than that you are safe and alive. *Nothing* matters more. And I—God, it's not you that I don't trust, don't you see?"

He let go of her, strode away to the bank of the river. Above, a crescent moon glistened a stripe of light across the water where the trees parted in its midst.

She was slow coming, and he realized she'd stopped to don her gown, and perhaps to think, for she was no longer angry when she came beside him. She threaded her fingers through his and tugged at him so that he sat along with her on the mossy rock.

Her gaze was upon him, serious and deep. "Tell me about Angelette."

He knew it took much for her to mention Angelette. It was a subject none broached in his presence, and he preferred the silence of it. But

Gwyneth was not that easy; she would not allow him that silence. She would not allow him to hide.

"You know the story," he said grimly. "You know—"

"Not from you."

"You know it just the same."

She shook her head. "No, I want to know it from you. I *have* to know it from you. Because I think you blame yourself for her death. And I think that you're wrong."

The look on her face bound his chest tighter. The last thing he wanted to do was talk about Angelette because to speak of her was to feel the pain all over again.

But looking at Gwyneth now, he realized that *not* to speak of Angelette could hurt *her*. He had to make sure that didn't happen.

"We had occupied the Chateau Voirelle," he began slowly, staring away from her, his gaze far away, in the past. In France. A time of both war and love.

Gwyneth watched the tension of his jaw, his hard profile shielding any display of emotion from her view. But the emotion was there, she knew.

Would he ever free himself enough to let it go instead of holding it so deeply inside?

"It was her sister's home. The lady of Voirelle had just given birth to twins, and Angelette had gained leave from her father, the lord of Saville, to visit her. He was a cruel father, possessive and severe, and she was giddy with the freedom of her life at

Voirelle. I think she almost welcomed the occupation, for it extended her stay at Voirelle.

"She was not eager to return home. She didn't know that in the end, it would be the difference between life and death."

His hand was still in hers, near, and yet his voice was distant. She squeezed his hand, and he looked down at her. She glimpsed the black pit of his guilt, and it was all she could do to bear it.

"It was the time of the Saint Valentine's feast," he went on in that same distant tone. "She was young, and exuberant, full of life and herself. She knew she was beautiful—and she reveled in it. That night, she danced and she played and she enchanted—sorcery that was innocent. She was young, younger than you are now, Gwyneth."

He looked at her, and his gaze was all torment.

"I was the one who should have been strong, wise, restrained. But I was entranced, and I did what I knew I should not. She was my enemy's daughter, and it was danger to both of us—and yet I let my pride overrule my head."

"You were young, too," Gwyneth pointed out.

He went on as if she hadn't spoken.

"Eventually, she was returned to Saville, part of the endless back and forth negotiations in the war. She didn't want to go back, but she had no choice. Before she left, I asked her to marry me.

"There was no way we could be together. Her father would never allow it. His daughter, his precious daughter, would not be permitted to wed the enemy. I knew that, and she knew that, and we both ignored the reality that had doomed us from the start. Through her maid, we began to exchange secret letters. And secret plans.

"It was simple. She would switch clothes with her maid and then walk out the gates of her father's chateau. Straight out of Blanchefleur, in plain daylight. It was so bold that it worked, but that's where her luck ended."

"What happened?" She knew much of the story, he was right about that, but she was hearing it now for the first time from Rorke. She didn't want him to stop.

"She planned to meet me in an alley behind a tavern. It was a place known to whores and beggars, no place for a lady. She was young and innocent; it was all adventure to her. I knew when I read her last letter detailing the alley where she would meet me that it was reckless, but I was as reckless as she. I thought we had something that could not be stopped, something bigger than time or country or any man. It was impulsive and naive, and I was the one who should have known better. But I was as blind."

He met her eyes, and he looked drained, as if the story had already cost him much and he was not even half-finished.

"You loved her very much." It was difficult for Gwyneth to say, but she had to get it out in the open. She was as haunted by Angelette, in her own way, as Rorke. She felt Angelette's presence between them, and she knew there had to be honesty now. She had to know if there was room in his heart for her, or if he would always love Angelette more.

She wasn't sure she could bear his answer, but she knew she had to have it.

His look was terrible.

"We were young," he said. "To her, I was excitement, peril, rebellion. And I thought I was a hero. I was going to save her from her father. It was love, but it was a lot of other things, too. And it was not worth her life."

Gwyneth felt a strange mix of emotion: a tremulous hope, and a yawning bleakness at the same time. Guilt drove him . . . not love?

Did that mean he could love her now, or did the guilt mean he would never love anyone again?

He went on with his story now: "The night we were to meet, the king ordered me to participate in a joust. There was no way I could refuse, but my mind was so full of Angelette that I wasn't careful. I was preoccupied and she paid the price. And she wasn't the only one."

"You were nearly killed yourself!" Gwyneth argued. She knew this part of the story only too well. It was here that her brother's fate had become entwined with Rorke's and Angelette's. Rorke was wounded terribly in the joust that day, and he had sent Damon in his place to meet Angelette.

Damon had arrived too late. Angelette had been beaten, savaged, in that tavern alley. She was barely alive when he'd found her.

Her murder had been brutal, a haunting nightmare. Its reach had spread over years, still spread. Damon had carried Angelette, still clinging to life, to Blanchefleur. But she'd died by the time he'd made it to her father. And the terrible chain of events had continued with Damon's false imprisonment. Ranulf had protected the true murderer, Father Almund, and masterminded Wilfred's execution in his place so that he could seize Penlogan. The destruction of that one terrible night had reached over all their lives, all these years.

Now Rorke, still blaming himself, couldn't accept that Ranulf was dead.

"I wanted to believe her murderer had been punished when Wilfred was executed by Saville. I *needed* to believe it. But it was wrong. All that time, Father Almund continued to live and to murder other young girls in his madness. And Ranulf continued to protect him and to exploit Wilfred's death to his own gain. And I—I did nothing to save those young girls. They died because I gave up, because I didn't find the truth."

"You saved me," Gwyneth said quietly. She squeezed his hand, and he looked at her, his gaze filled with sadness that she didn't know how to wipe away. "You came to Castle Wulfere, and you trained me to fight. I was a sad, lost little girl, and you gave me confidence and hope. You didn't know about the other girls. You couldn't know."

"But I should have known," he countered grimly. "It was my responsibility. I owed it to Angelette, to Damon, and to Wilfred and Graeham."

"No one wants to believe evil like that exists, especially among us," Gwyneth argued gently. "Damon believed in Wilfred's guilt, too. And he believed in Ranulf's friendship. Everyone did. You can't blame yourself."

But she could see that his guilt was powerful, a

constant self-torturing that had dwarfed everything else in his life for so long that it had become part of him, as natural as the beat of his heart. He was a fine and noble man, a good man, but the darkness overshadowed the light in his eyes.

She felt helpless to change it.

"So many lives were damaged by my recklessness, my arrogant pride," he said.

She thought of all the times she had accused him of arrogance, and felt regret. He was not arrogant. He was a good, valiant man, and she only wished he believed it.

"I thought I could do anything," he continued. "I was the king's champion. I was wrong. And I won't give up again."

He was speaking of his hunt for Ranulf, she knew. The mad quest that had begun the night Ranulf had leaped from the tunnels of Penlogan into the sea.

"He can't be alive," she said.

"Oh yes, he can," he said.

She wanted to plead with him, to rail at him, but how could she fight a guilt that spanned years when vengeance was all he'd had? He would not let go of it easily, for it had sustained him through the pain. She could only offer her heart and pray that it would suffice.

"You can't bring Angelette back," she said quietly. "You can't bring Wilfred back. You can't replace the lost years when Graeham had to hide in the woods because he'd been dubbed a traitor. And you can't take away Damon's scars. Father Almund is dead. And Ranulf—"

"—went over a cliff and disappeared," Rorke inserted. "His body was never found."

"The drop was severe. He couldn't have lived. No one thinks he could have lived."

Rorke said nothing for a long moment. "I can't give up."

"Can't—or won't?" she whispered over the lump in her throat.

"It doesn't matter."

Gwyneth squeezed her eyes tight for a painful beat. "It matters to me," she said softly, and lifted her gaze to him.

He looked down at her, and touched her face with his other hand. A tender caress, sad.

"I love you," she said thickly.

She knew he wouldn't return the words, that the dark, yawning pit inside him wouldn't give him permission. He was punishing himself. She read him only too well now.

"I don't even know how long I've loved you," she said. "Years, maybe. And I need you. The past is gone. There's nothing any of us can do to change it. The day I came to Manvel and ended up in your tent, it could not be anything but the hand of fate. It was meant to be, and I thank God for it. I never thought I could fall in love—and maybe that's because I was in love with you all along."

She gave him a tremulous smile. "There's only the present now, and the future to nourish. Can't you see that?"

"Gwyneth." He shook his head, emotion blazing in his eyes, then his mouth crushed hers in a kiss of torment and longing unleashed, and she knew he felt things he wouldn't say, or couldn't say, and in that heartbeat, she didn't care that they were left unsaid.

They were felt.

"You make me want to see it," he said finally, when he had released her. "You are a drop of hope in this black world. You are all that is rare and precious and wonderful to me. If anything ever happened to you—"

"Nothing is going to happen to me," she promised him.

He laid her down on the mossy ground under the black velvet shadows of the tree-lined riverbed and he made love to her again. And she didn't know if he would stay, if he would give up his mad quest, and she didn't ask.

She didn't know if she could ever heal all the pain that was inside him, but for tonight she treasured the touch of his hands on her body and the heat of his mouth on her lips. And for a glinting bubble in time, it was enough.

Twenty-three

"She's here, my lord. I've found her." Ryman called down to Rorke from the spiral stone staircase leading to an upper room in the east wing.

Rorke took the steps in bounds, his heart pounding. Three hours he had been searching for his wife! Three hours!

And all the while she had been in this lost, dusty upper room in a section of the castle she was not supposed to be in practicing at swords with a bunch of women!

She would be the death of him yet!

"Damnation, woman, are you trying to send me to an early grave from worry?" he demanded as he strode into the chamber with his justified ire. It was a wide, open chamber that had once been used as a scriptorium during its days as part of the abbey.

Women balancing mugs of water on their heads while at the same time attempting to thrust and parry gaped at him, and their mugs clattered in unison to the floor.

"Why, my lord," Gwyneth said, pivoting from her swordplay rehearsal with the young girl, Lily, who would don the role of Saint George in the evening's Midsummer's Eve festivities. "I had no idea you were looking for me! We were simply trying to stay out of the way. The hall is quite busy today with the preparations for tonight. The men were at work in the guardroom, and it's been drizzling on and off all afternoon. So we came here to practice. What's wrong? Did you need me?"

Heaven save him. He needed her. Too much. And damn her, nothing was wrong except that he had missed her and not been able to find her—and he had panicked.

"I didn't know where you were," he said lamely.

She stared at him, puzzled, and then she laughed. "My lord husband, you cannot always know where I am. And as you can see, I was not alone. I would not come to this part of the castle alone. Not since—"

"Not since what?" He was instantly apprehensive. This was not a part of the castle for which even he held any fondness. He'd never believed the old section of the castle, that which had been part of the monk's abbey, was haunted, but it was dangerous. Repairs had never been undertaken, and it had long ago fallen into disuse. It should have been torn down years ago, and he vowed to himself now that he would see to it that it was done.

That would be an end to the tales of ghosts.

The thought brought a lightness to him. He had long shirked his duty to Valmond, had never felt quite right about the inheritance that should never have been his to claim, especially in the aftermath of so much death from the plague.

Valmond had been a place of sad memories. Gwyneth was changing that.

Mayhap it was time to take his rightful place here. Seeing Gwyneth's work with his people had inspired him. It was the least he could do for her, and for his people.

He wasn't sure what impact it could have upon him. It was one thing to tear down stone and mortar to build anew. Guilt was not so easily dismantled, and hearts not so simply repaired.

"I made the mistake of coming here my first night at Valmond," Gwyneth explained, stepping away from Lily to speak with him in private. "I was rash. I wanted to find you, talk to you."

Rorke listened, surprised. He remembered how close he had come to seeking her out that night.

"I told you to stay out of the east wing," he reminded her.

"I don't do what I'm told," she flared back, and he was reminded that his wife was not to be ordered about. It was something he liked about her—and it frustrated the hell out of him at the same time.

"Gwyneth—"

"What are you going to do about it, lock me up?"

"I should!" he bellowed.

She just laughed. Then she tipped forward suddenly on her toes and kissed him. "Only if you promise to lock yourself up with me," she whispered. "We'll make love all day and all night. I will be your prisoner of love. Will you be mine?"

He was melting. And getting very hard at the same time. Gwyneth had taken to lovemaking like a robin to spring, as enthusiastic and brazen with her sexuality as she was about her swordplay.

"Wait a minute." He shook himself. He was still missing something. "You said that you had come here the first night. What happened?"

Gwyneth sighed. "I panicked, that's all," she said. "I lost my way and ended up in the old monk's cells. I dropped my candle, and in the darkness I thought I heard something, but I'm sure I was wrong. It was my imagination. Somehow, I backed into a cell and in my confusion, I thought I was locked in. That couldn't be, because there are no locks on the cells."

"What happened?"

"I thought I heard someone telling me to leave, to go away. And then nothing. It was my imagination, I'm telling you. Who else would have been there that night? Or any time? And I just lost the door in my confusion. I fell asleep and when I woke, I found the door and it was open. I came back to my room. That's all."

"Promise me you won't do that again."

"I told you—"

"Promise me. This part of the castle is in disrepair. You shouldn't even be here in daylight in the company of others. You will not be here at night, alone."

He could see she did not like his authoritarian tone, but she shrugged. "I will not, because I think it's right, not because you order it." She lifted her chin at him, so pugnacious always.

"Thank you," he said, deciding to ignore the latter part of her comment. "Now would you tell me what's going on here."

She smiled again, the brightness quickly restored

to her face. "Why, we're practicing for tonight—Lily and I. And the women are learning to balance themselves while they move. Just as you taught me, my lord husband." She kissed him again, and with an impish grin she went back to her business.

Rorke returned to the doorway where Ryman stood watching the women. He leaned against the stone doorframe, amazed at his wife and the laughter and the sheer joy that one lovely, determined, outrageous woman had brought to his life and his home and his people. She was undaunted by him, by anything.

"My lord, I never thought I'd see the day that we'd have women training at Valmond," Ryman said beside him. "And I never thought I'd see the day that I approved of it."

Rorke gave a look at his friend and comrade. Ryman, for all his rough edges, had become quite enchanted by the widow Melia and her feisty daughter, Lily.

As for Rorke, he was a bit enchanted by all of them, and all of them were clearly enchanted by Gwyneth. She had lifted the gloom from his castle, and no one was more surprised than he that he didn't mind. The desolation of Valmond, for so long, had fit his own mood. He hadn't sought to change Valmond—or himself.

Now . . . Change had come, and he wasn't sure what it would bring. He was only sure that for the first time there was a part of him that had begun to crack open and breathe.

But there was darkness amidst the light. Today,

when he hadn't known where Gwyneth was, he'd torn the castle apart to find her.

The more his heart opened and breathed, the more a fear inside him grew with it. A fear that something would happen to Gwyneth, and that it would be his fault.

"You're taken with the mistress Melia," Rorke commented.

Ryman's eyes flared. "Could be," he admitted.

Rorke noticed the way Melia glanced over at Ryman occasionally, flirting with her eyes and her laughter. Ryman didn't take his eyes off her in return.

"Might be a bit dangerous," Rorke said, watching Melia's swiping sword cuts.

"Loving women is always dangerous, milord. I'll take my blows for the rewards that wait at the end."

Rorke felt something inside his chest tighten, close to breaking. He wanted to live his life as free and full as Ryman. But he couldn't shake the feeling that something terrible was about to happen, and that it was just waiting for him to let down his guard.

He pulled Gwyneth close to him that afternoon in their bed. *Their* bed, it was now. They shared the huge lord's chamber.

She lay, flushed with lovemaking, her satin skin gleaming in the gray light that poured in from the tall windows. Her head was tilted back in satisfaction, her eyelashes drifting down on her pale cheeks. He couldn't stop looking at her face, her breasts, her stomach, her hips, and her long, slender legs.

"You're so beautiful," he whispered to her, not expecting her to hear him, thinking her asleep.

She opened her eyes and gazed at him very seriously. She looked so young, suddenly, and in that moment, embarrassed as he had not seen her before. Surprised, he watched her sit up, tug at the furs at the bed to cover herself.

"Are you chilled?" he asked.

"No."

"Then don't do that. I like looking at you."

She looked strange. "You don't have to say that. I'm not a simpering lady who needs flattery to survive."

"It's not flattery. You're beautiful. I love looking at you. I want to say it." He was puzzled by her attitude. It was as if she was irritated with him for noticing that she was so lovely, and he didn't understand it.

"You're mocking me," she said quietly. Accusingly.

Rorke was appalled. "No. Wait." He took hold of her as she started to rise and push him away. He held her there beside him, the furs twisting down her shoulders. "I would never mock you about that. I would never—you have to believe me, Gwyneth. You are all I could ever dream about in a woman."

"When you came back here, you didn't even seem to notice how I had changed: my clothes, my hair, everything. I know it was silly of me to ever think that I could be like other ladies—and truly, I don't wish to be, exactly—but, maybe, there's a part of me that likes the gown and the ribbons and the rouge, and—" She bit her lower lip and looked away from him. "I hoped you would like it, too."

"Oh, Gwyneth, I do. I did." He took her chin in his hand and pulled her gaze back to him. "But what you are forgetting is that I thought you were beautiful before. All of this—the trappings of fashion—they don't matter to me. You are beautiful. You."

Unshed tears shone in her eyes. He kissed her deeply, and pulled her down onto the bed and held her for a long time and told her exactly how beautiful she was to him. He realized how much she needed the words that came so hard to him.

She felt so small in his arms, despite her strength. He rested his hand on her belly and thought again of how slender she had grown in the past months since she had come to Valmond.

He thought of something he had overheard her little maid, Magwyn, say just that morning. She had asked Gwyneth if she felt well today, or if she needed her special tincture of herbs.

"Have you been ill?" he asked her suddenly.

Spooned against him, she turned her head to look up at him. He noticed anew how pale her face had grown, and for the first time that there were shadows under her eyes.

"No. I mean, not truly. I had a lot of trouble sleeping at first, and I was ill to my stomach. I think it was the change of environment." She frowned. "I began working with Prior Bruin to develop a physic garden, and he and Brother Arnulph provided me with the herbs I've been planting. Prior Bruin gave me the recipe for a special tea of his own brew. He has served it to me there, and I instructed Hertha how to make it for me here. It calms the nerves and soothes the humors. I've been feeling much better."

She rested her head back down on her pillow, snuggling into his arms again. "Prior Bruin has been very kind." She looked back at him again. "Did you know that Hertha and Burnet's son, Godric, is a lay brother at the monastery?"

Rorke nodded. "Yes, I had heard that. I haven't seen Godric in many years."

"He's ill," Gwyneth said. "Mad, Brother Arnulph told me. It's sad. I keep wanting to speak to Hertha and Burnet, but I don't know what to say. I don't know if they know, or how to comfort them if they do. They seem very worried, and I fear it is about Godric.

"I met him one day," she said, and her voice sounded sleepy now. "Before he was quite so ill. He was in the physic garden workshop. He was very kind, I thought. But I thought—" She opened her eyes now and stared back at him again. "I thought he followed me to the gate and told me to go away. I thought it sounded like the same voice I had heard that night in the east wing. But of course that couldn't be. I imagined it. It was very strange, when I first came to Valmond. I felt ill, and I was restless and—I did everything wrong in the beginning. I lost Prior Bruin's book of herbs, and I killed the lavender. The villagers wouldn't speak to me.

She closed her eyes again. "Perhaps it was a good thing you weren't here then. I'm getting much better at playing the lady."

"I think you are quite wonderful," he said softly, and kissed the top of her head. She fell asleep, and he watched her and the something inside him that was afraid of losing her grew tighter in his chest.

It was a deep and chilling thing in him, and it was impossible for him to judge. He didn't know if this fear was any more real than Ranulf.

"Green is gold. Fire is wet. Fortune's told. Dragon's met." The children, hands joined, chanted the traditional Midsummer's Eve verses rhythmically as they moved together around the ring of candles in the center of Valmond's great hall. To Gwyneth's disappointment, an outdoor bonfire had not been possible due to the weather. But in spite of that small setback, the sight of the hall—dusty and forlorn only a few months ago—now clean and decorated, teeming with villagers, touched her heart.

She had done something here. She had made this happen. Pride and hope formed a tremulous combination inside her chest.

Beside her, Rorke's hand found hers, gripped it. She looked up at him. They sat at the high table, lord and lady over the mass of revelers. It felt so right. How long would it last? When would he return to his search for Ranulf, his quest, his haunted vengeance for the crimes against Angelette and Wilfred and Graeham and Damon—and a host of girls murdered by the hand of Father Almund and protected by the vile greed of Ranulf?

How long?

His eyes tonight were shining and she saw the same tremulous hope that was in her own heart. Or did she only want to see that, imagine it?

Doubts were inescapable. For all that she was starting to believe that their love could vanquish the past, there were still dark clouds just beyond the horizon of Valmond.

Waiting.

The premonition of gloom bothered her, even on this special night. She wanted, needed, to push the darkness aside.

"Thank you," he said, and his words required no explanation.

She bit her lip. Emotion swelled.

"You're beautiful," he added, for perhaps the tenth time since she'd emerged from their chamber.

He couldn't seem to tell her often enough now and she was starting to believe him because he said it whether she was undressed with her hair wild and no powder, or whether she wore the finest gown and had her coif ribboned and her cheeks painted—as she appeared tonight, after Magwyn's enthusiastic ministrations. It truly didn't seem to matter to Rorke, either way.

She was falling so much more deeply in love with him all the time. How could she have been so lucky to find a man who accepted her for who she was— wild and strong and vulnerable and lost—all the parts of her, Rorke knew and understood.

He made her whole. She only longed to complete him the same way and experienced a lingering apprehension that she never could.

The children completed their seventh round of chanting the riddle-laden verses and the leader, Thacker, guided the serpentine procession away from the candle ring and to their places at the long tables with their mothers and fathers and other villeins and knights. Soldiers and farmers, servants and craftsmen, maids and stablehands all sat down together this night.

There were faces Gwyneth had come to recognize over time, and others that were new to her. She had heard that people were coming in from their forest cottages, hunters and former villagers, inquisitive, eager to see the new lady and their long-vanished lord.

People curious to see if the stories were true: that Valmond had come to life and the old days of happiness were back.

The sound of a horn's blow interrupted the laughter and toasting and general cacophany as Burnet entered, followed by a young man carrying the customary wassail. Burnet, holding a huge cloth-covered basket, approached the high table.

He set the basket down before Rorke, bowed low, and drew back the cloth to present the Saint John's humney.

The steward's face was lined with worry, one of the few faces this night that exhibited no joy. Gwyneth stared at his drawn face, and felt a chill creep up her back.

Then Rorke reached for the bread.

Long and graceful, the sweet seed-filled bread brought back fond memories to Gwyneth. She looked at Rorke, awaiting his cue. Throughout the hall, other lads carried bread baskets to other tables, and the games began.

Burnet moved away.

Rorke tore off a piece of the bread. "How many years until I—"

Waiting, he let her finish the question. She thought fast. "—realize that I am right about everything?"

He broke open the bread and counted the seeds. "Eight."

He tore off another piece. "How many months until I—"

"—get a sense of humor?"

He actually laughed, so she hoped that maybe, just maybe, she was making more progress on that front than it seemed.

"Five."

Another piece. "How many hours until I—"

"Make love to your wife upstairs?" she whispered mischievously.

"Hold on." He put back most of the piece he'd torn off so that he only held what amounted to a large crumb in between his fingers. "Two," he said, as he counted the seeds. "And that's two too long," he said, tossing the bread back into the basket.

He kissed her, right there at the high table in front of everyone, and when he let her go, there was a cheer that filled the entire hall.

And she thought of the question she really wanted to ask him. *How long will this last?* But she didn't know if she wanted to hear the answer.

By then, Hertha and a slew of maids had brought out the cuckoo-foot ale and the festivities went on.

The children gathered again under Melia's direction to sing the cuckoo song, to the crowd's enthused response. The noise in the hall grew and, while not deafening, did make soft conversation impossible. The meal was laid, fish and boiled eggs and cheese with vegetable dishes of onion, peas, and carrots. Rows and rows of people ate and drank and talked, and Gwyneth took it all in from the dais, lost in the awe of it, when Rorke stood, drawing the attention of all in the great hall to him.

He lifted his goblet.

"To Valmond," he said. "Home for us all—again."

The people cheered, then quieted down as they realized he was not done.

"And to my bride." He looked down upon her, and his gaze was hot and bright with the fire of the hundreds of torches that lit the hall. "Who brought her strength and her light and her determination here and made this night happen."

Again, the crowd roared, and Gwyneth felt tears spring to her eyes as she realized the roar was for her, and it was welcoming and appreciative. She nodded her head, too full of emotion to think of anything to say or do. She felt her cheeks flame.

Rorke drained his goblet along with the crowd, and at her side, Gwyneth felt a tug. She turned to find Lily there.

"He likes you," the little girl whispered. "He really likes you."

Gwyneth laughed, and hugged the girl close. "I hope so," she whispered against her hair. "I hope so."

Then she allowed Lily to lead her away, eager for

Gwyneth to direct the mumming play of Saint George and the dragon.

"A terrible dragon has been menacing a kingdom!" Valora began.

The children were perfect, down to the last line, the last sword thrust, the last bows and the last procession around the candle ring at its end. Gwyneth returned to the high table, flush with pride.

"It has been over two hours," Rorke reminded her, even as he nodded at his guests. He held her hand as if he couldn't bear to let her go, and they waited their traditional turn—every guest must leave the hall before the lord and lady.

And then he would wait no more, and he scooped her into his arms before the last straggling soldiers and carried her across the torch-lit hall and up the winding stairs to their great, plump-cushioned bed. He made intense, possessive love to her and she fell asleep in his arms, content and dreaming of dragons slain and kingdoms saved.

Rorke fell asleep with his arm around his wife. He heard her whispering to him, but it seemed as if the voice came from far away. And then he understood that the voice wasn't Gwyneth's, it was Angelette's.

She was in the tavern alley and her throat was bruised and her body beaten. *Help me, help me,* she whispered. And then the face changed, and it was Gwyneth's face, Gwyneth's voice.

Help me, help me. And he wasn't holding her anymore. He was far away. He couldn't help her. He had failed her. He had let Ranulf get away and this time it was Gwyneth who had died.

"No!" he shouted, sitting bolt upright, something pulling at him, holding him down, and he realized it was Gwyneth.

She had her arms around him, holding him close, stroking his hair, his face.

"What is it?" she cried, eyes wild, frightened.

He wrapped his arms around her and held her close. "Nothing," he told her. "Nothing."

But it wasn't nothing.

The clouds gathered up and stormed over Valmond.

Twenty-four

The trail of Ranulf's ghost was endless, cir-
cuitous, twisted, overlapping and overwhelming.
It had begun at Penlogan, the night he had gone
over the cliff. And it had traversed the whole of England by now. Soldiers, tramps, thiefs, beggars.
Cripples and outcasts. In woods and towns, caves
and cities.

Rorke had been everywhere, with and without
his men.

Rumors were tempting sirens.

Walcott had gone on from Redmund alone, following yet another siren, while Rorke and Ryman
had returned to Valmond.

The news the knight brought to Valmond the
morning after the Midsummer's Eve feast was not
unexpected or new. But something about the tim-
ing hit Rorke in a way that was different.

Fate, perhaps.

Walcott had followed a lead back to Wildevale,
the tiny hamlet by the sea at the foot of Penlogan
Castle. It was there that the story had begun. It was
there that Father Almund had perpetrated the majority of his crimes, killing and brutalizing the
young girls of Wildevale. They would disappear,

never to be found, their bodies tossed to the hungry sea when he was finished with them.

The village had recovered in the past three years. Graeham and Elayna were gentle masters of the land and people too long defiled by Father Almund and Ranulf.

In the beginning, there had been fear and superstition among this simple people who made their living primarily from the sea. It took time for them to understand that it was their own priest, not a night-winged specter, who had truly haunted their village. They had spoken in the same terms of the phantasmic apparition that had flown from the cliff that night.

An evil merman, one had claimed. A devil's serpent, others had reported. A figment of nightmares and mad visions. Some said he'd crashed upon the rocks and falcons had flown down to consume him, leaving nothing behind, not even bones.

Others said he swam away, whole and unearthly, untouched by the sheer fall as if by sorcery.

The only known fact was that he was gone.

Rorke had begun the search in an ever-widening circle around Wildevale. Reports were rampant, and led everywhere and nowhere.

One of the most intriguing at first was the one that had led him to the physician.

Ainsley of Dormead had been a physician of the king's court at one time, or so he said. He had many stories. He had served in France. He had ministered to the Queen. He had attended the Black Prince himself.

It was rumored that his penchant for drink had

led to his downfall and now unhappy banishment to the small town by the sea. A well-to-do burgher's wife in London had died under inexplicable circumstances while under his care. Only a large donation to the town's justiciary had allowed his escape from trial.

Whatever the truth of Ainsley's past, Rorke had never been sure and it hadn't really mattered. He knew only that Ainsley was a drunk and that the townspeople in Dormead despised him. Yet he had, for whatever reason, come to reside in their small sea town, and for a chicken or a pig or a basket of leeks—or better, a bottle of drink—he would extract festering teeth, apply medicaments to open wounds, or let blood to allay ill humors.

Mostly, his patients lived, and so they suffered his drunken arrogance and insults.

It was in Dormead that the first trail out of Wildevale had led. There was one fisherman that fateful night whose story was different. He wasn't of Wildevale. He was from downshore, from Dormead.

The fisherman of Dormead had kin in Wildevale, and slowly, the connection had been made, and followed by Rorke and the men who had ridden with him at that time. He had gone to Dormead and found the fisherman in his poor cottage. The story he'd told had been fantastic if true.

He'd found a man on the shore that night. The man had lain in desperate straits, near death. His body was broken in several places—both in arms and legs. But he could speak, and he had begged to be taken anywhere but to Wildevale. He'd offered money, lots of money, for aid.

The fisherman had carried him to his boat, and from there downshore, to Dormead. He'd brought the physician, and together they'd managed to get the man to the physician's house.

What happened after that, the fisherman didn't know. He only knew that there had been no money forthcoming. When he'd heard of Rorke's hunt, he had come to him. He had saved the man's life, or at least gotten him as far as the physician. He wanted to be paid. He deserved to be paid.

Rorke had gone to Ainsley. The physician had denied any knowledge of a stranger from the sea. No one in Dormead had seen any stranger carried up to the physician's house.

It wasn't the last time Rorke was fed a story with no evidence, a story that didn't hold up, a story that was a lie. The fisherman of Dormead's story was simply the first of many, and in a way, it was the fuel that had fired his mission, or madness, some would say.

Rorke had returned more than once to Dormead. There were no clues he hadn't followed twice, or three times, or more. Every once in a while, a new rumor would surface, and he would go back.

A new rumor had come to Walcott's ears in Redmund.

A fisherman had died in Dormead. There would have been nothing unusual about it, even under a physician's care, if not for the fact that the family had called it murder, and the physician was so despised that the town provost had actually put him on trial, toasted his feet over the fire till he had confessed, and hung him on the gallows. This time, there had been no escape from justice for the drunken physician.

His worldly possessions had been dispersed to the victim's family, minus a portion that had been saved for himself by the zealous provost, and finally, the fisherman's wife claimed, the fisherman had received what had long been his due.

But the fisherman's wife wanted more, and she had gone to the lord of Penlogan with a story that was not new, but was for the first time accompanied by the promise of evidence.

Evidence she would share only with the dark lord who had come so often to Dormead in the past.

It was Graeham who had sent messengers seeking Rorke, trailing him to Redmund, finding Walcott instead. Graeham's missive was one of doubt; like Damon, he had long ago deemed Ranulf dead. Walcott had taken the time to follow up the lead before taking the information back to Valmond. But like Graeham, he had found the fisherman's wife stubborn, unwilling to deal with anyone but Rorke. Her husband, she claimed, had been cheated already. She would not be cheated as well.

"I hope I have not made a mistake, my lord," Walcott said now, exhaustion from a long night of hard riding drawing his face in sharp lines. "I caused a delay by following the lead myself. I did not want to trouble you—with your new bride and this old business of Dormead."

Rorke shook his head. He couldn't blame the young knight. Walcott had ridden with him faithfully for long enough that Rorke trusted the man to have done whatever he thought best at the time.

"I left you to make your own decisions," Rorke said. "I won't fault you now." He read again Graeham's letter, the scrawled words on the sheet of folded parchment burning into his brain.

There was a deep, aching part of him that yearned for a new beginning, a new day, here at Valmond. But the past reached out its ever-hungry fingers to claim him.

If not for that first trail to Dormead, would he have begun this mad quest at all? He thought of all the times his closest friends, even Ryman who had been his constant companion on this mission for longer than any others, had looked him in the eye and told him it was madness. He had persevered. He couldn't give up. He had given up before, and more people had died.

He had punished himself for Angelette's death, and then for Wilfred's, and for the loss of so many girls of Wildevale. He had punished himself for Damon's imprisonment and Graeham's banishment.

Gwyneth's love gave him hope, and he had to give her something in return. She deserved a man who was whole.

And he was not. The black pit called to him. What if this time the trail held truth?

What if?

It was an impossible lure that had nearly destroyed him.

"You are weary," he said to Walcott. "Rest. You have done your job."

MY LADY KNIGHT 271

Rorke assembled a small group of soldiers to accompany him. He preferred to leave the majority of his contingent here at Valmond, especially the men he most trusted: Walcott and Ryman.

He couldn't shake the grip of anxiety that came upon him whenever he thought of leaving Gwyneth here alone. She had a bold spirit and an impulsive heart. He couldn't bear the thought that she would be hurt in any way.

Especially by him.

The sun was glinting the first rays on the tall, narrow windows of the large bedchamber he shared with Gwyneth when he entered it again. The maid Magwyn was lighting the hearth. He sent her away.

His wife lay sleeping still. He didn't want to wake her, but he would not leave her without a good-bye.

He gathered her into his arms and kissed her awake.

Her eyes were pensive in the pale light of the dawn.

"You're going away," she said.

He nodded. "I'm leaving Ryman and Walcott here," he told her. "If there is any trouble, any worry, you are to go to them. I would trust them with my life. I would trust them with you." *She was his life.*

"If you stay, you wouldn't have to worry," she said, muffled against his chest where he held her. He didn't want to let her go.

"I can't stay."

How could he make her understand that he had

to go? How could he promise her it would be the last time? Even he wasn't certain.

She read him easily, always. "It's over, Rorke. You can't change the past. There will always be one more lead."

Misery swamped him. He kissed her, hard, and held her a long, long moment.

The deep wound inside him screamed for the only solace it had known for three years.

"I have to go," he said.

And she said, "I know."

Gwyneth pushed open the window of her chamber. In the courtyard below, she watched Rorke mount his horse. He called to his men, signaling them. The pounding of their horses' hooves filled the air.

The beat of their departure echoed emptily inside her heart.

He was gone. It was no consolation to her to believe that he cared for her, maybe even loved her. The darkness inside him had won. She wasn't as strong as Belle, or Elayna. She couldn't save her own dark lord with the light of her love.

How could she save him then?

She dressed, eschewing Magwyn's aid. She donned a simple gown, and went to the guardroom. The men were, for the most part, asleep, lazing away a morning-after sluggishness following the night's feast.

Sword in hand, she thrust and parried, but in

time, she stopped. There was none of the power she often felt in such practice. Not today.

She could not slay a ghost.

Putting the sword back, she returned to the hall. Time. Was that all she could hope for—that time would heal Rorke?

How much time? Too much time, for her, at least. The day passed in painful increments. The children played; the women sewed. Gwyneth was restless.

Night fell, and she slept fitfully. By the early predawn, she decided a good distraction was what she needed, not self-pity.

Her thoughts turned back to the practice the children and women had enjoyed in the old scriptorium. Rorke had mentioned tearing down the old abbey section, the east wing.

Maybe she could convince him to restore it instead of tearing it down. The small cells could be used for her women, her band of lady knights. She was becoming quite attached to the idea that Rorke had tossed out as a joke that long-ago day at Castle Wulfere. The scriptorium would make a perfect practice room, apart from the guardroom the men used.

Her mind lit with ideas.

She wondered if she could find plans for the old abbey.

Burnet would have them, if anyone did. Still dark at this early hour, she took a candle and headed for the steward's office. There was no sign he had been there of late. In fact, she hadn't seen him all day, not since the night of the feast.

He was old, and according to Hertha, not in good health. Perhaps he should be retired. They would take care of him, of course. But with Valmond coming back to life, a steward with more vigor was surely required. She would speak to Rorke upon his return.

She wouldn't harbor any thought but that he would be back soon. And somehow, she would convince him to stay for longer and longer periods. Together, they would defeat the past.

Suddenly, she felt quite hopeful.

She set her candle on the worktable and walked around Burnet's office. The shelves were full of bound parchments. Books of accounts, documents, letters, lists of orders and villeins and soldiers and sheep.

On the very top shelf she found the drawings. Architectural renderings of the various phases of Valmond Castle. They were dated. The abbey was built late in the eleventh century. The first plans for the castle itself were dated 1118.

She recalled Rorke had explained that the abbey had been in the hands of the church for only about twenty years.

There were other drawings—plans from later in the twelfth century, and again, in the early part of this century when Rorke's own father had added a portico and new gatehouse.

But no plans for the east wing, the old abbey.

Frustrated, she returned the plans to the shelf. She went to a dusty chest, lifted the lid, and dug through stacks of parchments.

Did Burnet ever dispose of anything?

"Milady?"

Gwyneth jolted so that she struck the top of her head on the lid of the chest.

Hertha loomed over her, the look on her face strange in the dim-lit room.

"What are you looking for, milady?"

"I—" Gwyneth stood, rubbing her head. "I was interested to see if there were any plans of the east wing. I'm thinking of how it might be restored. Burnet wasn't here, so—would you know of any such plans in existence?"

She had to restrain herself from apologizing for going through the steward's office without his permission. Hertha had a way of making her feel like a wayward child.

"No, there are no plans. The east wing should be torn down. Destroyed. Forgotten."

The housekeeper's voice was so intense, Gwyneth felt a tingling coldness creep up her spine. She forced herself to shake it off. She remembered the night she had arrived, and Hertha's eerie behavior as she'd led her up the tower stairs to her chamber.

She refused to be intimidated now.

"I disagree." She straightened her shoulders. "Where is Burnet?"

"He is indisposed, milady."

"He's in your quarters?"

"He can't be disturbed."

Gwyneth stared at her. "Then take me to him. I've been studying under Prior Bruin. Perhaps I can lend him some aid in his illness."

Something unreadable was etched in Hertha's dark eyes. "Milady—"

Gwyneth didn't wait for her.

The steward's quarters were in the blocklike tower that connected through a corridor from the west side of the great hall. She had her own set of chatelaine's keys. She didn't need Hertha.

The rooms were very, very cold. She shivered as soon as she entered them.

No one was there. The bed was empty. No Burnet. She whirled. Hertha had followed her and stood in the doorway now.

"Please, milady," she said quietly, her look peculiarly fragile. "Please go away, Lady. Go away. Go away!"

Ghost words. The night in the dark east wing passage, and then again at the priory.

Gwyneth's mind reeled as she watched Hertha's shoulders sag. What was going on here? Why had she lied about Burnet—and *where* was Burnet? He was never around. It was almost as if he had an entire other occupation, quite apart from the stewardship of Valmond. He always looked exhausted, bent over, as if he could hardly go on, and yet he never seemed to lift a finger in his office.

There were stacks of parchments on a table in the corner by the one window. She could see from here that they were more accounts and lists, but there was also something she recognized.

Just an edge. A gilded, red edge. The leather tip of a corner of something she knew.

She crossed the room, her candle in one hand, and pushed away the parchments with the other to find the book of herbs that had come from Prior Bruin. The book that had disappeared. She opened it up to be certain it was the same book, and inside the front cover she found a letter, folded, the seal broken.

Unfolding it, she saw it was the letter from Rorke. The one he had questioned her about, and she had assumed it must have gone astray and never arrived at Valmond. But it had arrived. Burnet and Hertha had concealed it from her. She thought of all the strange occurrences, and wondered how many of them could be explained right here, with Burnet and Hertha.

She whirled on Hertha.

"Tell me what this means," she demanded of the housekeeper. "Why would you conceal Rorke's letter from me? Why did you let me think I'd lost Prior Bruin's book?"

Her thoughts reeled.

"What else were you and your husband responsible for? The ruined plants? The nights I woke and thought someone had been in my room? The missing things, the ruined clothes? The voice in the dark in the east wing?"

She wondered what other evidence she would find if she searched their quarters. But what she wanted most was an answer.

"Why do you want me to go away?"

The housekeeper crumpled. It was like watching a stone wall hit by a mangonel. She seemed to fall in on her own bones.

"Forgive me, forgive us both." She hunched over on the rush-strewn floor, sobs shaking her body. "We were only trying to save him. We would do any-

thing to save him. Don't you understand? Anything."

"Save whom?" Gwyneth pleaded. She set down
her candle and took hold of Hertha around the
shoulders, feeling almost as if she were keeping the
woman together.

"Godric!" Hertha lifted her red, tear-filled eyes.
"They're going to kill him, don't you see?"

"Who's going to kill him?"

"The monks!"

Twenty-five

It took some moments for Gwyneth to get the story from the hysterical steward's wife. Not that what she could glean made much sense. The tale was filled with ghosts and treasure and jealous monks in search of retribution for all that had been stolen from them so long ago. It came out between bursts of sobs.

"Calm down," Gwyneth ordered Hertha.

The older woman took a gulp of air, and seemed to steady somewhat. "They've killed him. I know they've killed him. He failed. We failed. We couldn't find it. We couldn't—"

"Find what?" Gwyneth couldn't make sense of the scrambled story.

"The treasure!"

"What treasure?"

"They want it back! It's theirs. It was always theirs."

"They? Who are they?" This was going too fast. She didn't understand.

"The monks, Lady!"

"What monks?" The only monks she could think of were hardly killers. Prior Bruin didn't look as if he could squash a spider. Brother Arnulph—well, that could be another matter, but still. The man spent his days growing lavender, for saints' sake. If he wanted to kill people, he wouldn't have left the battlefield.

"I told ye, Lady—I begged ye," Hertha whispered, glancing over her shoulder as if afraid they'd hear her from across the meadows and river that separated Valmond from Millbridge Priory. "Why didn't ye listen to me? They want Valmond. They want the treasure. It's theirs. They left it here, and they've come back for it! It's the curse. The lords of Valmond are being punished."

Gwyneth recalled Godric's story about the monks of the old abbey that day in the workshop of the physic garden, how they'd stolen from travelers. *They took their gold and jewels, whatever they had, and they murdered them for it. They had convinced themselves it was their holy duty to take from the rich and give to God. They were certain they would be made saints some day for their charity. It was a madness of course, and the treasure they'd built up was the beginning of the wealth of the lords of Valmond. That's why they're angry and jealous to this day. That was their treasure, theirs! And they want it back!*

Oh, blessed saints. The woman was a wheel short of a wagon. She'd spent too much time creaking about Valmond. She'd started to believe the legends, the curse.

Was she dangerous? Gwyneth didn't like the idea of leaving her here, alone. At the priory, they'd locked up Godric. No wonder.

Where was Burnet—really?

"Has Burnet been searching for treasure in the east wing?" she asked.

"I'm so worried for him!" Hertha cried. "What if he's gone to them? He was out of his mind with worry for our Godric. And he's been working, night after night, with their maps and their orders, in the east wing. Digging, tearing down walls, examining every cellar, every secret dungeon. He's so tired, Lady, so—" A sob caught her throat.

Gwyneth's head hurt. But the urgency in Hertha's voice bothered her, and she appeared to be on the verge of a complete collapse. "Try to be calm." She helped the older woman to the bed. "I'll take care of everything."

She wished Rorke were there, but she went instead in search of Walcott or Ryman. She'd promised Hertha that she would do something. Finding Burnet was the first priority. She went to search for Rorke's men. She would send someone to the priory.

The practice room was empty. It was early. The men were still abed, except those on watch duty. It was barely breaking dawn, not even truly light yet. She thought of the many times she'd visited the priory, escorted and unescorted. Still, Rorke had been so serious about her not leaving the castle unaccompanied.

She'd been unbearably touched by his concern for her, but she was annoyed at the same time. She was fit enough to take care of herself, and she wasn't worried about ghosts. She was worried about an old, frail man who was quite possibly insane and lost, maybe even hurt.

She would wait a few more moments, but no more than a few. The men would be up, breaking their fast, very soon. Or she would wake them.

She went back to the hall, then to the tower. She found Melia kindling the hearth in the large sleeping room she shared with Lily and several of the other children and women.

"Melia, would you take several of the women and attend Mistress Hertha in her quarters? She's quite unwell. I'm going to the priory. I don't want her to be alone."

Gwyneth didn't want Hertha to be alone—or unwatched. Might the housekeeper be dangerous? The idea troubled her. There were children at Valmond. She was responsible for their safety.

Melia's expression was confused, but she must have sensed Gwyneth's impatience for she went straight about her task.

Gwyneth paced back down to the great hall. Her vaguely formed notion of gathering a few men to accompany her to the priory—Walcott and Ryman—trailed away as she considered other possibilities. What if Burnet were in the east wing? She needed confirmation of Hertha's story, and she was worried about the elderly steward. What if he were in the east wing now, hurt, and that explained his absence?

If Burnet was hurt, time was of the essence. It would only take a few moments to check.

Candle in hand, she headed for the east wing.

She hadn't forgotten how dark it could be in the lower passages of the east wing, but she *had* forgotten how cold it could be. It might be early summer, but in the damp chill of that corridor, one wouldn't know it.

The keening noise of the wind outside, the smell of dust and damp, surrounded her immediately.

"Burnet?" she called out. "Burnet!"

There was no answer. She forged ahead, slowly, carefully, remembering the uneven nature of the stone, and that there were sections in disrepair.

Shadows flickered against the narrow walls of the corridor in the spill of the candlelight. Ahead was only blackness.

She stepped onward, always cautious. Then she heard it.

A sound unlike the wind. A breath, a whisper—

Then there was the sound of something moving in the air, but she was barely aware of it striking her head. There was no more cold, no more voice, no more rushlight.

The world was silent and black.

Rorke hurtled back to Valmond across the darkling dawn landscape, his long night ride almost ended—but seemingly endless. His mind gripped on his goal: getting to Gwyneth. He had to know that she was safe; then he would see about Ranulf.

After all these years, all this searching, all his mad focus, it was happening again. Someone he loved was in danger, and he had let it happen.

He had been searching the entire country for the past, and all this time the past had been in own land, waiting for him, stealthy, murderous, thieving. All this time . . .

The man he'd faced last night had been quite possibly the filthiest man Rorke had ever seen. He'd been holding a sickle, glaring at him across an open, muddy, dark field as if he expected Rorke to jump him at any moment. Beyond him stood a tiny cottage. The fisherman's cottage. Here it had all begun, and here he hoped to find a way to its end.

Rorke had left his men in the town, seeking shelter at one of the taverns. He'd decided that he would be more effective at gleaning information if he came alone. A band of men could appear intimidating to poor villeins, and he wanted answers this time. Finally.

He dismounted, gave a low word to his battle-trained steed. The horse wouldn't move till he bade him so. He held up his hands, well away from his sword hilt.

The man lowered his sickle.

"I am Rorke of Valmond."

"I know who ye are," the man said.

He looked vaguely familiar to Rorke. "And who are you?" he replied. "Are you kin to the fisherman, Tobin, who once lived in this cottage?"

"I'm his brother."

"I seek his widow. I understand she has word for me."

The man shrugged. "Mayhap. What have ye for her?"

Rorke wasn't planning to waste any time. Watching the man carefully, he reached slowly for the small cloth purse at his belt. He unlatched it, and tossed it at the man.

The fisherman's brother caught it one-handed. He slipped open the loose knot. The gold within, glinting in the moonlight, appeared to satisfy him.

"Come with me." He turned and marched across the dark field. Rorke followed him.

Inside the cottage was no less dismal than without. It was naught but four walls of dried grasses and a thatched roof lit by a low-burning central hearth. As he entered, Rorke's eyes burned from the smoke that had no escape.

Several children slept rolled together in a tattered blanket in one corner of the hut, and an elderly woman lay on a thin mattress in another. Another woman, the fisherman's wife, rose at the entrance of Rorke and her dead husband's brother.

The man held out the purse. She took it and examined it.

From the pocket of her dress she withdrew a crumpled parchment, much handled and refolded, based on its state.

"No one would ever believe him." She held on to the folded parchment while she spoke. "He gave up, finally. He even trusted them. They said he would get his share. What did he care where it came from? He'd earned it. He'd saved the man. But in the end, he figured out that the doctor wasn't going to give it to him, after all. He was going to go to the provost with his story. He went to the doctor one last time, but it wasn't for treatment. Oh, he claimed he'd asked for treatment! Claimed it was all for Tobin's sake. But we proved it. Proved he'd not been ill."

"What happened to Tobin?" Rorke wasn't sure

he wanted to know, but the widow seemed eager to talk, to tell someone her story. And he still didn't have the parchment, the proof, whatever it was that she held in her hand.

"The doctor said he came to him for a malady of the head. He gave him his drugs, cut open his skull, straight down the middle," she said in a low, hoarse voice. The smoke in the suffocating hut seemed to intensify as she laid out her gruesome tale. "He killed him. But we got the doctor in the end. Now he's dead, too. They should all be dead, every one of them that had a hand in it."

Now she thrust the folded parchment at him.

"It's a treasure map," she said. "Or that's what the doctor said. He promised Tobin part of it, when it was dug up. But his promises were nothing but lies. You can have it now."

She held the bag of coins close to her breast. "Take it away from here. I never want to see it again!"

Rorke couldn't make out the parchment's contents inside the dim hut. He left the woman and her husband's brother and the rest of them to inhale the fresh, damp sea air outside.

In the moonlight, he had gazed down at the parchment, the end returned to the beginning, and he knew he'd been right all along. But right didn't help now, not if he'd failed Gwyneth.

Twenty-six

"When you're dead, he'll go away. We can go back to searching for the treasure. We'll find it, eventually. We are very patient."

Her head ached with a regular, pounding rhythm. She didn't know where she was. She was stretched out on something hard.

The east wing. She had been in the east wing.

Gwyneth opened her eyes. She had trouble focusing. Above her, she could only see darkness. Lower, the walls were lit by some kind of light, revealing cobwebs and filth. It was all rather fuzzy.

The smell of the place was fetid.

"You are wondering where you are."

Yes, she wanted to say, but her mouth felt thick, her tongue heavy.

"Never fear, you are still at Valmond. You have been too curious, Lady, and now your curiosity will be satisfied. Are you happy?"

She'd been looking for Burnet. Hertha was having some kind of mental breakdown. The events of the morning came back to her.

And so did the source of the voice by her side.

"Brother Arnulph?"

She heard the movement, then saw the shadow

towering over her. There was a light somewhere in the room—a candle on the floor, maybe. She had no idea what had happened to her own candle. She assumed she'd dropped it when she'd been struck.

There were no windows in this room, and she sensed that they were below ground level. Below the abbey. This foul chamber was nothing like any of the cells she'd glimpsed in her brief foray into the east wing.

"Yes, my lady. You are so right. And so nosy. Poking your head places it shouldn't be. You should have heeded your warnings. You had plenty. Burnet and Hertha didn't do their job, did they? They were supposed to get rid of you, scare you away. They failed."

"Why would they do that? Why would they help you?" But she already knew, suddenly. Godric. Brother Arnulph had put Godric away in the bloodletting room. He had said he was mad.

But who was mad now?

Hertha was right. Godric was right. Oh, God, it had been Brother Arnulph all along.

"Now, you will have to be eliminated," he continued as calmly as if he were explaining yet another medicinal use for fennel. "Another sad note in the long, unpleasant history of the lords of Valmond."

"Your poor lord husband," he continued, and she could almost believe he was genuinely concerned. "He will be destroyed by your death. No doubt, he will abandon the castle yet again. We will drive off all the villagers, as we did before. The simple people are easily incited to superstition. And then, it will be ours. We will have all the time we need."

"Time for what?" Gripped by panic and fear, she only knew she had to keep him talking. Keep him from taking whatever action he planned.

"Time to find the treasure, you foolish girl. Now get up."

She didn't want to get up. She had a feeling that anything he wanted her to do wasn't going to bode well for her health.

"How did you get in here?" she asked, not moving. "I don't understand."

"There has always been an abbey entrance on this side of the castle. It was sealed up. Or so they thought. We took care of that a long time ago. It's taken three years to come this far. If only Lord Valmond had stayed away. If only his pretty bride had not wandered about where she had no business. Tonight was an especially bad time, my lady. We had to deal with Burnet. Now we will deal with you—sooner, later, it doesn't matter."

Oh, dear heaven. What had he done to Burnet? What was he going to do to her?

"The stories—the legend—you're saying it's true, that there's a treasure."

Arnulph chuckled, but his humor didn't go so far as his patience. He jerked her upright by the hair.

She let out a small cry and pushed herself up with her hands, trying to avoid any more pain than necessary.

Her palms felt filthy from whatever she'd touched on the bare stone floor where she'd lain.

"Where are we?" she said, on her feet now. He let go of her hair, but he had hold of her arm now. He was impossibly strong.

She could barely see anything for the shadows and the hair tangling in her eyes and the pain thudding inside her head.

"The abbey cellars," he said flatly. "Dungeonlike, almost, you might say. Full of steep steps and tiny secret storage rooms where a lady with a wanderlust could easily fall and break her neck. Pity, there will be no one to hear her cries."

Gwyneth's blood froze, but she tried to think. She had to keep her mind working.

"Where is the treasure?"

A new voice answered from the black depths of the chamber. "Now, if we knew that, my child, we would not still be here."

Gwyneth's stomach dropped. "Prior Bruin?" she whispered.

"Nay, sweetling, don't you remember me yet? I've been wondering, waiting, knowing you would know me." The dark, crooked shape of the crippled man came closer. "After all, we were as good as family once. Would have been family, indeed, if that traitor scourge Graeham of Penlogan hadn't ruined everything."

He kept coming. The light was behind him, illuminating his form but not his face.

Gwyneth shoved at the hair in her eyes. Arnulph never let go of her.

"You look so much like your sister," the crippled man whispered. "Elayna. God above, I loved her.

She should have been mine. Now you're mine. But you have to die. Too bad."

He was so near now, she could see the fierce mad glow of his eyes. She began to make our his features.

He was Prior Bruin. At least, he was the man she had known as Prior Bruin.

But she knew now that he was not. He was an imposter. She had never seen it. She had never even thought of it. She had seen what she had expected to see, what she had been told to see. But now it was so plain.

Recognition stopped her heart. "Ranulf," she breathed.

"Oh yes," he hissed. "Yes."

"What happened to Prior Bruin—the real Prior Bruin?"

Ranulf laughed, an eery, echoing sound. "He was quite delicate. Even I could kill him, in my somewhat reduced physical state. I didn't need Arnulph for that."

The grip of Arnulph's arm tightened on Gwyneth's arm.

"My man Arnulph has been a steadfast friend." Ranulf smiled thinly. "More so than your brother."

"My brother was your friend! You let Damon rot a year in Saville's dungeon! You allowed Wilfred to be executed for Father Almund's crime, and you allowed Graeham to spend years branded a traitor—all so you could possess Penlogan. You never had any right to any of it."

"I earned it. On the field of battle, Lady. And off it. I deserve a castle. I deserve a lordship! I will take it, if I have to, but I will have my due. Rorke told me years ago about the treasure beneath Valmond, and when he took Penlogan away from me, I saw no better vengeance than to take Valmond in its stead. I found Brother Arnulph—that's all you need, you know. One good man."

One evil *man,* Gwyneth thought.

"It's a story," she said aloud. "There is no treasure."

"There is truth behind every lie," Ranulf's hard voice spat. "There is treasure here. There has to be! I won't stop until I find it."

Gwyneth thought of how Ranulf had schemed his way into possession of Penlogan years before. He'd gone over the cliff rather than be seized for his crimes, and he had begun immediately to conspire to take control of another castle.

She reminded herself to keep her wits about her. It would be finished now, one way or another.

"Rorke will come looking for me. I will be missed."

"Rorke is gone, Lady. Away on his mad quest for me." Ranulf laughed.

"You hated them, didn't you?" she said suddenly. "You hated them all. Rorke, and Graeham, and Damon. They were all different from you."

"They had titles and lands and castles," Ranulf ground out. "They didn't earn them. They were given them. I earned everything I've ever had. I deserve everything they had!"

"No, they were noble and good and true. You hated that about them."

"Shut up."

Without warning, his hand reached out and smacked her hard across the cheek. She reeled backward, only remaining upright as a result of Arnulph's firm grip.

"There is no treasure!" she whispered hoarsely.

"Get rid of her," Ranulf ground out. "I have no more patience." He withdrew something from the interior of his monk's robe. Arnulph's grip changed to a locked arm around her chest, which held down both of her arms; with his free hand, he seized her chin. She didn't understand until she saw what Ranulf held up.

A vial—greenish-black glass—shiny with some liquid.

"Never will you be able to say I was not considerate of your pain, my lady," Ranulf said softly, and for a moment, he sounded eerily like the kindly prior again. "This will ease your path into the next world. Take it. There is no point in struggling. It will be better for you this way."

He held the vial to her mouth. She shut her lips tightly against the cold tip of the glass.

The smell was peculiar and sickening. She wished she'd had more time to learn about herbs. Apparently, Ranulf had had plenty of time while he'd been playing prior at the monastery and plotting his evil will against Valmond.

"I am actually sorry about killing you, Elayna."

Gwyneth blinked. He'd called her Elayna. Was it a slip of the tongue, or was he so mad that in this desperate moment he had confused her with her sister?

"Open your mouth," Ranulf ordered now, his

voice completely changed from the kindly prior back to the cruel soldier.

When she didn't comply, he slapped her so hard her face slammed back against Arnulph's shoulder. In the beat it took for her to make an involuntary gasp of pain, he uptilted the vial against her lips. She spat, but Arnulph held her mouth closed, his clamp on her face spinning new pain through her.

"Good-bye, Lady," Ranulf said, the sound of his voice strange through the resounding ache all through her head. "Good-bye."

He turned, and his crippled form moved away, the *clack-clack* of his cane on the stone floor reverberating in the deep, desolate chamber.

Arnulph spun her around, shoved her toward a narrow opening. She had no idea where it led, and she dreaded finding out.

They were alone now. Ranulf was gone. Arnulph pushed her through the narrow opening and she reached out for support, finding nothing but cold, wet stone. How deep under the castle were they?

"This is where the monks housed their travelers in bygone days," Arnulph was telling her.

"The travelers who didn't leave, you mean?" Gwyneth gasped as she half-fell down three or four steep, winding steps in the pitch black.

The candle had been left far behind in the larger chamber where she'd been poisoned. For poison she assumed it was. She felt a strange calm move over her, and the painful haze and panic eased away. Maybe it was the drug, she couldn't be sure.

For now, her mind was clear.

She remembered everything Rorke had ever

taught her about focus and breathing. This was no sword match. She had no weapon. But she had her body, her wits, her strength, and she was used to being underestimated.

Arnulph continued pushing her down the seemingly endless winding steps. She could feel the suffocating dank air thickening with each step, and she knew they couldn't be far from the bottom. And at the bottom waited the nightmare world of the mad monks.

He pushed her down the last steps, and she stumbled. He had both her arms twisted behind her, but her feet were free. Hair tangled damply in her eyes, but it didn't matter. It was too dark to see anything.

She felt a void with her foot as he pushed her one last time, and she lurched backward. They were standing upon some kind of precipice. She couldn't imagine what lay below in the evil black. A pit, perhaps. Would there be bones of long-dead travelers murdered by the monks? *Pray God, Burnet is not down there,* she thought suddenly.

The thought of Burnet reminded her of the people of Valmond, and Rorke. She had so much to live for. This was her last chance.

"You don't have to do this," she said steadily.

"I want to kill you," Arnulph said. "I enjoy killing. I enjoyed it too much. It was upon the king's orders that I went into the brotherhood. He thought it would cleanse my soul.

"I like to hurt things and see how long they cry," Arnulph said. He had pulled her back against his chest, twisting her arms harder.

She knew he wanted her to cry out, and she didn't want to accommodate him.

"You're a healer," she gasped as he twisted her arms more.

"Healing, killing, they are two ends of the same pole, are they not? I control life and death. It's what I do."

He pushed her forward now, to where her feet barely had purchase on the slick stone. The precipice awaited.

Her involuntary scream brought a low laugh, and he hauled her back. He was enjoying this moment too much to hurry it.

"Frightened, Lady?" he hissed by her ear.

She gave him a moment to think he was right. He chuckled to himself and his grip of her lessened for just a breath. She pivoted, ignoring the pain in her wrists as he tried to clamp back down on her. There was no point in delay. He would either kill her, or she would save herself. But she would not go down into that pit without a fight.

She had just enough time to kick him, hard, in the groin. He swore loudly, the sound unearthly in the deep underground chamber. Then she felt something cold wash over her, from inside. The poison.

But his astonishment at her blatant attack gave her one more breath of time.

She ran for the slick, winding stairs. She screamed again when he chased after her, clawing at her legs as she reached the first bend. She kicked at him, panic coming back as she felt more and more coldness coursing through her veins.

There was little time now.

He slammed her headfirst onto the stone steps as he dragged her down. She couldn't lose focus now. She scrambled back up and made it up a few more steps before he hauled her down to the stone again. The pain of her cheek hitting the cold rock was meaningless at this point.

She aimed another kick and heard a thud and a gasp as she made contact with his face. Flipping, she took her chance to kick him again, aiming at a shadow in shadows. She thought for an instant that she could see his eyes, but that was impossible. How could she see his eyes in this black void of ice-cold and damp? But she knew what they would look like. They would be mad.

With a hoarse shout, she sensed his movement— away from her, his scrambling, clawing hands gone. She couldn't see his fall, but she could hear it.

And then she heard nothing.

Rorke stormed through the gates of Valmond, shouting orders as he went for a contingent of men to mount up and ride with him to the priory forth-with. He swung down from his horse in the open bailey before the hall.

He found Ryman inside, at the tower steps, ques-tioning Melia.

"Where's Gwyneth?" he demanded.

Ryman pivoted, his rough-hewn face drawn in lines of concern. "She's missing, my lord. Since early this morn. When her maid arrived to light her hearth, she was not there. I sent out a man to the priory immediately, but he returned with word that she was not there."

"But I know she went to the priory," Melia said, insistent. "She was with Mistress Hertha. Something happened, I'm not sure what, but Lady Valmond woke me and asked me to stay with her in the steward's chambers. Mistress Hertha is in a terrible state. Something about the monks and Godric. Burnet is missing. Lady Valmond said she was going to the priory."

Rorke didn't wait to hear the rest. Pricking dread filled him. He had brought Gwyneth here, left her in this environment where he had believed her to be safe. There had been men here to protect her. And still, she was gone.

If anything happened to her, it would be his fault. Just as it had been with Angelette. And this time, he knew he wouldn't be able to go on. No vengeance would satisfy the loss of Gwyneth.

She could even now be in the hands of the man who would like nothing more than to kill anything Rorke loved.

He burst into the steward's quarters and found Hertha incapable of being any help. The older woman lay stretched on her bed, staring at the whitewashed stone ceiling.

"They're going to kill him. It's no use." Hertha sobbed over and over.

Rorke burned with frustration and apprehension, but he resisted the urge to shake the woman.

"If you should find Gwyneth at Valmond"—and how he prayed she would turn up, safe, and at home—"keep her under your personal watch," he told Ryman when he left the housekeeper to the tending of the women.

He was already calling to his men as he hit the steps down into the bailey.

Gwyneth had to be safe. Everything that had driven him for so long burned away in that moment. He knew what mattered now. The future. Gwyneth.

He prayed he still had them both.

Twenty-seven

Rorke gave little notice to the cry of the priory gatekeeper as he swept through with his men, continuing on horseback straight into the open cloister.

He dismounted, flinging orders at his men. "Search everywhere. I want Prior Bruin—and I want answers."

If the prior had been harboring a traitor and a murderer in his midst, even unwittingly, he would have a lot of explaining to do.

The cloister was amazingly empty. Rorke had known how many of the monks had died in the plague years but had not been here in person to visit and see the decimation of the once-bustling order. He had been aware, vaguely, that the order had been rounded out primarily by lay brothers in these last years.

What foul conspiracy had taken hold of this once-pure brotherhood?

His father had worked side by side with Prior Bruin creating works of herbal lore. Had Prior Bruin, long renowned for his dedication and almost mystical earthly sainthood, so lost touch with his monks that he had allowed such devilry to go on beneath his nose?

He remembered from childhood where the prior's office was. He sent men scattering in all directions, some for the physic garden, where he knew Gwyneth had studied with Brother Arnulph, and others to the chapter house and various buildings that made up the small enclave.

If Ranulf was here, he would not escape.

A few brothers came out of buildings, but no permission was requested as Rorke's men set about their business.

The prior's office was straight ahead from the cloister center. The low building was modest; its whitewashed interior was clean. The building was square-shaped, with the cloister mead forming its center and other paths winding off by narrow cobbled ways.

He walked as quickly as he could into the prior's building. In his tunic, he carried the parchment provided him by the fisherman's wife. The parchment her husband had witnessed before his death—a map drawn by the injured man they had reclaimed from the sea.

The map depicted Valmond, the old abbey section, and scrawled words that outlined the legend of the jealous, angry monks who had cursed the lords of Valmond for centuries for taking their abbey, stealing their treasure, digging it up to make it their own.

Rorke recalled revealing the legend to Ranulf during their journeys together as comrades. It had been a joke, a way to pass the time. Had Ranulf in his greed suspected that it was truth, not tale?

Had the die been cast so long ago, even farther

back than when Ranulf had gone over that cliff at Penlogan? If Angelette had not set out that fateful night and been murdered by Father Almund, would Ranulf yet have returned with Rorke to Valmond and begun his own quest to find the legendary treasure?

At one time, the two men had discussed returning together to Valmond. They had talked of many things, many possibilities, traveling as brothers and friends.

The prior's building was still, empty. The arched wooden door set at the end of the central stone corridor loomed huge suddenly to Rorke as he paced toward it.

He didn't know what he expected to find. How could Prior Bruin have been unaware of what was happening here?

How could he have let a stranger come into the priory, an evil lurking among them, waiting to destroy all of them as well as Valmond? For Rorke didn't doubt that Ranulf would have no compunction killing any monk who came to suspect his purpose here.

There was no time or mood for knocking. He opened the door. The prior's office gleamed with light that stroked in from tall windows set against a garden backdrop. It was there in that private garden that Rorke knew his father and Prior Bruin had striven together to work on their herbal.

He could hear a *snip-snip* from the garden. He paced across the office, out into the sunlit mead.

Prior Bruin was at work clipping his roses.

The crippled monk turned slowly. His cowl covered his head.

"Lord Valmond," he said, nodding. "How wonderful of you to visit my humble garden. How long it is since we have met."

His voice was low, raspy, kindly, but his mouth was twisted in a leer. The shadowed portion of his face became clear when he used the hand not holding the shears to push the cowl back.

Rorke's vision wavered.

"So you have come to me," Ranulf said. "At last. Your search has ended, has it not?"

Rorke would have wondered why Ranulf was so calm in the face of his arrival if at that very moment he had not felt the tip of something sharp upon the back of his neck. At the same time, his sword was whipped from its sheath and tossed away.

"I am always prepared for visitors," Ranulf said. "Please, make yourself at home here in my office—for, after all, I certainly intend to make myself at home in your castle when it becomes mine."

"How long have you been acting as Prior Bruin here?" Rorke asked. His mind spun with the realization. What had happened to the prior?

"Oh, a long time, my friend. Nigh on two years now. This tiny priory with its poor monks, off any main roads of travel now, maintains little contact with the outside world. Poor Prior Bruin. He wasn't much missed!"

Ranulf's expression was faintly piteous.

"He spent much time preparing himself for sainthood," he went on. "Well, now his preparation has been put to use. I only speeded his way to his saintly destiny—and set myself on the path to my own."

"Your destiny is to fry in hell for all the people who have died because of you," Rorke ground out.

The painful tip dug a bit deeper into the back of his neck. The man behind the dagger was bald, burly, thickly set.

Rorke had another moment of shocked recognition. He was one of the men who had attacked him in the forest, dressed now in the common robe of a priory lay brother.

He wanted to ignore that tip digging into his neck, put his hands around Ranulf's throat and strangle him if he didn't tell him exactly where Gwyneth was right now. But he needed more information before he made his move. His men would come searching for him soon.

Ranulf didn't seem to understand yet that Rorke had not arrived alone.

"He will have a knife in a secret pocket at the back of his tunic," Ranulf said. "Remove it."

The bald man slipped his hand inside the neck of Rorke's tunic and retrieved the dagger.

"For three years, I've imagined what it would be like to kill you," Ranulf said. "Ever since the night you took away from me everything I'd worked so hard to gain."

"Penlogan didn't belong to you," Rorke reminded him. "You got it through lies and murder and treachery."

Ranulf ignored his points. Rorke knew that his old friend had never seen it that way. The second son of a poor knight, Ranulf had set out by fair means or foul to gain the kingdom he believed the world owed him.

"Valmond doesn't belong to you," Ranulf countered.

Rorke took in the physical state of his old comrade. Ranulf was as tall as ever, but he was bent, broken. Whatever damage had been done to his body when he went over that cliff, the ministrations of the drunken doctor of Dormead had not repaired it completely, nor had the further tending of the priory monks.

No, Ranulf's strength now was in the vile cunning of his mad mind, not in the power of his once-invincible battle arm.

But the burly attacker from the forest was another matter.

"Valmond was—is—the rightful property of the monks of Millbridge Priory," Ranulf continued. "And I, as its prior, will retake it when you are dead. I've been researching the history of the commitment of Valmond into the hands of your ancestors by the king all those years ago. It seems the actual documents, which I discovered here in Prior Bruin's archives, read such that if a lord of Valmond dies without an heir, the lands, castle, and old abbey revert to the monks."

"You aren't a monk," Rorke pointed out, amazed at Ranulf's audacity, his ability to adapt and take advantage of any situation.

Ranulf tut-tutted. "A minor detail. The point of the matter is, people believe I am a monk. People see what they expect to see. I am Prior Bruin. And any man in this monastery who could not accept that has already been eliminated. Except for Godric. But he had his uses. That is now at an end, however. His parents' usefulness has also ended. I have been a patient man, but my patience has its limits. Progress must be made. Everything was going fine: We'd driven off the villagers. We had the castle to ourselves. Our secret entrance. The digging and the tearing apart of walls has gone on for some time now. Then you had to get married. Your wife had to bring people back to the castle. She brought you back. And so things must change again. Plans must be revised."

He clipped a rose, as if his conversation were completely sane, simply a routine discourse. As if he had not a care in the world.

And perhaps in his mind, he did not. He stood far enough apart from Rorke that if Rorke made a move, the bald man could slice his throat before he would ever reach Ranulf.

He sniffed the rose, then dropped it in a basket on the turf beside him. "Now, where were we? Ah, your unexpected arrival today. You know, I have many times sent men to track you, and to kill you, but you always escaped. As I escaped you. Yes, I knew that you tracked me. Oh, how I knew. The doctor at Dormead was quite a problem. Should have disposed of him long ago. But that might have created more suspicion, so we let him live. A drunk. And that fisherman—who would listen to him?"

Ranulf was right, Rorke thought dully. He hadn't believed the fisherman's story himself three years ago.

"I always had my fortunes along with my downfalls," Ranulf continued. He had stopped clipping the roses now and stared with his ice-mad eyes at Rorke. "The physician had his uses. He was greedy, and he saw right away that we could work together. Taking Valmond was always an alternative for me, in fact had been my plan before the seizure of Penlogan fell into my lap."

"You mean, before you helped Father Almund cover up the truth about Angelette's murder."

Again, Ranulf ignored points he didn't want to consider as part of his historical view.

"When I woke up in the physician's house that morning after my fall from Penlogan, I immediately began to plan," Ranulf said. "You chased me over the cliff that night. You made me what I am, in body. Did you think I would not avenge that loss?"

"You made yourself what you are," Rorke replied, realizing again how little need he felt now for vengeance. This broken man before him was not the evil ghost he had chased for three years.

Ranulf was pitiful, twisted and tormented in endless schemes to take what didn't belong to him. The blackness of his existence was horrible to perceive, and it was a punishment that Rorke could never hope to exact in equal.

"You belong in a dungeon for the rest of your life," Rorke said quietly. "You belong where you can think every day of every person whose life you were a part of taking, and where every day you can live with the broken pain of your body."

Ranulf laughed. "You would put me in a dungeon at Valmond, would you? Or perhaps Wulfere or Penlogan? Perhaps my former comrades could share me throughout the year."

His grin was miserable to see. How had they never seen his vile sickness all those years ago in France?

"No, I don't think so," Ranulf finished, no longer laughing. "I have no intention of languishing in a prison. You would have died soon enough, and I was half-expecting for some time that you would put things together, hear the whispers on your lands, and visit the priory one day. I have been ready to kill you for a long time."

"You are a broken, pathetic remainder of a man," Rorke pointed out. "You can't kill me. Your minions can't kill me. Even now, there are a dozen of my men combing this priory. Your time has come, Ranulf. This time you will face your sins at last."

He could see the bald man from the corner of his eye. When he'd mentioned the dozen soldiers on the priory grounds, the man had immediately flinched. He was looking over his shoulder, then back at Ranulf as if he didn't know what he should do—and as if he was wondering whether protecting Ranulf was important enough to risk his own life at this juncture.

Rorke returned to his attempt to put together the pieces of the puzzle.

"How long have you been tormenting my faithful servants to do your will?" Rorke demanded.

"Ah, Godric and his parents," Ranulf said. "They were easily swayed to my service once they realized their son's continued health and well-being were at stake. Unfortunately, they failed to completely drive

away the people of your lands. And even more unfortunately, you had to make the problem worse by
bringing home an all-too-curious bride. I enjoyed
toying with her at first, especially since she was
Damon's little sister, not to mention your lovely
bride. It was a game—everything is always a game,
my old friend. What greater game was there than to
host my dearest enemy's bride each week. I could
have killed her at any time, any moment I chose. I
always knew I would kill her—fast or slow, it didn't
matter.

"How much of my potion to give her each time
she visited was always a new decision, a new play in
the game," he said slowly, coldly. "I watched her
with each visit. I enjoyed seeing the effects. She lost
weight, grew pale. But I always held back. She re-
minds me of Elayna, you know. Sometimes, I
thought she was Elayna. It was the only thing that
kept me from killing her sooner, I think. Of course,
that's over now. She's quite dead, you know. This
time, the dose was complete."

Ranulf smiled thinly, watching Rorke's reaction.

No, Gwyneth, Rorke thought bleakly. He refused
to accept Ranulf's words. His hands fisted. He
heard the sound of voices in the building. They
were coming fast, from the corridor, through the
open door into the prior's office.

"Where is she?" Rorke demanded, and he gave
no heed to the burly, bald lay brother who had so
vilely served Ranulf. Rorke could have fought off a
thousand of him with the strength of his need for
answers. He didn't care anymore about the treasure
or Ranulf's plans or his own life. There were a hun-

dred questions, a thousand, that had haunted him for years. How could Ranulf have betrayed their friendship? How could he have let Damon suffer in Saville's dungeon for twelve months? How could he have let Angelette's killer go on to kill more women, the people he had vowed to protect on the lands of Penlogan?

But none of those answers mattered now.

All that mattered was Gwyneth.

He knew there were men pouring out into the mead from the prior's office, and in his side vision he could see the bald lay brother sprinting for the garden walls. He wouldn't make it, but that was of no concern to Rorke.

Ranulf grunted as Rorke smashed into him, knocking him down easily. Rorke was on top of him, ripping the shears from Ranulf's grip into his own. He thought of how many times he'd dreamed of killing his enemy.

"Where's Gwyneth?"

Ranulf's nostrils flared in his lean, cruel face. He laughed.

"I could kill you. I've thought of nothing but killing you for years. Tell me where my wife is."

"I will not be taken," Ranulf hissed. "Don't you know that yet? I am the taker! I am in control. I will always be in control. You were born to it. I take it!" His words were those of a raving lunatic, but his gaze was focused.

He placed his hand on Rorke's over the shears at his throat.

"I'll tell you where she is," he whispered. "She's

with Angelette. She's with me. Live with that, friend. She will be with me."

Rorke didn't have time to ponder Ranulf's meaning. What happened next was a blur. He was oblivious to the shouts of his men behind who had seized the bald lay brother and were even now coming to their lord's aid. He pressed the sharp point of the shears against Ranulf's throat.

"Tell me—"

He didn't finish the question. Ranulf pressed his hands harder against Rorke's on the shears, and pierced hard. He gurgled, blood spewing out of his mouth.

Rorke stared, reeled. He let go of the shears, and they stuck in Ranulf's throat, blood bursting everywhere. Ranulf's hand fell away, lifeless.

It was over. It was difficult to take in, and he couldn't for some moments. After all the pain, all the deaths, all the years of torment for so many, Ranulf was dead. And Rorke felt no joy in it. Ranulf's death couldn't save him from his pain.

Only Gwyneth's life could do that.

He spun on his men, praying they had found her safe and sound. "Where's my wife?"

Their empty looks destroyed him.

Twenty-eight

He fought the rising panic inside him with a steely force. The thunder of his horse's hooves, the heavy gray of the sky, the dread of his heart, all blended together.

Behind him, he left the destruction of the priory and the body of a man who'd done everything he could to destroy his world. He prayed Ranulf had not succeeded.

Godric, at least, had been discovered, weak from more bloodletting than any man could normally withstand. Rorke had left men behind to round up the monks and lay brothers left in the priory. The other attacker from the forest had been found to be part of the evil group Ranulf had gathered when he'd taken over Prior Bruin's role. Every man in the priory would be held to account for the doings of the past few years since Prior Bruin had been murdered.

There had been no sign of Gwyneth, or Burnet, in the priory. And a quick assessment of the membership of the priory revealed there was one monk missing: Brother Arnulph.

Immediately on arriving at Valmond, Rorke was swarmed with people—villagers and children, craftsmen, stableboys, soldiers—all asking about Gwyneth. All had stopped what they were doing as they became aware that she was missing. It was easy to see in that moment that she had won every heart in Valmond by the caring she had lavished upon them since arriving at Valmond.

What he could not see now was how he had ever ridden away and left her here alone. He would not leave her again.

First, he had to find her.

But it was the child Lily who did that. Fear hung like a stone in his heart as he stormed into Valmond, and he almost shoved her away unseeing, feeling only a tug on his tunic, but when he looked down, he found the girl who had sworn to protect her lady panting, dirty, eyes wide.

In a heartbeat, he was not shoving her away but running along with her to the east wing, down unlit black corridors, into a secret level belowground he'd never known existed.

Rushes held aloft by men who'd followed after them lit the scene and that was the very moment he almost lost all reason. He found Gwyneth, collapsed on the damp stone stairs, blood seeping from her temples, her face bruised and her body so still, where Lily herself had found her after sneakily following her into the east wing that morning.

"Your lucky star," he told Gwyneth when he lifted her carefully into his arms. "Lily. She followed you. She protected you the way I should have protected you."

"It's not your fault," she whispered, opening her eyes. "I am fine," she told him over and over as he carried her out of that dark filthy cellar, up into the light of Valmond and to their own bedchamber. "I am fine."

But he could not believe it, not at first. There was so much blood. One side of her face was covered with it. He issued a curt command that was instantly obeyed by women eager to do anything to help.

He had seen worse, far worse, on the field of battle, he kept telling himself. He insisted on tending her himself, pushing back her tangled hair, cleaning away the blood to find the torn flesh where her head had struck the stone during what he knew had to have been a terrible struggle. But his Gwyneth, his strong fairy-warrior, had won. She had saved herself, but just barely.

Fortunately for them all, it had turned out that Ranulf's efforts at concocting slow poisons were better than his ability to concoct a fast-acting one. The potion had left her sick but not dead. It was the blood that Rorke feared now as he had lifted her away from that place where she'd been left to die.

At the bottom of those dark steps they'd found the body of Brother Arnulph, his neck broken. They'd also found Burnet, injured and unconscious, but alive in the gaping pit that Rorke had never known existed. It was Valmond's violent past come to life—the oubliette, the pit where the monks of the old abbey had secreted their murdered travelers. Bones upon bones were there. He had left men behind with ladders and strong backs to climb down into that nightmare and bring back the old steward. Even now, he was being nursed, and he would recover.

But it was Gwyneth who held Rorke's attention and his heart. And it was her blood, which no matter how many worse wounds he had seen made this one the most terrible.

Her hands felt like ice when he held them, but she never wavered in her belief that the future was theirs and nothing would stand in their way. She had always been that way—so full of faith. He hadn't trusted her faith, and he'd been wrong.

"It's just a scratch," she promised.

The cut was actually quite small for the amount of blood, and he was chilled to think how close she had come to death in that dark cellar. If Lily hadn't followed her, if the cut had been deeper or wider, or Ranulf's potion stronger, or—

There were so many possibilities that could lead him back into a nightmare, but he clung to the fact that he had her in his arms and that he would never let her go.

He stayed with her all that long day. He gave her a mixture of herbs he'd known physicians to give men who had been wounded in battle, knowing rest would help her recover faster. He held her all that day and night, listening to her breathing, changing her bandage when needed, checking on the stitches with which he had carefully closed the wound, and whispering of his love to her when she roused enough for a little broth, or another dose of the sleeping herbs. She was also fighting the after-effects of the poisoned potion Ranulf had been giving her, and they could only give it time to go through her body and pray it would leave no lasting damage. She was determined and so strong. It broke Rorke's heart to see her suffering, but she didn't complain. She was focused on the future, as she had always been.

"You are my life, my heart," he kept telling her. The emotions that had been impossible for him to express for so long couldn't be contained now. She had freed him. It was her life, not Ranulf's death, that had changed everything. The love he felt for her was so huge, he could scarcely express it. He knew now that what he had felt for Angelette so long ago had been a youthful love. His love for Gwyneth was mature and deep and forever. "I love you," he told her. "I cannot live without you."

And in the long night, she promised him, "You won't have to," and he believed her.

The festival of the Michaelmas moon was a glorious sight at Valmond, and there was nothing more glorious than the goose procession into the great hall teeming with peasants and soldiers, family and friends.

The autumn festivities rose around the high table where Rorke and Gwyneth stood smiling, hand in hand, to signal the commencement of not only a night of joy, but a future of hope.

Beside them on the dais stood everyone who had reason to celebrate this new beginning just as much as Rorke and Gwyneth themselves. Damon and Belle, with their children, Venetia and Ryen. Graeham and Elayna, with Sebilla and Sabrina. And

Lizbet and Marigold. Gwyneth looked out on her family, so dear to her, and she felt tears prick her eyes. Happy tears. She was closer to them than ever as they all realized how precious life and happiness could be, how easily it could all change.

The people of Valmond had come back in full force over the summer. Recovery was slow, but it was there, for them all. Valmond would be a great castle again. Rorke had already begun the tearing down of the east wing. Gwyneth had agreed; she had no desire to use its foul rooms now. Her idea to found an order of lady knights had not been abandoned, though. They would rebuild with that goal in mind. Rorke had not taken much convincing. He knew better than to think he could sway his wife from anything upon which she'd set her will.

No treasure had been found. It had been a story, nothing more, and a nightmare, but it was over. Rorke had his own true treasure right beside him, he said often these days. His Gwyneth.

Life, Rorke had told Damon upon their arrival, would always be interesting with Gwyneth. Damon hadn't disagreed. He had simply offered his amused condolences.

Gwyneth took Lizbet's hand as her sister stood beside her.

Kenric was there, too. He was Ranulf's brother, and no matter how they all had suffered, the guilt he shouldered for his brother's crimes was worst of all and they had insisted he come to Valmond for this celebration.

Gwyneth had noticed Lizbet watching him, and she suspected it would not be long before her falconer sister confessed that there was something more than birds making her heart fly. Another wedding at Castle Wulfere, Gwyneth thought. But for now, there was today.

"Lackwit," she whispered to Lizbet, who dragged her furtive gaze from Kenric's stern profile.

"Dolt," Lizbet returned, falling into the easy teasing camaraderie they had always shared.

Yes, everything in her world was right and whole again, Gwyneth thought. There was just one thing left unsaid.

"To Valmond!" Rorke declared, his goblet raised, his other hand still firm in his wife's. The crowd cheered. "To family and friends!" His gaze swept the dear people who stood with him on the dais. "And to my wife!" There were more cheers, and beneath its covering roar, he said, "I love you."

Gwyneth smiled, overjoyed every day she looked into the eyes of the man she had always known was locked inside, sometimes still disbelieving herself that he was here, with her, and that the pain was finally gone. She knew there would always be a core of darkness in her dear husband. He had lost much, and spent years trapped in a hell that she could only imagine.

Nothing would erase the past, but the memory of it was not as horrible as before. The destruction wrought by Ranulf over the years was a scar they would never forget, but it had not been a mortal wound. They had overcome. They had a future. Even the fact that his sword arm had never quite recovered wasn't a matter of any import to Rorke now. His desire to fight battles was long gone—except for the sweet battle of living with her, he had teased.

"I love you, my sweet dark lord," she returned softly. She let go of Lizbet's hand to turn fully to him. "To our love," she said lightly against his ear. "And," she added happily, "what came of it—our baby."

His face was bright, his eyes glowing, and he crushed her mouth with a kiss that brought the crowd roaring once more to their feet. And the light of Valmond was their light. The future had arrived.

COMING IN JANUARY 2003 FROM
ZEBRA BALLAD ROMANCES

—BELLE OF THE BALL: The Graces
by Pam McCutcheon   0-8217-7456-5 $5.99US/$7.99CAN
Belle Sullivan is a tomboy—and darn proud of it—until she over-hears the local swains mocking her and her sisters. Determined to make the men pay, she vows to become a beauty and ensnare them, one by one. She then hires handsome Englishman Kit Stanhope to teach her the art of flirtation. Before long, she is a veritable heart-breaker. If only she didn't yearn to use her skills on the very man who taught them to her!

—THE TRUTH ABOUT CASSANDRA: Masquerade
by Laurie Brown   0-8217-7437-9 $5.99US/$7.99CAN
A willing spinster, Anne Weathersby has set aside her own needs to care for her siblings. But debts and good deeds take their toll. To make ends meet, Anne embarks on a secret, scandalous career as a novelist.

—THE MOST UNSUITABLE WIFE: The Kincaids
by Caroline Clemmons   0-8217-7443-3 $5.99US/$7.99CAN
Drake Kincaid's parents' will stipulates only that he marry by his thir-tieth birthday, not that he marry *well*. And no one—including Drake's grandfather, could possibly think tall, bossy Pearl with her ragtag sib-lings and questionable "cousin" Belle would make a good wife.

—WHERE THE HEART LEADS: In Love and War
by Marilyn Herr   0-8217-7447-6 $5.99US/$7.99CAN
When Rachel Whitfield's brother is taken by French Canadian ma-rauders, she persuades brawny trader Jonah Butler to take her north to rescue him. It's a battle of wills from the beginning, but soon it's something more—a journey into the secrets of desire . . .